EMERGENCY SHIFT

BOOK 1 OF THE FULL MOON MEDIC SERIES

DANIEL POTTER

FALLEN
KITTEN
PRODUCTIONS

To Seria M.
A mom, paramedic, trans woman and possessor of one of the largest hearts I have ever known. Her life has never been easy, but she navigates it with an inspiring combination of both bravery and kindness. I'm honored to count her as a friend.

THE CROSSROADS

For centuries magic has been in retreat; confined to the deepest shadows, allowing humanity free reign in the world. But now the time of hidden secrets is ending and the seals that protect the mundane world are starting to crumble. As the realms of Death and Dream extend their fingers into mortal lives, ordinary people find themselves caught between the end of their age and the birth of a new one. Some will arise more than mortal, while others will find themselves on the menu. Welcome to life in the crossroads.

Twilight Run details Abby Night's first encounter with magic. It is in no way required to enjoy *Emergency Shift* but is a great prelude. To read it, join my mailing list.

1

"Dearie, there's nothing wrong with my heart," the old woman insisted, despite the fact that it wasn't beating. I heard nothing through the stethoscope pressed against her chest. She breathed, but only right before she spoke. Days like these made me wonder if the rapture my Aunt Betty always babbled about had come and gone without anybody noticing.

"You called complaining of chest pain, Mrs. Weatherby. You're saying you don't feel any pain now?" I asked with a professional smile as I glanced at my partner, Cindy, who towered over me with the stretcher at the ready. She had her arms crossed as she waited. She shook her head a little, declining to state her opinion.

"I feel better than I have in years, Abby," Mrs. Weatherby said and flexed her gnarled hand. "Even the joints stopped complaining. It's so nice. The man in the suit was very kind."

I gave up trying to find the heartbeat. From her blue lips to the coolness of her skin, she gave every sign of being a corpse, and I smelled the evidence of a Code Brown. As a paramedic, I should be administering CPR while Cindy readied the defibrillator to shock her back to life. But she watched me with alert eyes. A Code Z was a post mortem patient that continued to move, but the usual symptoms included trying to bite chunks out of paramedics. "Man in the suit, ma'am?" I asked.

"Oh, he came right before you two got here. Wanted me to come with him. But I turned him down. I have things to do today. Told him I'd be right along after I finished some... business." She laughed as if that had been a clever joke and she pulled her shirt closed.

"Mrs. Weatherby, why don't we give you a ride to the hospital? Just to be safe. Let the doc check you out," I asked her, offering my hand.

Her eyes narrowed with suspicion, "No, Abby. I think it'd be best if I stay here. No need to get poked and prodded for nothing."

"Uhh. Your blood pressure is very low. I'm sure your doctor would appreciate it if you got yourself checked out, Mrs. Weatherby," I said with a bit more force. "As your neighbor, I would really appreciate it."

The smile came back, warm despite her deadness. "You have nothing to fear from me, Dearie. So sorry for troubling you and," she looked Cindy up and down, eyes squinting at her name badge, "Colin."

"You're refusing transport, ma'am?" Cindy asked with a voice steeped in professional disapproval.

"Yes indeed. I won't be one of your frequent fliers anymore." She responded with more firmness than I had ever heard from her. The fluttering anxiety that I heard at my door every time she'd gotten a new prescription was completely gone.

Cindy looked at me. I looked at her. We had no procedure for a talking code Z. We're not cops; we don't take anyone any place they don't want to go unless they've got life-threatening damage. Cindy presented Mrs. Weatherby with a refused transport consent form. In less than a minute we were wheeling a stretcher with only our medical bag on it past my apartment door. Cindy stopped, "While we're here, could I use your bathroom?"

I winced. "Err, can you hold it? I haven't had a chance to clean up..."

"From the full moon?" Cindy finished with a bit of a smirk.

Warmth crawled across my cheeks and I looked at my door. Cindy was the only person who knew about my... blackouts, and she had that curious shine in her eyes that would make her difficult to dissuade. Besides which, now that she'd mentioned it, I also needed a piss. The toilet worked, at least.

With a grumble, I pulled out my keys and opened the door to the ruin of my apartment. Cindy took two steps in and froze with a muttered, "Jebus crust. You weren't kidding."

The apartment had never been fancy. Now it looked like it had hosted a wild animal on a bender. The door opened into my living room area. The old leather couch's upholstery was more duct tape than leather, the coffee table sported a jagged split down its center, held together by a section of lumber nailed to its underside. The heavy old entertainment center I'd inherited from my parents bore deep parallel grooves in the wood and no TV. Unpatched fist-sized dents were scattered over the cheap plaster walls.

I closed and locked the door. It had two deadbolts, one of which had a keyhole on this side.

Cindy was turning in place, examining both the damage and my half-hearted repairs. What was the point of fixing stuff or getting new stuff when you knew it would happen again? It had been two months since the weirdest call we'd ever been on. We'd pissed off Death, been chased by skeletons, and Luna, the moon herself... bit me. She'd promised to guide us out if I let her touch me once, and awed by her beauty I'd agreed. Her teeth sliced deep, each so cold that they burned. "With this first touch of three, know my anger, Abby Night," Luna had whispered. Now my arm bore a circle of tooth marks, but worse, a piece of her had stayed in the wound. A spark of cold rage is nestled next to my heart. Waiting. On the full moon, it burns away everything but rage. The first time, I convinced myself I'd been burglarized in my sleep. The claws, the snarling, the rage had to have been a dream. Waking up to my TV being smashed into my kitchen sink forced me to admit it the second time around. In addition to zombies, vampires and a wannabe necromancer, Portland now had at least one werewolf: a paramedic named Abby Night. Me.

Cindy measured her large hand against a hole in the wall. It would have been a bit high for me to punch, but Cindy had nearly a foot of height on me. Six foot two with broad shoulders, a square jaw, and a well-kept uniform, only her brightly-colored nails might clue you in. We'd worked together for two months before she'd asked me to call her Cindy instead of Colin, though she wasn't out to the entire company. Most simply assumed she was gay, which caught her enough flack. "Looks like these were more scooped out instead of punched in. Do you get bigger?" She asked.

"I don't know." My voice had a trace of a whine to it. I tried to shrug off the sensation of being the subject of a nature documentary. "Don't remember much other than getting really pissed off." Not entirely true, I remembered the claws, wickedly curved and sharp.

I went to the kitchen and started filling up the brand new coffee pot. My old one had suffered a fatal collision with my TV. I'd been using my phone for most things in the week since the last full moon, but phones still couldn't brew a cuppa, no matter what app you installed. "Bathroom's through the door there." I pointed towards my bedroom.

"It doesn't look like you try that hard to get out. So at least you're not a monster that hunts down everyone you know and love." Cindy still spun, looking at the damage.

"Cindy, stop fixating and go pee!" I finally yelled.

"Heh, sorry." Cindy ducked her head and moved towards the bathroom. "I just keep thinking it could have been me. If I had been lead that night, you know." She called out as she went into my bedroom. "Aww, Abby, are you sleeping on that mattress? That can't be good for your back."

"Leave it, Cindy!" I called, jabbing my coffee pots On button. It made terrible coffee, but it made it fast. And there was nothing wrong with the mattress, I'd shredded the foam the first night but once I'd collected all the bits into a sort of nest, it was more comfortable than before.

"Okay!"

Cindy was wrong about that. The spark hadn't filled me with a mindless animal rage. It had inflamed my own useless anger at Jimmy. Had Jimmy not been ten years gone, I would have broken down my door and hunted him to the ends of the earth. He was dead via a bullet fired from the gun that I'd bought him for his 18th birthday. The same gun that killed my parents and nearly three dozen others. I might be a werewolf or something now, but in high school I was definitely a worse monster.

In a few minutes, pit stop complete, we were back on the Bus. That would be the ambulance. Cindy drove as I mulled over the paperwork from Mrs. Weatherby. Code Z, plus refusal to transport would be a whole new kettle of fish for the powers that be. I wasn't clear on who made those decisions. Far as I knew, only Portland had a problem with the restless dead. They were more a nuisance than an apocalyptic threat. I'd had several coworkers who'd been bitten, but nobody'd caught anything nastier than when you get bit by a meth head. Which is still gross.

"So, got New Year's plans?" Cindy asked me as I sent the report.

"No..." I ventured, Cindy had been awfully quiet as we drove. It was getting on towards sundown. Not that you'd know from the perpetual gray clouds that had been hanging over the city for the past week. Portland winters weren't particularly snowy, but they were wet and dismally gray.

"You should," Cindy said with a bright smile. "You could be a real party animal with the full moon so close."

"Oh, definitely not!" I shivered. "That's not funny, Cindy. That's not safe at all."

"Maybe you're angry because you're trapped in the apartment," Cindy said as we pulled onto the freeway, patrolling our normal route on the west side of the city.

The radio crackled to life. "MICU 12. Please report."

I grabbed the handset mic, eager for a change in topic. Even though a call for a report instead of a general call to local ambulance units was never a good thing. "MICU 12 copies, over." I replied.

"MICU 12 you are being recalled to base." The dispatcher said with a tone that almost said sorry.

"En route, Dispatch," I responded and looked to Cindy.

Cindy spread her fingertips on the steering wheel. "This is way too early to get called home. I haven't even chipped a single nail. How fortunate that we are heading in that direction already. Almost as if I knew this would happen as soon as you sent in that code Z transport refusal."

"How very psychic of you, Madam Cindy." I rolled my eyes.

In the twenties, Portland had drastically overhauled its emergency response infrastructure. They halved the number of traditional cops in the city and rebranded the firefighters as the Civic Response Force or CRF, usually pronounced serf. I still call them firebugs, which most of them appreciate. The firebugs do everything that cops used to do that doesn't require a gun: direct traffic, ticket speeders, and talk down rowdy drunks. Suddenly the firebugs who were used to spending the hours between beating the ambulances to calls and polishing their fire engines were overworked, stressed and making mistakes. After a few botched calls during the second plague, the city blamed the ambulance companies instead of their newly minted serfs. They pulled the contracts from the half-century-old ambulance companies and opened bids to the public. There are now nearly a dozen ambulance companies in Portland. Many rent space in old firefighter stations as CRF outgrew them and either built new buildings or took over former police stations. This is a long way of explaining why we were stationed in the old Hillsdale fire station in southwest Portland.

It's a small two-bay firehouse with a peaked roof. Sadly, there is no upper story, so no fire pole to slide down from the bunk house. The company, Northwest Life Response (NLR) is a small one, with only four ambulances. In the old days, they would relegate an operation like this to running back and forth between nursing homes and elderly care facilities. But NLR played hard; their ambulances were top-of-the-line, fully-equipped mobile life-support units, plug-in hybrid models. Maybe in another half-decade it would start getting the tired sensation of a small ambulance company, but right now, it was the best place I'd worked in a while... If you ignored the dysfunctional father-son drama.

As the garage door came up, Cindy let out a groan. "Oh, Jeeebus... Mr. Clipboard's here in all his glory." Mister George Gifford stood in the middle of the bay, a lean black man with a grizzled gray buzz cut, trademark clipboard clamped in his armpit. I could already hear him in my head. You gals got some explaining to do. Well, he wouldn't say gals. Cindy was very strictly Colin to Mr. Gifford.

2

"Can you two not be the weird ones for once? I swear you're the biggest weirdness magnets in the whole damn city." Mr. Gifford rapidly tapped his pencil on the metal clamp at the top of his clipboard. "We've got the damn brass on their way here. You two better clean up nice."

I groaned as I stepped out of the ambulance, "Brass?" Mr. Gifford had been a Marine and it bled into everything he did. "You're talking about Dr. Wiggins, I presume?"

Mr. Gifford jerked his thumb upwards. "Higher, much higher."

"Higher?" I stopped. My knowledge of who handled code Z stuff stopped at the back dock of the OHSU hospital. I assume there's another doctor who handled the code at Legacy Hospital across the river, the other major trauma center in Portland, a city of not even a million people, but with enough action to keep two emergency departments hopping at all times. And it's not even a plague year. "No idea, chief."

"Andrew Millar ring a bell?" he asked gravely.

I swallowed. Yeah, a big one at the top of a cathedral.

While the man perhaps wasn't the absolute richest in Portland, he was the one that spent the most. Notably, buying up all of Legacy Health System a few years ago, and wielding major influence in the OHSU system after flooding the university with money.

Gifford nodded.

I had my first urge to rush into the locker room and put on makeup since high school. The man was as close to royalty as Portland gets. I wondered if sneaking a call to my Aunt Sybille, who's on the city council, would be wise. Cindy and I hit the showers. A black limo had pulled into the garage by the time we were out. I had no idea what to expect as Cindy and I stood there in the doorway to the crew quarters, waiting. Mr. Gifford stood with a rigid back as the uniformed driver circled around and opened up the passenger door. Dr. Wiggins popped out first, a handsome man with bronze skin and a wide nose. "George! Good to meet you, finally." He turned towards Mr. Gifford and offered his hand. They shook firmly, with Wiggins smiling warmly and Gifford nodding with grave solemnity.

"Good to put a face to a name." Mr. Gifford agreed.

As the two exchanged that handshake, the chauffeur reached into the limo and helped a man who had to be Andrew Millar stand. He sported a wispy goatee that was nearly white, and his knees shook slightly until he locked them. He had the withered look of a cancer patient. Perhaps there was a personal reason the man had been pumping money into the city's healthcare system. It didn't look like it was doing him much good.

"Allo, Abby and Colin! Nice to see you without the whole hazmat suit for once, eh?" Dr. Wiggins had released Mr. Gifford and was advancing towards us with his hand extended like a shark's fin.

"Hello, doctor," both me and Cindy murmured, and shook his hand.

"I thought we might see you rather soon, but," I looked in the billionaire's direction to finish the sentence, but he snared my eyes with his own hard stare.

"Don't worry, I'm not here in any official capacity. The Doctor and I were in a meeting together when he got your alert. I couldn't turn down the chance to meet the famous Abby Night." He made his way over, leaning heavily on his jet black cane.

My mouth went dry. I was famous for one thing and one thing only. My name was forever burned into history as the girl who gave Jimmy Libbey his gun. He thumped towards me, and after reaching us, looked me up and down.

"Thank you very much for saving Victoria Quentine's life." He turned to Cindy and flashed a smile. "Both of you."

I blinked; he knew Vicky? "Uhh, Just doing our jobs, sir." I managed to stumble out.

"All in a day's work." Cindy added.

He laughed, a dry rasp. "A very nonstandard day of work from what Victoria remembers of the incident. And yet you got her out."

"Any of us would have done the same." I said, even as the memories of that night flowed. The strangeness had started that night. As we responded to that call, Cindy and I had been pulled into a dark place that had not been the Portland we knew. Everything smelled of decay, and Death had howled for our patient.

"I doubt that, Miss Night. Victoria is a very special person and it would be a true loss to humanity itself if she had passed that night." He pulled out two business cards from the inside pocket of his jacket and spread them towards me and Cindy. "If either of you run into trouble in these... Uncertain times, feel free to give me a call."

Carefully, I took a card from his hand. "Thank you." Yet I felt his gaze stare at the circle of pale irregular scars on my forearm and I cursed myself for grabbing a short-sleeved shirt after my shower. The scar tissue was nearly moon pale, in stark contrast to the light copper of my skin.

"Is that a tattoo?" he asked, threadbare eyebrows pinching together.

"Misspent youth." I said, pocketing the card and stepping back.

"I wish I could say the same." He laughed as if it were funny. "Now that this old man's social inquiries are done, I'll let you all get back to your important business. Apologies for the intrusion."

"Good meeting you, sir." Cindy said.

He nodded and turned slowly back towards the limo. He moved towards its waiting door with a deliberate pace, the cane acting as a third, independent, leg rather than favoring one or the other. I suppressed the urge to recommend he use a walker instead of a cane. He'd get around so much faster and have less chance of winding up in the back of an ambulance because of a fall. Although perhaps that would be a more merciful end than whatever was eating his body. Dr. Wiggins quickly filled the gap that Andrew had left.

"Well, he is my ride back to the hospital, so I'd better make this short. The mayor has recommended that when emergency personnel encounter a code Z without cognition impairment, that they be transported for observation."

I snorted, "We're not cops, Doctor. She refused transportation."

He blinked. Like most doctors, Dr. Wiggins always seemed to be under the impression that he held some sort of authority over the EMTs. They don't. "Well, then, you should alert dispatch."

"I'm not calling cops on a patient!" My voice rose and his mouth gained a stubborn thrust to it, "Look if you put it in writing, I'll call in CRF mental health counselors but I'm not calling in the cops."

"If they're dead, they're not patients anymore, Miss Night. They could be a serious threat to life and limb." He attempted to loom self-importantly, but the man had all of two inches of height on me. He gave it up as Cindy and I closed ranks with a huff. "We are dealing with the unknown here. We have to be cautious."

"You know what makes me cautious, Doctor? A client with a gun. That's my line for calling the blue. No code Z even holds a candle to that." Although the skeletal knight who'd ripped off the roof of our ambulance came close. "Mrs. Weatherby was calm, rational, and a lovely, if slightly nosy, neighbor. She refused transport. End of story, doctor. You want to do a follow up call with her, then go knock on her door. How about doing something useful, like tracking down the source of all the sudden-onset anemia we keep seeing downtown."

"Anemia? That's not really my department, Abby." Dr. Wiggins said, and I suddenly realized I didn't know what sort of doctor Wiggins was. I'd only met him after we started bringing in moving corpses. I had assumed he'd been the poor sod drafted out of the emergency department to handle code Z, but apparently not. If he wasn't plugged into the hospital gossip network, then he had to be an outside academic.

Cindy laughed, "Go to the emergency department and ask them about the double-barreled mosquito."

Dr. Wiggins frowned as if he tasted something unpleasant, probably the limits of his authority. "I... will follow up on that. Thank you." Another round of goodbyes, and he ducked into the limo along with Andrew Millar. Everyone in the garage let out a breath as the long vehicle expertly threaded out the bay door and pulled into traffic.

"Dayum." The side door to the bay had opened and the large frame of Mr. Gifford's son, Cliff, filled the doorway, grinning lopsidedly, a beam of sunshine in the gloom. "Looks like we pissed off real money this time, Dad."

Mr. Gifford regarded his son with a sour expression. Cliff's smile didn't waver. The two men were odd mirrors of each other, nearly identical faces on wildly different bodies. The elder lean, almost honed, military discipline etched into his very movements. Cliff stood bigger in every dimension, but had a catlike ease to him. The pair ran the NLR's office; the senior covered the days and junior the nights. Overlaps didn't happen every day but when they did, there were always sparks. Sometimes the sparks caught and ignited into shouting matches that me and the rest of the employees loved to speculate about.

"You're early." Mr. Gifford said instead of hello.

Cliff patted the duffle slung across his chest. "Got some new parts for Big Red. Wouldn't want to work on it on company time."

"Be sure the paperwork gets done." Mr. Gifford turned on his heel to retreat into the office, but paused to look at me and Cindy. "You two restock but don't bother heading out. I'm calling an All Hands when the night shift comes in at six."

"Yes, sir." I answered as he disappeared into the office.

Cliff shook his head, tsking at us, "You two kicking at hornets' nests again?"

Cindy chuckled deeply, "Nah, we're upgrading to kicking

at fairy mounds. Those were the fairy godmothers coming to tell us off."

"What? They wouldn't let you into their party? Forget your wings? Or did they take one look at Abbs here and slam the door?" He strolled our way, grinning that grin that had been the first thing that had made my heart flutter since forever. Too bad it lived on the face of my boss's son. It never failed to root me in place.

"And what's that supposed to mean?" I protested, crossing my arms as Cindy and he performed the EMT high five, touching elbows.

"I don't mean nothing, Abby." He said with smooth ease. "But you're more of a leather and whips vibe. Colin here would rock the sparkles better. He's already a fairy."

"You know it." Cindy said with an exaggerated bravado and quickly changed the subject before I could get at the whips comment, jerking her thumb at Big Red. "So what treats you got for your pet?"

Cliff's eyes lit like headlights and he cast a longing look at the ancient fire truck that sat in our care. The engine grinned back at us from the end of the bay with his massive radiator grill. The small bubble-like headlights always seemed to have a gleam of mischief to them. Big Red, as we called him, was a vintage fire engine from the 1950s. Part of the lease was that we let him rust in peace here. Someone somewhere in the city government had an attachment to the old beast of a machine. "I finally found an alternator with the right voltage. Might actually run this time."

I laughed, "You say that every time you get a shiny new part." The firebugs who had cared for the engine previously had religiously kept the engine shiny, but nobody had maintained Big Red's guts in twenty or thirty years. Cliff had been attempting to resurrect him since he got out of prison two years ago.

"Ya never know what's gonna be the keystone to bring her back to life." He said.

"Probably because you've replaced every single other part?" Cindy asked.

"All except the engine itself," I added.

Cliff shrugged, pleading no contest.

"So much work to get us slapped with an environmental fine." I scoffed, not entirely jesting. Sure the fire engine was pretty, in that ugly 1950s way, but once Cliff got it running, then what? It rusted all over again?

"Hush your mouth." Cliff said with a laugh. "Sometimes the old ways got it right."

His dad opened the All Hands meeting two hours later with the exact same sentiment. "Sometimes the old ways were the best ways."

We were all gathered in the center bay of the Firehouse. All four ambulances were in house, which happened only in the half hour between the 12-hour shifts which, with prep and debriefing, worked into 13-hour days. With 4 ambulances, there were 12 paramedics in total with a few more semi-retired on call in case of sickness or vacation. Us regulars worked three or four shifts a week, depending mostly on Gifford's personal whim. Cindy and I had just been upgraded back to four. The ambulance that the knight had made into a convertible had taken some time to repair. We stood uneasily in the crowd facing Mr. Gifford. Cliff lounged in a metal chair, sipping a coke, in earshot but not at the meeting.

All the medics glanced at each other nervously. There were lots of old ways for Mr. Gifford to pick from. Some could be good, some were definitely not.

And he let us squirm before he smiled. "Who here has heard of the firehouse model?" Everybody looked at him, and a rustle went through us as our collective eyebrows raised. The firehouse model was one of those things that had been ground away by corporate efficiency long ago.

Mick, a beefy barrel of a man, spoke first; he usually did. "Hell yeah. That's where you get paid to sleep."

Mr. Gifford nodded, smiling coyly, "When it's not busy, at least. There've been meetings with the city over code Z and other things that don't quite have codes yet. Whatever's going on, weirdness is definitely on the rise. The city council has asked for a company that's willing to develop an expertise on the subject. I dropped Northwest Life Response into the hat with a bid and they accepted."

"What's that got to do with the Firehouse Model?" I asked.

"Heh." He nodded. "Good question, Miss Night. Because in exchange for getting priority on every call that smells weird to dispatch, we get the Firehouse Model. Taking priority will build our expertise, and the model ensures we have a deeper well of personnel should something really bad happen. Starting next week, we're going to start transitioning to twenty-four-hour shifts. Two in a row. 16 of those are slumber hours, half pay unless you're on a call. Works out to forty hours. Optional third day over pure overtime. Particularly while we're staffing up to fill out the schedule."

Hands shot up, Mr. Gifford took all the questions one by one. The long and short of it was: this is what we're doing. Yes, it's probably dangerous. There will be openings in other ambulance companies if you don't want your spot. Talk to Cliff for schedule adjustments, which made Cliff nearly snort his soda. It was kind of mad, Gifford was essentially making sure he had four medics for each ambulance.

Which meant... he was taking Cindy's and my account of what happened in the Twilight very seriously.

He closed the meeting, "The world is going to get weirder and more dangerous. Those who have kids, better make your peace with that before you stay on."

Now, I have to wonder if he had any inkling how right he was.

3

I took all the overtime Mr. Gifford offered. Every moment in my trashed apartment just felt like waiting and it was a good excuse to avoid my aunts. That, and Mrs. Weatherby had begun to stink, although the one time I saw her in the hallway she didn't look bloated and rotten. Cindy didn't take the overtime, so I got paired up with a few others, but I was back with Cindy when the weirdness hovering around the edges of my life stepped back into the open. The moon had waned to a thick crescent in the sky when it peeked out through a hole in the expanse of gray cloud determined to wash the city away before Christmas. Her sudden appearance made the scars on my arm itch.

We had begun our second tour in the bus in what amounted to a forty-eight-hour shift. We were cruising down near Burnside as we waited for the usual drug or alcohol overdose call. Tuesday nights tended to be slow. Cindy filed her nails as I drove aimlessly, trying not to think about Jimmy or wondering if things would have gone differently if I hadn't tossed my phone out the window en route to Aunt Betty's. If I had read those screaming texts and warned somebody, maybe things would have happened differently. Since then I've been trying to repair the hole he ripped in the world, that I had helped along. I'd planned it with him, scouted out the ladders. I used to have the names of everyone Jimmy killed that night memorized, repeated them to myself like a rosary prayer. They didn't help. Only calls help, the ones where we pull someone back from the brink. They're scattered between befuddled elderly, hypochondriacs, and addicts that don't have a single unbaked neuron inside their heads. People who need and want help because they're hurt. It took me four years to get out of my head enough to do anything again. Now, I've spent six years prowling the night for people to save. It still doesn't make up for Jimmy, but every night I spend in the bus, I feel like I'm a little closer.

"Code double-U code double-U, MICUs do you copy?" The radio squawked, running me off of memory lane and back to the present.

Cindy swore, blew across her nails and grabbed the palm-sized microphone and held it up to her lips. "MICU 12 here. Over." She said in a bored tone, voice lowering from its usual falsetto.

"Code blue, Code blue, MICU-12, We have a mass incident; at least thirteen vics, all but one certified deceased. Respond." The center display in the dash flashed into GPS nav as it plotted the route. We weren't far. Two miles and we didn't even have to drive over a bridge. I hit the lights and the siren.

"You want point on this one?" I asked Cindy as we launched through an intersection.

"Hell, no. You've still got four years on me," Cindy quipped before squeezing the mic, "Copy that. MICU 12 is responding. Is the scene secure? Over."

"Scene is not secure, but caller reports no current activity or firearms use." The dispatcher paused, not saying "over." "Caller reports one of the patients is... glowing. You are at your discretion MICU-12. Over."

Cold dread leaped down my throat and splashed among the full contents of my stomach. Cindy's eyes met mine; we nodded. "Copy that." She pulled her finger off the talk button. "That's not a code Z."

"That's why they called it a double-U." I said, slamming on the brakes as a self-important asshole took his sweet time to pull out of the way. He got the hint only after I laid on the horn. Then it was a straight shot. The electric engine's whine rose through the rumble of the pavement. The address wasn't a house, but an underpass. A homeless encampment. No matter what the city council said or what program they passed, the tent clusters still bloomed like flowers along any patch of unclaimed grass or like mushrooms, beneath dry bridges. Over time, I've been to most of the major ones.

Not this underpass, though. This cluster of tents sat too near downtown to be tolerated for long. Their natural colors were painted out by the strobing red and blue lights of the cop car that had beaten us to the prize. Only one, at least.

By the sound of it, that would change in less than a minute. Cindy jumped out the door before I even stopped the bus. I slid into the rear space of the ambulance, and slung our medical bags onto the stretcher as Cindy popped open the rear double doors.

"Eeh," A cop on the far side of his car greeted us as we pushed the gurney out. "Not sure you gonna-"

"We'll see it for ourselves." I cut him off.

He stepped into our path on the sidewalk; behind him

stood a rough hole cut into the chain-link fence, "Listen, Med. Something's—"

"Go go go!" The wheels of the stretcher clattered onto the pavement and we barreled directly for the entrance to the encampment, Cindy facing me, pointedly not looking where she was going. Facing Cindy's six foot two with an unadvisable BMI, the cop wisely moved out of the way. We rushed into the camp and a sour scent slapped my nose. Another cop stood with his back to us, holding one of those mace-like flashlights above his head, illuminating the scene. In his light lay a field of dismembered bodies, a jumble of misshapen limbs, like a game of twister gone horribly wrong. They were not human, All the hands possessed either too few or too many fingers, ending in gnarled claws. The sightless eyes stared out of heavy-browed heads with wide mouths that were more accurately termed toothy maws.

All dead. Dead but not still. The leathery skin swelled with blisters and boils that popped with the sharp snaps of good bubble gum, hurling puffs of green vapor into the air.

"I don't think that shit's healthy," rasped the cop.

But we didn't have a choice. In the center of the carnage a woman lay clutching her stomach, her back towards us, her labored breaths making her shoulders heave. A long braid of golden hair glowed softly with a warm light. An armor of interlocking silver scales sheathed her body. The light of the cop's flash light gleamed on the long blade that lay next to her.

"Go grab respirators?" Cindy asked.

"Hold your breath?" I responded, and she gave a little nod of her head. Together we hoisted the stretcher into the air and moved across the battlefield. Whatever the monsters were, it was too late for them. The sour scent wormed into my nostrils even as I refused to breathe. Movie props? My mind suggested feebly as instinct ran through the procedures. We both nearly collapsed next to the woman. "Portland Medical Services," Cindy gasped as she kicked a green limb further away, its skin boiling in slow motion.

I stepped over the woman and turned. She grunted when my headlamp shined in her face. Model-perfect teeth locked together in a grimace of pain. "Nice night for cosplaying." I kept my tone casual, flippant. Her eyes focused on me, irises glowing with the same soft light as her hair. They had contacts that could do that, right? "Can you tell me what happened?" my mouth said as I spotted the shine of blood flowing across her midsection.

A cat hissed behind me, then a high pitched voice echoed the threat, "Get away from her!" I whirled, my headlamp catching the flash of animal eyes as a silhouette dodged behind a concrete support pillar with a frightened meep.

"We're here to help," I called out at whoever was there, before turning back to the injured woman. "Watch my back," I whispered as I knelt, telling myself not to get distracted.

"Copy that." Cindy opened up our medical bag. "What do you need?"

I panned my gaze up and down the vic's body. Blood leaked between the scales of her shiny body suit. She had one hand clapped over her side right on the edge of her ribcage, the other staunching the flow of blood from a wound above her thigh. "Okay ma'am, we have to stop that bleeding first thing." I pulled a pair of thick, heavy scissors from my own toolkit.

No response. I glanced up at my partner. "There a zipper back there?" I asked.

Cindy shook her head, "Nothing. How the hell do you go to the bathroom in this?"

"Heh." The woman laughed, her grimace of pain momentarily flirting with a smile.

"Get the bleed kit." I tried to slide the blade beneath the scales but the weave resisted. It was as if the gaps between the scales sealed themselves as the blade approached.

"You will never pierce this armor with your iron, mortal," the woman declared.

We'd see about that. I grabbed her wrist and moved her hand from her side. A quarter-sized hole gaped in the armor and through her flesh as well. Dark blood, blue black by the light of our LED headlamps, flowed swiftly from the wound. "Stick it there!"

Cindy shoved a white cylinder of cotton and coagulation agents deep into the wound. Swiftly it swelled from a quarter-inch thick to three, its maximum girth. Not good. I needed to see the wound itself. At the edge of the hole I got a blade of my scissors between her skin and the armor and heard sizzling accompanied by the woman's hiss of pain. Still, the armor slowly yielded to the slicing blades, but it was like cutting through an aluminum can. After two cuts, it felt like my fingers were about to give out, but I managed a six-inch long slit. Cindy grabbed the two edges and strained to pry them apart. I peered down into her side and all my breath left me, momentarily forgetting how to breathe it back in.

They had ripped her wide open beneath the armor, a gaping crevice in her side. Blood usually obscured everything with trauma on this level; if you could see deep into wound that big, it meant they had little blood left. The light of my headlamp penetrated deep, and what greeted me wasn't remotely human. Where I expected kidneys and loops of intestines, were strangely shaped crystalline organs that shone with the same soft light of her eyes and hair.

"Transport." I heard myself croak. "Transport now." Whatever she was, she was well beyond what we could do beneath this overpass. I grabbed every cylinder in the anti-bleed kit and stuffed it into the wound. Scrambling into position I grabbed her shoulders and Cindy her hips, and with a smooth motion we lifted her onto the stretcher.

"Where are you taking her!?" Demanded that same voice from before. This time it belonged not to a shadow, but to a young girl, no more than ten, in a tattered black dress; black cat ears lay back flat against her head. The insides of her slitted eyes shone in the light of my headlamp. Shoving it into one of the many compartments of my mind marked, "later." The kid wore an absurdly realistic cosplay, nothing more.

"To the hospital," I said as we lifted the armored woman into the air. Both Cindy and I shared a surprised expression. The woman, probably as tall as Cindy, weighed barely anything at all. "Is she your mother?" I asked the girl. We moved back through the field of belching limbs, not waiting for an answer.

"No," the girl answered, catching up to us as we exited the field of limbs. Her hand latched onto the edge of the stretcher as she ran to keep up.

I tried again as we slid the woman into the back of the bus. "Is she your guardian?" Letting myself glance back at her was a mistake. Her face was a soul-rending blend of feline and human misery. Tears shining in her cat's eyes, her lower lip trembled.

"Yes." She said before letting out a plaintive meow, as if words failed. Little fangs bit into her lip as she swallowed and tried again. "Can you make her better? I can't lose..."

"We're trying." I pulled myself up into the spot beside the stretcher. Pausing, I glanced up at the still bewildered-looking cop staring blankly at me. Technically, she should go with him.

I'm not big on technicality.

"Come on." I extended my hand to the girl, making a decision that would completely upend my life.

4

The girl's feline eyes flicked to her guardian, her ears half back, uncertain. I read it as a moment of calculation. My arm began to falter, but her tiny hand slapped into my palm and my fingers closed around it. Dimly I was aware that my gloved hands were covered with the woman's blood stuff. I pulled her up beside me; she had more weight to her little body than the grown woman. "Don't touch anything." I warned her in a clipped, hollow-sounding tone.

She nodded timidly and sniffled. It had that wet, bubbly quality that stings my heart; she was about to fall into wracking sobs despite her best effort. A small piece of me shouted to do more for her. "Hang on, darlin'." The words coming out of my mouth echoed my mother's. I turned away from those wide eyes before my own memories flooded in. Memories I did not need on the job.

"Watch that tail." Cindy said as she closed the double doors.

Course she had a tail. Neither of these people was human. But only one was dying. Deal with that later. I could feel the evening's events already straining against the locks in my head. The woman's golden eyes had dimmed, but still watched me with a clarity that anyone as damaged as her should not possess. "Okay now," I told her and sniffed, a sound very similar to the girl's. Fuck, I was gonna cry after this one. I held up my fingers in a V in front of her face. "How many fingers am I holding up?" I asked. She had blue blood, glowing jewels for internal organs and my scissors had burned her. All my medical procedures were out the window, leaving only keeping her calm, keeping her conscious, and giving her hope.

"Two, mortal," she said, her tone still imperial as a small flower blossomed on her pale cheek, pink with veins of blue. "Why are you not afraid?"

"I'm doing my job," I said, as Cindy fired up the sirens and pulled into the street. "We're taking you to the hospital. You just hang on until we get there. It's not far."

She smiled; one of her front teeth had sprouted tiny legs and was trying to pull itself free. "I am not important, but the girl is." A tiny shoot of green wriggled through the white of her eyeball.

"You're going to be fine. Stay with us," I lied. It's an easy lie to say. It's part of the script. Once in a great while, it becomes true. I reached out and squeezed her hand; the bones in it squirmed in my grip. Cindy took a corner hard. The girl gave that little meep of surprise I'd heard earlier as she grabbed hold of my arm for stability.

After we rounded the corner, the girl didn't let go. Little arms circled my arm and squeezed. Face buried in the fabric of my uniform, she began to cry the promised tears with small, quiet sobs.

"Ssssshh," I soothed as my own emotional barriers

wobbled. "Almost there. It will be alright." My voice sounded prerecorded.

"She must go to the Queen." The woman's voice pulled my attention back to her. The little shoot pierced her iris and golden light was flowing down her face, draining from the eye. A tiny forest sprang up on either side of the golden stream. "Please, fearless mortal, will you promise to bring her in my stead? Protect her."

"Yes," I said, without a doubt getting in the way. "She'll be taken care of. But you'll take care of her yourself. Once you are better." Last requests are rare but I always agree. It's simply part of keeping the patient calm. Usually it's a small thing, like "tell so and so I love them." I try to do those. Once I promised a gunshot victim to get the guy who shot him. That one I never followed up on.

With one half of her face resembling a miniature mountainside, dotted with trees and her teeth bounding away like sheep, the other half smiled, "Titania's grace shine on you, Abigail Night. I bind you to your promise with my last breath." Her chest rose and fell with a shudder.

Something in my chest twisted hard, a spike of pain like a pierced nipple left me clutching at my heart and grasping for breath. "Jesus fuck." I cursed.

"Abby?" Cindy called back. "What's going on back there."

I looked over the bed of the stretcher. Flowers and tiny trees were competing for territory over the woman's collapsing body, springing from underneath the scales of her armor. "It's going to be a DOA," I said, massaging my left breast as the pain slowly subsided. Dead on arrival. "Also tell them it's a new code. Docs might want to look at this anyway." Normally, I'd simply start CPR, but the weirdness had finally exhausted my professionalism, and I could only watch the transformation progress. Cindy killed the siren but kept the lights.

What was happening to the world?

As I unraveled into numb shock, the girl let go of my arm but stayed close. Wiping her nose across her sleeve, she only surrendered her grip on my arm in exchange for being beneath it, leaning against my side. My hand initially brushed across the curve of her ears, they were warm and moved beneath my fingers. Real. My hand retreated down to her boney shoulder. Safe, human.

We rode in silence, me wondering what child protection services would make of her. Surely Portland's foster care services, bastion of liberal thought, wouldn't be as bad as the rest of the country.

As we turned into the hospital, she spoke. "You shouldn't have done that. I'm very bad luck."

I said nothing. Child protection services would count as protection, right?

There's an entrance specifically for code Z cases. It was back by the loading docks; that's where dispatch sent us. City hall was keeping post mortem animation quiet for the moment. There were betting pools among emergency services as for how long it would last. I'd already lost my bet three weeks ago. Underestimated the power of denial. Other than a few local tabloids that nobody sane believed, nobody was screaming about zombies in the media. Just a few twitter threads that most in the emergency services industry monitored religiously.

Two figures wearing yellow hazmat suits waited for us at the dock. One tall, one squat. Doctor Wiggins and Nadia, the coroner. Behind them stood half a dozen large men in scrubs, each welding the catchpoles that are usually used by animal control officers. Why were the coroner and the doctor the only folks who got the hazmat suits? I could only assume there was an invisible line on the hospital's salary scale that marked the expendable from the difficult to replace. The men with the catchpoles and the paramedics were both under the line. The girl maneuvered herself behind me as I moved to open the door.

"Hello, miss Night." Dr. Wiggins waved amicably, his voice muffled by his plastic shield. His handsome face and gray speckled goatee were framed perfectly in the plastic window of his face shield. I always wondered how he'd wound up with the family name of Wiggins; had his parents assimilated so hard that they'd jettisoned their heritage like my mother had? Or had it simply worked out that way?

I'd never asked; it was my own little hangup, so I forced a smile. "I don't think you'll need the brigade tonight, Doctor. No animation at all."

"Have something new. Yes?" Nadia stepped forward, her Russian accent thick and her dark eyes glittering with excitement as she leaned down to peered into the ambulance. "Let us see it! Chop chop." She hadn't given up on her origins at all but leaned into them. Nadia loved her job, and her naked eagerness always sent shivers down my spine.

"Gimmie a moment. If you'll take the front," I said, turning, expecting to maneuver around the girl, but she wasn't there. I had felt her little hands pressed on my back a moment ago. Now the space behind me stood empty.

"Oh, hi there," I heard Cindy coo from the front. The girl must have scrambled into the front seat.

Nadia's tongue clicked impatiently, and I hurried to grab the rear of the stretcher. Together we lifted it onto the slightly-too-high loading dock. Both Wiggins and Nadia stared down at the mass of greenery and brightly colored flowers. "What is this, Miss Night?"

"Ten minutes ago, it was a person." I crossed my arms, suddenly feeling defensive. "Massive trauma to the torso, wearing a weird skin tight armor." Wiggins turned to me, thick eyebrows arched in a skeptical manner. I plowed on, "We found her in a circle of dead monsters. She had blue blood and definitely odd organs."

"Are you telling me this is- was an alien, Miss Night?" Dr Wiggins had seen at least thirty cases of post mortem animation in the last three months, but apparently post mortem metamorphosis strained his limited imagination. Nadia remained bent over the corpse.

"Alien of a sort, Doctor. I think the word we're looking for is fairy." It sounded so silly, did she have pointed ears? I couldn't remember.

He snorted, "Did she have wings? Is there golden dust?"

"Her eyes and hair glowed." I said, stepping up onto the dock and staring him down. It didn't work as well as it had back at the station; this was his turf.

Wiggins opened his mouth to object again, but Nadia cut him off with, "Doktor! Look at this." She held something small and white that wriggled at the point of a pair of long forceps.

Scowling, Wiggins turned away and leaned over to peer at the white thing. He tried to adjust his glasses but a hand rammed into his faceplate, knocking them further down his nose. With a curse, he grabbed the fingers of his left hand and pulled the arm into the torso of his suit, readjusted his glasses and squinted. "Is that a bug?"

I moved closer, and the little thing gave the tiniest bleat of distress. "It's a sheep, doctor." Nadia announced with a slightly less pronounced accent. She was right. A fluffy sheep no bigger than a tooth. Doctor Wiggins blinked, then shook his head, sucking in his doughy cheeks as he stepped back.

"I want a report, Miss Night." His voice wavered a moment. "As detailed as you can make it."

I nodded, "If you can put in the request with dispatch, I'll get right on that." Gently reminding him of the actual chain of command.

"Yes." He said, staring off into the future, probably at whatever award he'd win for discovering whatever this was. "I'll put in the call immediately." His right hand grabbed at his pocket, but only got suit. With a sigh, he wiggled around until his left hand appeared in his bubble hood with a very large iPhone.

"Have fun, Nadia." I said, but she didn't acknowledge me, still poking and prodding with her forceps. I stepped down into the ambulance and closed the doors. A giggle came from the front.

"Some help you are, Cindy. Making me deal with Igor and Mrs. Schwarzenegger out there all by myself." I complained once the doors were safely shut.

"You're senior and you took lead. The docs are your problem." Cindy said, "Besides, I had to entertain our little guest. You are So cute! Yes you are!"

"Hey don't patronize the kid." I said, shoving some supplies back onto their shelves.

"What kid?" Cindy asked, reaching into the passenger side seat and fiddling with something. "Oooh! Almost got it! Too slow!"

I peered over the back to see not the girl but a small black kitten batting at Cindy's shiny nails. She reared up, little claws extended.

"I have no idea how she got in here but she's sooo CUTE!" Cindy's fingers made for the kitten's exposed belly.

The kitten screamed the tiniest battle cry "Meeeuuu!" and attacked Cindy's hand with gusto for its impertinence.

"Ow!" Cindy exclaimed as the sharp teeth latched on to a digit. "Oh you're a little biter, aren't cha? Aren't cha?" The kitten and the hand locked into a life-or-death wrestling match. It didn't go the kitten's way. The hand bowled her over and Cindy gave no sign of further pain from the claws and teeth.

"Cindy, I don't think she likes that." I commented, noting the kitten's ears were folded back as she gnawed ineffectively on Cindy's thumb.

The kitten stopped attacking and looked directly at me. Her eyes were the girl's. "Mew!" She pleaded.

Cindy continued to roll the kitten who was definitely the girl, side to side. "Aww, course she does! At this stage you have to show them who's boss or else they become little terrors." She smiled at her captive. "Adorable little terror! Yes you are!"

The kitten kicked free, ran up the back of the seat and launched herself at my chest before I could react. She impacted my left breast and clung there as if they made my Portland medical services jacket out of Velcro. Her claws penetrated right through it, my shirt, and my bra like tender flesh-seeking needles. "Ouch. Watch the claws!" I exclaimed, reaching for her.

"Mrrrph," she answered, scrambling up to my shoulder and leaping off behind me. I heard the thump of something much larger hitting the ground behind me.

"Aww," Cindy sighed, "I guess she likes you better. Does your apartment allow pets?"

I turned to find the girl with her arms crossed, eyes narrowed with a sour pout on her lips as if Cindy were my fault. "Let's just get to the station, Cindy," I said shrugging at the girl.

What the heck was I supposed to do with her now? If she was a cat when child protection services showed up, I'd look like a nutcase.

5

The girl did not want to talk. My gentle "Hey," and "Are you okay?" met only silence as she stared out the back window. Occasionally the light of the street lamp would hit at the precise angle that her inhuman eyes reflected in the window along with the lines of tears that ran down her cheeks. I asked her why she was crying once, and she simply wiped her eyes on her sleeve and remained stubbornly silent. At a loss, I let her be.

Mr. Gifford was back-lit by the yellow light of the bay as the garage door rolled up to admit us. The clock on the dash read just after eight. He'd probably been a few minutes from heading home when Dr. Wiggins' request for our immediate relief and debrief had filtered in from dispatch. He shook his head and moved to the side, waving us into the bay. Dang. I'd much rather explain this to Cliff. No other ambulances were in the station, so Cindy rolled us up to the supply cabinets in the back of the building.

I had expected the girl to be a cat again when we stopped, but she was the one who opened the rear door and stepped out of the bus in full view of Mr. Gifford. He stopped mid-step as the girl hopped down to the ground. His stern face softened into incredulity, eyes shooting from the girl to me and back again. "And who is this?"

"Uuuuh, a stray we picked up on the last call. It's... complicated." I said, standing above her on the rear bumper of the ambulance.

"I think you've got something more important to do than the reports they're yammering about." He quickly closed the gap and knelt down to the girl. "Hello, sweetie, I'm Mr. Gifford. What's your name?"

The girl jerked her head to the side. "I can't tell you that."

"What the?" Cindy had come around the side and winced as if she had a sudden headache. "Oooh. Right. This is another weird call." She muttered to herself.

"Do you have a nickname then?" Mr. Gifford, totally nonplussed, probed gently.

The girl balled up her fists and I watched her black tail lash with effort. "I'm a... Normal little girl and I'm..." she gave a little growl. "Sssssupposed to be here!" Her head snapped up to look Mr. Gifford right in the eyes. Something rippled through the air between them, and Gifford's head recoiled a fraction of an inch. He blinked rapidly as if dust had flown into his eyes.

"Right..." He said with a heavy breath. "You're... a normal little girl and supposed to be here. Of course. Just for a little while, that's okay. But her name?" He looked up at me.

"Uh... It's a secret because." I fumbled over the parts of my brain that were screaming WTF! "Because that's her nickname, Secret. Call her Secret." I nodded to myself. Secret is a perfectly normal name for a black cat and... she was close enough to one of those. Right?

Mr. Gifford stood up and scratched the corner of his nostril with a thumb nail as he peered into the ambulance. "You left the stretcher at the hospital." He observed.

"I'm happy to let them decontaminate it. We don't have an autoclave big enough." I said.

"Make sure they give ours back and don't swap it out for one of theirs." He grumbled and thrust the clipboard at me. "Take inventory, clean, and resupply." He yawned, "I'll go punt Roger and Mick out of their bunks. When you're done, come get me and I'll check it."

I took the clipboard from him and watched him stride back towards the office, slightly stunned and annoyed. Like we needed him to double check our resupply. The girl's trick had put him in a foul mood. He'd hovered over us like a grumpy mother hen for a month after the Twilight run, but I had thought we were clear of this bullshit.

Cindy and I shared a roll of our eyes before I slipped down next to... Secret. She leaned against the bumper and breathed as if she'd just run around the block. A proud little smile sat on her face, her slitted irises wide enough they almost looked human. I lowered myself to her eye level. "What did you do to Mr. Gifford?" I asked.

"Tell me my name again." Her voice soft but demanding.

"I called you Secret. It's-"

She flew at me, slamming her body into my chest and wrapping her arms around my neck. Had I not had a hand braced on the bumper, she would have knocked me flat. "Thank you! I didn't even have to ask for a name. I love it." She pressed herself against me and I felt the vibration of what could only be a purr. My body went stiff with surprise. I looked up at Cindy.

"You named it, now you gotta keep it." Cindy winked and mimed a hug.

My arms folded around Secret and my insides wobbled. Before I realized what I was doing, I'd picked her up and stood as if I'd had children clinging to me my entire adult life. She practically melted against my chest. "Don't think I'm not noticing you dodging my question, Secret." I scolded feebly. The manipulative little git purred louder.

"Should I ask the firebugs across the street if they have a jaws of life lying around? I think she's attaching herself permanently." Cindy grinned.

"You-," I grunted, "You're no help at all. Isn't this supposed to be your department?"

She put her hands on her hips, "And what is my department, huh?" She glanced towards the office and dropped her voice to a whisper. "Yes, she makes the ovaries that I don't have hurt, but it's clear she likes you better. I'd take her as a kitten."

Secret turned and struck out her tongue at Cindy. "You play mean."

Cindy crossed her arms, "Cats need to earn their keep and know the pecking order. I'm more of a dog person."

Secret's answer to that was to turn to me and say, "I'm hungry. Is there tuna?"

I laughed, "We'll see what we can find."

Despite our move to the Fire House model nobody had embraced cooking meals for everyone in the station yet. Since the onset of my full moon troubles I got even worse about cooking for myself, either buying my meals on the road or skipping them entirely if we got swamped. The kitchen proved to be a bit of desert in terms of unclaimed foodstuffs, the fridge populated entirely by reusable shopping bags labeled with black sharpie. No tuna, but I found a neglected looking bag of gold fish crackers shoved in a drawer. Secret took it with gusto, shoveling handfuls of the salty snacks into her mouth, chewing once or twice before swallowing. After demolishing the majority of the bag, she discovered the fishy nature of her snack and soon a pair of them were swimming through the air, propelled by her little hands. With her distracted, I Googled the number for the Oregon child protection services. Finding it, I stepped out into the hallway with a sudden tightness in my chest.

I dismissed the sensation as nerves and thumbed the dial button.

With each ring that sounded I felt a finger curl around my heart.

"Oregon Child Protection Services, How may I be of service?"

"Hi, My-" was as far as I got before the fingers in my chest squeezed and pain stole my voice away. Mouth gasping open like a stunned fish, I fell against the wall and slid down it. Sharp nails, claws, were piercing through my lungs as fingers attempted to pull my heart out of my chest.

"Hello?" A tinny voice asked from my phone, still balanced on the palm of my hand.

I fumbled at the disconnect button and missed. Tipping the phone from my grasp, it tumbled from its perch and clattered across the checkered tile of the hallway.

"Is anyone there?" it asked in a whisper.

Letting myself fall to my side, it remained out of reach of my trembling fingers. Numb spread across my shoulder as my fingers clawed at the tile, straining to drag my entire body the inches they needed. Myocardial infarction, my clinical brain diagnosed. Heart Attack. The damn fairy was giving me a heart attack. Darkness closed around my vision, narrowing down my world to the phone's red hang-up button.

"Ma'am? Ma'am? Are you alright?" It asked as the world, only containing a single button, rippled.

A little finger stabbed the red from the darkness. The hand inside me dissipated instantly. Air flooded into my lungs. I gasped greedily as life spread back through my body, rolling onto my back so I could take it in more readily.

Secret gazed down at me. The happiness that had been on her face a moment ago was gone. Her feline ears drooped as her small mouth compressed into a thin unreadable line. "You promised." Tears brimmed along the lower lids of her eyes as they narrowed in anger. "That was very stupid. So very stupid."

"Secret. I don't-" I stammered and stopped. How was I supposed to say that I'd never intended to keep that promise? I couldn't... keep her. My eyes closed.

In the dark of my eyelids I heard the rustle of fabric over flesh. They opened to find the small black kitten standing on my chest. Still with drooping ears, she very deliberately laid down between my breasts and closed those yellow eyes.

My head fell back to the tile flooring with a hollow thud. I simply breathed as my fingers found their way to Secret's fur, and the reluctant purr that rippled out from her smoothed the echoing aches in my chest.

I needed to get up before someone found me in the hallway but I couldn't muster the will to move. My muscles felt full of sand. Yet, heavy footsteps were coming from the kitchen. Breathing I could do. Breathing felt good.

Two sharp finger snaps sounded as I neared the ledge of slumber. I managed a groan as my phone launched in the karaoke version of the Addams Family theme. Oh, fuck. Victoria. The goth queen of Portland had decided now would be a good time to talk.

6

Secret glared at me through half open lids as I shimmied myself along the floor so I could grab the phone. It sported a new crack from corner to corner. Cursing internally, I dragged my thumb across the green answer button.

"Abigail!" The voice that flooded out of the phone was so loud that the cat on my chest flinched, and I double checked to see if the speaker mode was on. It wasn't. "Are you having a heart attack?" she demanded as I dialed down the volume to a point that her voice wouldn't puncture my eardrums.

"No." My raspy voice sounded far less certain than I would have liked.

"Then what? Did you get stabbed? Are you in an ambulance!? Damnit, Abby, it felt like somebody was strangling me from INSIDE my ribcage!" She nearly shouted at me.

Cradling Secret, I sat up and braced my back against the wall. The movement drew pain across my heart like a bow across a string. I hissed through my teeth, Victoria made a similar sound.

"What did you just do?" She demanded.

"I sat up. It's fine Victoria. I'm going to be fine. We're

going to be fine." Risking a deep breath, I probed the pain. Definitely fading. Secret snuggled aggressively against my chest. Safe. Angry but safe. That somehow made it better.

"Bloody fucking ashes, Abigail! Tell me what the hell happened! What hurts you, hurts me. It's not fake. I have the right to know if you're in trouble," Victoria seethed.

"I'm always in trouble, Victoria. It's kinda what I do, remember? I gave you a blood transfusion. It's not special." Hot sticky resentment crawled up my neck. What I had told no one other than Cindy about the Twilight run was that it had been Victoria herself who had made everything so much worse. It had been her that had woken up the dang double-barreled mosquito that was stalking around the nightlife. A psychic connection did not give her the excuse to worm her way into my life like some sort of long lost sister.

Not that she'd take the hint. She launched into professional mode instead. "We had a blood transfusion in the twilight realm. At the nexus of life and death. It's different there. Our life energies are entangled. We share one part of our souls. Tell me what happened." Victoria's voice transitioned to wheedling exasperation.

"Whatever," I grunted. I did not want to share a soul with this woman. "It's over. Nothing you can do. It made its point," I looked down at Secret, purring contentedly on my arm, although her claws were extended and pricking through the sleeve of my jacket. Like Victoria, she'd entangled me in even more of this... Magic BS. As if sensing my gaze, she gave a yawn. The curl of her tiny pink tongue pulled on my aching heartstrings and I held her a little tighter. Unlike Victoria, Secret's cute kept deflecting my anger. Victoria wasn't cute; every time I thought of her, she was pale as death or attempting to strangle me as a code Z.

"What made it's point?" Victoria asked after a pause. "What have you found?"

I very nearly snarled. "Why don't you leave me alone and do something useful like hunt down that vampire you woke up."

"He made a rather pointed argument against me talking to him." Victoria's voice gained a hysterical edge.

"I don't want you to talk to him. I want you to clean up your mess and stake him. We're seeing a definite uptick of sudden anemia among young women downtown." I hung up. Let her chew on that. Victoria had confessed that she'd woken up an ancient Vampire with the blood of three hundred virgins. Seeing a chandelier full of empty blood bags, instead of 300 nubile virgins offering themselves, he'd gotten a mite offended and stabbed Vicky through the stomach.

Usually I didn't believe it entirely. Now, though, with a cat that was sometimes a girl in my arms, and pain in my chest from an attempt to break a promise, I did. My tank of disbelief about it had gone totally empty.

"I have a lot of questions for you." I told the cat. "Think you could change back for me?"

One ear flicked in response as she tightened her grip on my arm, remaining stubbornly asleep.

"I mean it. I have no idea what your guardian meant by bringing you to the Queen." I said.

If anything, Secret slept harder.

Sighing, I couldn't quite muster the willpower to peel her out of my arms. Instead I braced against the wall and pushed myself to my feet. If she would not talk, then I needed to go help Cindy with the sterilization and restocking of the ambulance. I'd put her down for that.

Back in the bay, Cindy had unloaded everything from

the ambulance: equipment and disposables, and organized it all in two rows, one for each side of the bus. They stretched about twenty feet from the yawning double doors. In her hands she held a hose with a sprayer attachment. I wrinkled my nose preemptively; the disinfectant always made my nostrils burn. A stink far worse than even Cindy's nail polish. She hadn't started spraying though; next to her stood Cliff jawing away.

"... telling ya Colin, you gotta go see They Live Under. Ya know it's gunna be a classic. Nailed the entire situation. Gunna be just like that." Cliff prattled as Cindy shook her head.

She'd donned a full bunny suit along with the respirator with big purple filters that jutted from the sides. Always called to mind the poison mushrooms from one of Dad's video games. The disinfectant we used could burn skin if you touched it. "Cliff, code Z's nothing like that. We just strap them down, or if that don't work," she nodded towards the rows of supplies, "We got the deanimator. They don't pull themselves back together."

I snorted, "Can we go one night without talking about the zombie apocalypse?"

Cliff turned his headlamp-bright smile on me. "Well that's the thing! It's gotta be a top secret government project. Nanobots that the hospital puts in ya. The dead will be a secret army when the Chinese invade, but sometimes they wake up early." Cliff's eyes shone with enthusiastic mania. I could never tell if he believed his latest theory or not. His grin tightened as he read my unamused expression. "Aw, come on, Abby, what's more likely, nanites," he held up a finger and shook it, "which ARE possible. Or maaaaagic." His hand turned to sprinkle invisible pixie dust.

"Magic," Cindy said definitely through her mask and

turned on her spray. Instantly the biting scent of chlorine and worse drove both me and Cliff back. Secret leapt from my arms with a surprised yowl, becoming a black streak in my vision as she dove beneath Big Red's chassis.

"What the hell was that?" Cliff asked as he pinched his nose, looking between me and Big Red. "That thing blended right in with your jacket."

"New station cat," I managed to say between coughs while Cindy advanced into the ambulance.

Cliff's eyebrows rose. "Oh? You clear it with Dad? He don't like cats. Much safer springing dogs on him. My sisters were always trying to smuggle kittens into the house. He never budged."

"When does he ever budge?" I asked as we ambled towards Big Red, both bending down to peer beneath it. Secret hid behind one of the tires, I could hear the occasional tiny snnt! of feline sneezes. Big Red had a lot of tires.

"The sergeant," Cliff's voice gained a sarcastic edge, "budges all the time, so long as you never call him out on it. That's how I got and lost a dog." Cliff's cheer drained a bit. "Worked out for the dog, though," he added forcefully, beaming his grin from the other side of Big Red, head held at an angle that struck me as a crooked crescent moon.

I had a butterfly-light urge to kiss him. Fortunately, he was well out of range, so it was easy to pluck off the urge's wings and cover it with a nervous laugh. He'd never want me anyway. Even if he did, it would end the moment he found out about Jimmy and what he'd tattooed on my hand. Swallowing down the bitter rise of memories I said, "Listen, let me find her. She trusts me. Since your Dad's still here, maybe you should actually do some paperwork for once?" I caught the shadow of movement around the last tire on my side.

He laughed deeply, "With him hanging over my shoulder? I think I'll skip that shouting match today."

I opened my mouth to respond but a clatter of a bell punted whatever I had been planning to say out of my brain. Then the buzz of the garage door motor joined in as I stood back up onto my feet and looked towards the rising metal shutter. It revealed a man dressed in red, a sack thrown over one shoulder as he shook a small silver bell back and forth so rapidly that its plasticky tones jumbled up on top of each other. "Merry Christ-mas! Peace and Goo-d will to meeen!" He hollered at us in a strangely choppy accent as he strode inside.

"Hey, man. Could you step back outside, please?" Cliff said, aggressively stepping forward so his bulk would be the first the man would physically encounter. The man continued walking towards us, wobbling as if drunk. "This is private property!" Cliff tried again, his voice a harsh bark, "No Soliciting."

"Did ya not hear me? I come in peace and good will. Despite the fact that you got something here that belongs to meee." He stuck his ruddy red nose into the air and inhaled a long breath through it. The light revealed that he wore the clothes of a salvation army Santa, but one who'd spent the season in an alley strung out on meth. A greasy gray beard cascaded down his front from a head that seemed too big compared to his sticklike limbs, and the bulge of his belly made him look more pregnant than fat. Only his long, red, pointed cap shone. Too red compared to the rest of his clothes, too clean. "Trying to hide her with foul perfumes. But the nose," he tapped said part of his face, "Knoooooows."

Cliff pulled a wrench that had been hanging from a loop on his overalls in a clear threat. "Leave. I won't ask ya again."

"There's nothing here for you." I balled my fists, teeth

gritted as if I were steeling myself to restrain a patient. Something about his man projected menace.

His eyes snapped to mine and brightened, "Ho, ho, ho, how little you know before the fangs grow, puppy girl." He sang off key as my entire body flushed with panic. He knew! How did he know? Spinning around on one leg, he performed a drunken pirouette and continued, "Kings and Queens will own all as the iron-cursed age falls. Black or white, spring or fall, mortals will kneel before us all."

"Take your drunken rantings down to Burnside. Now." Cliff demanded and stopped slouching. I had never realized he slouched until that moment. The large teddy bear of a man suddenly became an angry wall.

"Ha ha ha," the evil Santa stopped his spinning to size up Cliff. He tossed his bell into his too-wide mouth and simply... swallowed it. "Oh, look a knight appears! Brandishing steel most unkind. I promised peace when I entered this home, so peace will stay. But, let us have one dance before I am on my way."

"Then get going." Cliff thrust the wrench at the Santa who clearly wasn't, more as a prod towards the door than an actual strike. The Santa's body bowed away from the wrench, limbs bending like cheap plastic poles instead of solid bone. His hand clapped around Cliff's wrist like a snap-on bracelet. Pulling hard, he forced Cliff into his thrust and drove his shoulder into the much larger man's chest. Something in my mind screeched as Cliff's red tennis shoes left the ground and his entire body popped into the air. Not merely thrown over the creature's shoulder but tossed upward a solid foot. A silver blur arced across Cliff's stunned face as he reached the apex of his arc. He landed flat on his back with a heavy "oof." A single slash across his cheekbone bled.

The Santa bowed to the stunned Cliff, arm outstretched to the side, a silver blade clutched in his spindly fingers. "Such a lovely dance, sir knight. Another night, another time, we'll dance again and your blood will taste like fine wine."

There, down at my feet, among the medical supplies, sat the post mortem deanimator, otherwise known as a short-barreled shotgun. Loaded with a "less lethal" plastic slug. At the ranges allowable inside in an ambulance it still popped skulls as if they were water balloons. Swallowing, I stepped up to it. "Who are you and what do you want?"

"Hee, hee, hee," he chortled. "You do have manners, I see." He straightened, the blade disappearing in a flourish of his fingers. "Call me little Nick. I'll tell you plain, I seek the halfling pooka who dwells within this domain. Bring her to me before the sun does set and I will shower you with gems and gold." Opening his hands, revealing gemstones piled in one hand and shiny gold coins in the other. "But force me to hunt you down," snapping his fists closed, he squeezed the riches in his hands, "and we will have so much fun." Red ran between his fingers.

"Why do you want her? What will you do to her?" I asked. The gun was right at my feet. But he was so fast. The gun's safety was keyed to a bracelet on my wrist. It worked the last time I'd needed it. Would it this time? What if I missed?

He shrugged. "Here's the game. Three nights of blood. Three days of fear. Survive them all, and still the Wyld Hunt draws near. There is no way to win, for shame, for shame. But that's the way I play ball." His mouth opened, and he stuck out his tongue. The bell lay on it.

Taking it in his hand he rang out the bell's clattering sound. "Peace and goo-d will to men!" He hollered out as he pivoted on his heel and started marching out of the garage. "It won't last! But I grant you Peace and Goodwill as the morning comes to light!" He sang as the door closed behind him.

What the hell was I supposed to do now?

7

The immediate answer, staring at the garage door that had betrayed us, allowing that horrible thing that pretended to be a man into our lives.

Insistent meows broke the spell. Still, fear slowed me. Secret made it halfway up my pant leg before I plucked her off and hugged her to my chest. A little cowardly voice inside of me shouted that holding onto Secret as she trembled was the absolute wrong thing to do. I hit that little voice with the biggest mental hammer I could imagine.

Cliff moaned, "Da fuck. The fuck was that?!" He pulled himself up to a sitting position, rubbing the back of his head.

"Sorry." Cindy offered, "I, uh, should have sprayed him. Yeah. I should have done that." She stood right in front of the ambulance, with her hand holding on to the sprayer so tightly that her nitrile gloves had split along the knuckles.

"Dude, that old coot laid me out like I was nothing." Cliff dabbed his fingers at his cheek and grimaced at the blood on his fingertips. "No offense, Colin, but unless you got acid in that thing, I don't think spraying him would have helped a damn."

"It's pretty close to acid." Cindy muttered.

"Cind-," I started and her eyes widened, snapping towards Cliff, "Colin," I quickly corrected, "it's okay. He's gone."

Cliff still wrinkled his nose at the sight of his own blood. Maybe he hadn't noticed my slip. "Hey, Cliff," I said, louder than intended, "Let me get that bandaged," grabbing a medkit, eager for something I could fix. Obligingly, Secret climbed up from my arms and onto my shoulder, freeing up my hands.

Cliff stared at the cat as I approached him. "That her then? That's the pooka whatever?"

"It's a type of fairy," Cindy said as I knelt to look at the wound. Little Nick had cut through the skin and into the cheek muscle. I slathered it with disinfectant and taped a bandage over Cliff's cheek. "You better go to the hospital and get this stitched."

He grimaced, "Can't you just do it?"

"I'm not a doctor." I said firmly.

"If I go in now, I'll be waiting till sunup and they'll charge me a grand for five minutes of work." He said.

"You have insurance, Cliff," I countered.

"Yeah, it's the same as yours." He flashed me that grin of his, although with a trace of a wince. Grumbling under my breath, I went and got a box of sutures, along with a bit of local anesthetic.

"I didn't do this," I told him as I laid out a sterile cloth and a few tools.

"Course not. It was the stitching fairy. And if it's really ugly, I'll blame Colin," he said.

"Could you stitch his mouth closed while you're at it?"

Cindy countered without venom, her voice flat and tired as she went down the rows of supplies with the clipboard. I felt a pang of guilt, as I should have been helping her, but I was occupied with Cliff. Secret settled down on my shoulder and watched as I pulled the bandage off. The gauze was saturated with red already. I frowned at the cheek; it bled like a scalp wound.

"So, you two going to tell me the story of how you got a magic cat?" Cliff asked.

"Murf," Secret objected.

"As long as you stop talking so I can work," I told him.

He complied. Cindy and I filled him in on the events of the call. Cindy related the weird sensation of forgetting about the girl Secret when she saw the cat version. We left out the part where she had Jedi mind-screwed Cliff's dad and I didn't volunteer what happened when I tried to call child protection services.

"Okay so she's a pooka. That's a type of fairy. So is Little Nick also a fairy?" I asked after we had finished the tale. Cliff's brows furrowed, but I had a few stitches to go.

"Don't say his name!" Cindy scolded. "He might hear it." She paused, sitting down on the bumper of the bus. "But probably, he noted that Cliff's wrench was steel, so he might not like iron."

"So all we need to do is put Secret in an iron cage and he can't get her." I mused.

"HISSSSSSS!" Secret sank her claws into my skin.

"Ow! I was kidding! Mostly." I winced.

"Murf." she said, withdrawing her claws.

"If she's a pooka, I doubt being in an iron cage would be healthy," Cindy said.

"Done," I announced as I trimmed off the last thread of the stitches.

"You two are insane." Cliff turned away. I caught his hand as it rose to touch the wound.

"Hey, no touching! Let me get another bandage," I scolded. Blood still seeped from the wound at a worrying rate. Granted, he had two dozen puncture wounds to go with the slash, but the blood flow should have slowed more by now. I could super glue it, but the rate of seepage would muck with the bond. "And everything we said is true."

"That's not the insane part! You two had what had to be a magic sword right there and you left it there for the cops." He tsked, "I'm disappointed with y'all."

Cindy groaned, "This ain't no looter shooter, Cliff. We can't just grab folks' stuff because they died."

He laughed, "Magic, fairies, goddamn. Dad's gonna lose his shit. What you gonna do? Go to the cops? They know about the zombies, right?"

"Oh, yeah, that will work. I'm being stalked by an evil Santa Claus and need protective custody." I remembered the befuddled expressions on the cops at the scene where we'd found Secret. They weren't going to be of any help even if I could trust them.

"Then what are we gonna do?" Cliff asked. "We got till sundown, right?"

"I'll figure something out. He knows about this place. I've got a few people I can ask for help." I swallowed the bitter taste of having to take Victoria up on her offer of help. If she couldn't do anything, then my Aunt, "Brimstone" Betty would always be on board for a last stand against the forces of darkness. Wasn't sure what she'd make of Secret though, exorcisms were never fun.

"Did you not hear the 'we' in my last sentence?" Cliff crossed his arms. "He got the drop on me tonight, but he only gets that once."

"Cliff, it's not safe here. And you've gotta work." I said, "Maybe we can find some sort of holy ground."

My hands free, Secret jumped down into my arms. I held her up beneath her armpits and she stared back at me with her soulful yellow eyes. "I don't suppose you'd like to explain what's going on? Uh?"

She blinked very slowly.

"Go do whatever you do and change back so you can talk." I told her very clearly and slowly before placing her down on the concrete. "If you can't do it where we can see, then go to the kitchen." I gave her a little shove towards the aforementioned room.

Secret turned around and very deliberately jumped onto my leg, climbing me like a tree. I peeled her off and placed her back on the floor. Same result.

"Yep, definitely not a normal cat. No right-thinking cat would like you that much," Cliff said.

"What the hell's that supposed to mean?" I glared at him as I grabbed Secret by the scruff of her fuzzy little neck.

"MRRROWWW!" The kitten protested and my will to put her down collapsed. With a sigh, I offer her my jacket pocket, which she crawled into. She started purring immediately.

Cliff shrugged. "You just strike me as a dog person somehow."

I shook my head, not sure where he got the idea that I'm a dog person. I grew up with cats, but that fact didn't help against the evil Santa. "We get off at six. I'll take her home with me I guess, and try to figure out a plan. Maybe he's all bluff. If he was the one that sent those monsters after the knight, why didn't he snatch Secret before we got there?"

"I dunno. Let's see what sort of cold iron I can find. I'll

talk to Dad about it." Cliff pursed his lips and slowly, reluc-
tantly, turned and started walking towards the office.

Cindy sighed beside me. "If you need anything, it's
yours, Abby. All I got is a house, a semi-decent gaming PC,
and a bunch of clothing that won't fit you. But if it's guns
blazing," she swallowed, "something about that... Evil Santa;
I couldn't even move, Abby."

"I made the promise, so it's not your fight. I'll figure
something out. Let's just get this shift done," I said with a
sigh. Victoria really was my only hope on this.

Cindy shook her head, "If the rapture happened, you'd
tell the angel, 'let me finish this shift first.'"

I laughed nervously, "Screw that, I wouldn't go. I'm no
nun."

"Just a workaholic." She grinned, and I winced. Since
Mr. Gifford announced the reorg, I'd slept at home twice. I
really needed to do laundry. Mercifully, she switched the
topic from my unhealthy work habits. "I do have one idea
that could help, since he tracks by scent. But let's get
closer to shift end before we do something about it." She
looked down at my bulging pocket and held a finger to her
lips.

I got her idea immediately, "You're kinda cruel,"
managing not to chuckle.

"Tell me it's not a good idea."

It made sense and if we could throw Little Nick off the
trail, then I could simply hide out. He probably had to keep
a low profile.

We passed the shift, doing paperwork, napping, eating. I
had to change Cliff's bandage three times, but the bleeding
finally stopped. Secret stayed in my pocket and napped
almost the entire time. She devoured three whole cans of
tuna I'd fetched from the corner store. I feared her little

belly might pop. Afterward, she fell into a very determined snooze.

Mick and his partner were rolling in as Cindy and I commenced the "hide the kitty from the evil Santa's nose" plan. One thing you have access to in the medical industry is some pretty damn good soap. Guaranteed to suck all the oils, moisture and anything else that could possibly emit a scent out of your skin. It will also leave your skin red and flaking, but after being trapped in a box with a diseased fountain of projectile vomit that becomes a feature, not a bug.

Cindy filled the sink with warm water while I refolded some blankets. I've had cats who could detect a flea bath being drawn through three solid walls. Secret realized that something was up but merely popped her head out of the pocket to sniff at the air. Feeling a little guilty, I stroked her head. "So I just want you to know, what I'm about to do is all about protecting you and not motivated at all by a petty urge for revenge. After all, it's probably not your fault for endangering the lives of all my coworkers."

"Me-uw?" she asked as I quickly power-walked towards the kitchen.

She attempted to bail as I walked through the doorway, but I held the pocket tight around her shoulder. A yowl of panic split the air as I pulled off the jacket and held her over the bubble-filled sink. "Remember! Keep your eyes closed!" I said.

"Come here, sweetie." Cindy grabbed at her, her hand encased in a thick rubber glove. Secret hissed, spat, and bit at the fingers to no avail as they pried her out of my jacket pocket. She tumbled out and hit the water with a sploosh.

All the fight left her after that. We were able to lather her up and rinse her off without enduring a single attack.

Except for the pitiable look of wide eyed betrayal on her face that occasionally slipped into an ears-back glare that promised vengeance for this indignity. All in all, I'd rate her pretty low on the "difficult to bathe scale", maybe a two or three, with one being Gary, my old orange tom who loved water, and ten being Sassy girl, who was a "toss in the toilet and flush repeatedly" sort of cat. Either way, I made a mental note to clean everything breakable off the counter tops when I got her home.

She started growling when we bundled her into a towel, and continued to protest as I tucked her under my arm and made for my car. My ostensibly white hatchback waited for me right outside the fire house, parked right on the street. A nearly ten-year-old plug-in hybrid hatchback with batteries that I should have replaced three years ago. So long as I filled the tank it got me where I needed to go. If it were a sedan, then trunking Secret would have been an option, and since the growling bundle was too large for the glove box, I took a chance that she was too intelligent to murder me while I was driving, and just plopped her in the passenger seat.

My passenger stayed a growlurrito for about five minutes after I pulled out, halfway home. Then I heard that whisper of fabric unfurling next to me. When my eyes finally obeyed, there was a scowling girl in the seat. "You're the worst protector ever," she sulked. Curiously, while the fur on her ears and tail clung together in wet spikes, her tattered dress and long black hair were completely dry.

"I needed you to answer my questions hours ago. Important things like: can the scent that man is tracking you by be washed off? Without info, we have to experiment," I said. "Understand?"

Crossing her arms she emitted a small, disgruntled

meow before adding, "Meanie. Sometimes I don't wanna change."

"Does that mean sometimes you can't change?" I asked.

Silence answered me. I almost purposely missed the turnoff to my apartment building to give myself and Secret a bit more time to converse. I had a hunch that as soon as I had to deal with more people Secret would be small and furry again. Well, smaller and furrier than in her current form. Also, there was a black hearse parked near the door of my building. Which meant Victoria wasn't waiting for me to ask for help.

Cataloguing all the sarcastic things that would be unwise to say to Victoria, I pulled into the parking spot next to hers. I looked over and nearly had a second heart attack. First, there was a man at the wheel, looking hungrily at me, and second, judging from the way his skin had shriveled around his skull, he was very dead.

8

Secret slipped down into the foot well without a sound. The corpse's jaw moved up and down as it leaned forward. With a pop, the door opened partway and his nearly skeletal fingers wrapped around its top edge. The corpse heaved itself upwards, but only a few inches, a chain link collar around his neck and secured to the head rest stopping him short.

"NO! Bad! Get back in the car, Lenny!" Victoria's voice blasted through my car's mostly nonexistent soundproofing. She stood about ten feet away, by the entrance to my apartment building, thrusting something silver at the animated corpse. Her black leather trench coat parted to show a blood red t-shirt which matched her lipstick. Looking fabulous for someone who had spent three weeks in the hospital getting her guts sewn back together two months ago. The thing she held was one of a half-dozen pendants that hung from her pale neck. I opened my door and stood.

The zombie groaned inarticulately.

"I don't care if you're hungry, Lenny! You're dead; you don't get tips." Victoria's fingers changed their grip on the pendant, thumb in the middle of a small wooden cross. Threatening to snap it. "Back in the car. Don't you make me drive myself home!"

With a moan of annoyance, Lenny sagged back into the hearse's driver seat and shut the door.

"Good boy!" Victoria exclaimed, letting the cross drop back to her chest. "Now stay put!"

"What the hell is this, Vicky!?" I erupted. You'd think that getting stabbed through the stomach by a vampire would have deadened her appetite for the undead. You'd be wrong.

She smiled, showing her perfect teeth, "Hi, Abby. Don't mind my driver, he's new."

"He's got post mortem animation. He's dangerous." I could feel my eyelid twitch. What if somebody cut between our cars?

"Well, I needed to do something, when you got," her eyes scanned me, "injured? I mean, last night I fell over. Fortunately, onto my couch, but what if I had been driving? I could have died or killed someone else. It's unethical to take those sorts of risks until I know the situation. Lucky for us both, Lenny had availability." She shot me a proud smile.

"You could have gotten a self-driving car?" With the house she owned, she definitely had the money for one. Hell, she could have hired a driver since she was apparently precious to Andrew Millar.

Instead, the smile broadened, "Self-driving cars are death traps."

I winced, my jaws clenching so hard that they hurt. My mind growling at Victoria's sheer, no, gleeful, insanity. She had a zombie driver and was proud as hell. She was showing off. And Lenny... Lenny understood her, obeyed commands and complained! I hoped Mrs. Weatherby wasn't home, for her sake.

"You going to invite me up? Or are we going to shout at each other in the parking lot like two mad old biddies?" She adjusted her jacket, pulled out a vape stick and took a drag. Good thing the supposed link between us only went one way. I'd only be half surprised if she was inhaling embalming fluid. The thought of letting her see the state of my apartment made my stomach queasy, but I did not see an alternative.

I looked in the car to see Secret, still human, huddled in the well of the passenger seat. I held out my hand to her. "It's okay."

Secret looked up at me as if pieces of my face were missing.

"Victoria's going to help us. She doesn't have a choice in the matter." I said, keeping my hand outstretched.

"Excuse me?" Victoria protested, but I ignored her, beckoning Secret with my fingertips. Slowly, Secret unfolded herself and crawled forward to take my hand. Once outside she immediately cowered behind my legs, peering at Victoria, her feline ears back, the wet fur on her tail attempting to puff up. Victoria cocked her head curiously and blew out twin plumes of smoke through her nostrils. "Well, what do we have here?" she whispered to herself.

"We'll do introductions inside," I said, With Secret out in the daylight, it suddenly felt as if the trees themselves were staring at my back.

Secret kept me between her and Victoria, hissing when the necromancer got within two feet. We took the stairs, and Victoria took the elevator to the third floor. My cheeks started burning as I fumbled for my keys. "Apologies for the mess." I mumbled. "I was uh, burglarized recently." Sure, she'd buy that. Squeezing my eyes shut and grimacing, I opened the door.

A surprised "Oh!" escaped Victoria while Secret sniffed hard.

I had not progressed on the repairs. The couple days I hadn't spent at the firehouse, had been spent on a Hallmark Channel Christmas marathon. Turning, I found Victoria's eyes as round as golf balls as her gaze ping-ponged over both the damage and my hasty repairs. Secret stepped in, her wrinkled nose leading her. "Smells like... Dog. Do you have a dog?" She pronounced it as if owning a dog were a mortal sin.

That made me laugh a little. "No dogs here," I said, "There's one downstairs." All the ruinous state of my apartment, and she focused in on the scent of a dog that she could probably beat up in her cat form. It made me feel a little better.

Victoria sniffed experimentally, "Does it visit? There's a bit of a funk."

I shrugged; it just smelled like home to me. "Come on in, the couch should hold together as long as you don't jump on it. I'll make coffee; I assume you like it emo black."

"Ha." Victoria smiled tightly as she stepped inside, still looking at the room as if the furniture might leap out and shiv her. "Actually, milk and sugar, if you don't mind."

I closed the door behind her, its back side bearing a mass of parallel scratches as if something huge had been digging to get out. That hadn't been it, though. I only remembered striking out in sheer frustration. Bottling the image of claws carving up ribbons of wood, I marched myself to the kitchen and started coffee, Secret close on my tail. She peeled off to inspect the fridge, which I use as a very poor filing system. Bills and paperwork I had to fill out hung there until I got sick of being visually nagged and took care of it. Secret focused her attention on the one photograph that sat in the dead center of the door. A freshly printed photo of myself and my parents, all smiling in Sunday clothing, way back in high school, before I'd met Jimmy. I expected her to ask me about it when she looked my way, but she drifted to my cabinets, opening and closing drawers.

"Why are you still living here?" Victoria finally asked. "When did it happen?"

I sighed, debating if I wanted to tell her the truth but decided against it. Maybe Vicky herself would be cool but if she mentioned it to someone like Andrew Millar, then I could find myself in a cage under a mountain, or at least the hospital basement. "Rent's cheap." Which was true. "So, you know anything about fairies, Vicky?"

Victoria stared at me long enough to let me know that my changing the subject hadn't been subtle, but she was going along with it anyway. "I know enough about fairies that if I ever stumble onto a circle of mushrooms in the forest, I'm turning right around and going back the way I came." Her eyes drifted to Secret who was still peeking in my cabinets, although she had my can opener in hand now. "So the girl's a fairy, is that what you're telling me?"

"Yes." And I told her the story while the coffee brewed, including the bit with the phone-induced heart attack. I finished as I passed her a mug of coffee.

She hadn't said a word during the story, and now took a deep swallow of the caffeine-laced liquid as we sat on opposite ends of the couch. Holding my Red Cross mug with both hands, she stared at one of the holes in the wall. "You realize you're an idiot, right?"

My hackles went up. "Comfort is part of the job some-times! That means you lie occasionally."

"Oh come off it, Abby!" Victoria glared sourly at me. "You pulled me out of the land of the dead! Did it not occur to you that maybe other things are also coming back? You saw her insides! You knew she wasn't human! You have to be careful!"

"It was a dying request!" I protested. "I didn't swear an oath or sign a contract. All I said was yes. That's it! That shouldn't be enough to do... whatever..."

"Geas. She laid a geas on you. A magical binding." She shook her head and blew out her nose as if she were blowing out smoke. "The world is changing, Abby! Words are not simply vibrations of molecules against our eardrums anymore. Promises have power again and breaking them has conse-quences. At least those made to beings from the nether realms." She smiled, not a fake one at all, black-rimmed eyes sparkling. To her this was clearly an improvement in the world.

A small black cat jumped into my lap and nudged my hand with her nose. The bitter words that had been coating my tongue fell away as I stroked her still-damp fur. "Okay, fine. It was ill-advised, but what are we going to do about it? Do you know spells or something that could keep that Santa away?"

She pursed her thin red lips. "We can try the basics, circle of salt, put out a saucer of milk, look up some glyphs against evil."

"Vicky, You have a zombie driving you around!" I nearly shouted. "You have to know more than that!"

She laughed sharply. "I've got, call it a talent, which sorts out what bits of rituals used to work, and what got added as things stopped working. The dead want only one thing:

life... A few drops of blood and they'll do what you want. But fairies? Who knows what they want? I'm about as eager to try summoning them as I am an actual demon."

"Do they exist?" I asked, and then suddenly wondered if I actually wanted to know.

A smirk. "I don't know. I've been out of bed for a month. Necromancy is keeping me plenty busy before I go poking at evil incarnate." She adjusted herself to face me fully. "Looking at the texts, it seems that magic or whatever you want to call it went away slowly, starting over a thousand years ago. Calling stuff got harder and harder, until the door shut entirely sometime in the latter half of the eighteen-hundreds. Since the naughts it's been opening back up, but it's opening much faster than it closed. And no, I don't know why."

"That presence that pulled us into the Twilight said it was your fault the barriers were weakened. Wanted you punished for it," I reminded her.

She threw up her hands. "It shouldn't have weakened anything. I'd love to ask him, but he wasn't the talkative type." With a huff, she crossed her arms. "You'd think he'd be grateful."

This was interesting and all, but I didn't have the time to hunt down a vampire, although maybe he would have an actual clue. "So what do we do about the Santa?"

"I don't know... Yet. Hopefully, we have another night to figure it out." She stood. "I'm going to go get some supplies and do research. I'll be back here before nightfall. We'll use everything we can think of, and hopefully find something that works. He already admitted to being afraid of iron. So that's a start."

"So I'll just wait here?" I asked, not hiding my disappointment.

"That's probably best. This "Santa" promised not to come until nightfall but that doesn't mean he's not out there prowling around." She frowned suddenly, "Speaking of, maybe I should shower before I leave? No, that won't work. It's probably in my clothes at this point. Ah well."

My hand tightened on Secret's fur, "What do you mean, 'in your clothes'?!"

"You said he tracks by scent; this place definitely has a-"

A gunshot rang out. Close enough that my window panes gave a little shiver. I hit the floor.

To my surprise and horror Victoria ran to the window and peered down at the parking lot. "MY CAR!" She shouted.

9

"Woo! Got 'em!" Somebody shouted from below. "You get that, Nigel?"

"Fucking bastard ended Lenny!" Victoria bolted for the door, but didn't make it farther than the couch before clapping a hand over her midsection and slowing to a hobble, hissing like a snake in pain. Yet she kept moving, hunched and slowed. I risked a look out of the window. A burly, red-bearded man stood at the driver's side window of the hearse, reaching in through the broken window, the other gripping a pump shotgun. Bile rose. What the hell was a militia boy doing at MY apartment block? He wasn't alone, but the other wasn't wielding a gun, just a camera on one of those fancy steady mounts. Both shared the red-colored hair.

Only two of them. Two of them I could deal with. "Stay here." I deposited Secret firmly on the windowsill and strode out the door past the still-hobbling necromancer.

The pair hadn't left when I strode out the front door. Instead, the big one had grabbed hold of Lenny's wrist, displaying the ex-animated hand to his cameraman. "See! Look at this dusty, flaky crud, this man's been dead for years.

You saw it all. Lying in wait for an innocent bypasser." His smile parted the shaggy hair of his beard. Big in every dimension, open red and black flannel over a white T-shirt that read, Slade the Ghost Hunter, with a QR block stretched over his belly. "Now get this, Nigel," he put the gun down on the ground to pull a bowie knife out of his belt. "First one I've bagged in daylight, so we got plenty of light."

Gun down. I wasn't going to get a better invitation. "Boys!" I barked loud, channeling my Aunt Betty at her most fiery, "What in God's name are you two playing at here!" Both men flinched. Nailed it; they were from the country. "Discharging a weapon! You two got five seconds to explain yourselves before I call the law down on ya." Aunt Betty terrifies me and if a patient's got a slice of the country in them her angry tone never fails to get some compliance.

Slade's knife disappeared and he quickly displayed open hands, "Aaaah."

I focused on the smaller man. They were definitely brothers; where Slade had probably played football in high school, Nigel had a bookish look, a couple days' stubble and gold-rimmed glasses. Might be the glasses, but he looked older. His slash of a mouth broadcast, 'Shit, we're busted.'

"Are you filming me now? Turn that shit off now." I said, putting a fist on my hip and remembered I hadn't even changed out of my uniform.

"Keep filming." Slade said out of the corner of his grimace as if I couldn't hear it, before hitting me with a brilliant country boy grin. "Ma'am! We're here doing a public service! We know it sounds crazy but we're saving you from a plague of the Undead. The government's trying to cover it up but Slade the Zombie hunter is here to expose the truth! This here monster was lying in wait for you in broad daylight."

I crossed my arms. "I do not consent to being filmed." Immediately, Nigel pointed the camera at the ground.

"Nige!" Slade protested, "This could go viral! This is proof."

"Can't use the footage if she doesn't consent, going viral isn't worth getting demonetized over," Nigel said in a tone that sounded as if this was a refrain.

I kept in character as I heard the door swing open behind me, "Zombies? Is that what you're gonna say in Court? Looks like you just killed a man."

Slade brandished the dead limb. "He's been dead a long time. Don't you see? This is a public menace. Why else would a corpse be sitting in a car?"

"Because it's a decoration for my business! Which you just shot up!" Victoria snarled from behind me. "Do you have any idea how expensive that car is? And you just peppered shot all over its interior!" She strode past me, black boots stomping on the sidewalk. One hand pressing firmly on her stomach as if holding the contents in. In her other hand, she held a shiny short-barreled revolver pointed at the ground, but its threat was very clear.

Slade blinked, suddenly uncertain, "We... saw it driving here." Nigel looked about to flee, edging sideways.

"What do you think all those wires are there for? You two owe me a lot of money." Victoria stalked forward. "Give me your contact information, you'll be hearing from my lawyers."

Slade covered the QR code on his belly. "Bullshit, lady. It looked right at me."

Nigel grimaced and stepped between Victoria and his brother. "Look ma'am, maybe this is just a misunderstanding."

"It's real, Nige." Slade protested, "It's not some sort of cheap plastic."

"Well, then." Nigel gave a sly smile. "Then perhaps we both can agree to let things go. We don't get sued and you don't have to deal with questions why you're using human remains as a decoration!" He had a point.

"It's a very high quality fake!" Victoria huffed, "You can't go around shooting up my property! I demand compensation."

"Vicky, we have bigger troubles right now," I whispered at her.

Instead, she raised her gun. Both men raised their hands. "Clear out now!"

"Hey, hey, hey!" Slade protested.

"Live and let live till the count of five," Victoria declared. "One."

"Alright, miss." Nigel backed away, glancing towards a black pickup truck parking in another spot. "We're leaving."

"Let me just get my-" Slade bent for the shotgun on the pavement.

"Leave it!" Victoria pulled back the hammer with a click. "Two!"

"It's my gun, you crazy bitch!" Slade bared his teeth.

"Mine now! Three!" Victoria's hand did not waver.

"Come on, Bro!" Nigel urged.

With a heave of disgust Slade turned and ran for the truck. "You'll regret this, you... zombie lover!" He called back from the cab as he started the engine. Nigel was already in the passenger seat. They roared out of the parking lot. The side of the truck displaying Slade the Ghost Hunter, except ghost had been crossed out with red spray paint and zombie stenciled above it.

As soon as the truck pulled out of sight, Victoria

deflated, her posture hunching with pain as she uttered a quiet curse. "Stupid rednecks."

"Did you reopen your wound?" My medical instincts momentarily overwhelmed my bewilderment at what she'd just done.

"No..." She groaned, "It just really hurts when I move too fast." She sat heavily on the wall of a planter, carefully disengaged the hammer of her gun and clicked the safety on before shoving it into an inner pocket of her trench coat.

"I had it handled. You know," I said. "You didn't need to pull out your little friend. They were going to leave."

She shook her head. "I dated one of their cousins in high school. Trust me. The Higgins family are nothing but bullies, Abigail. Don't bother talking to them. You have to show them you mean business, or they'll walk right over you."

"Higgins," I repeated, that name was familiar. Victoria and I had gone to the same high school. She'd been one of the standard popular girls I'd been vaguely aware of, one grade ahead of me until her parents died in a car crash. There'd been a huge deal about it, flags at half mast, donation drive for Victoria and her sisters. Jimmy and I had been resentful of that; as the bottom of the high school hierarchy, we figured that if our parents died, nobody would notice. Thinking about Jimmy, I remembered seeing the name Roy Higgins on his top ten assholes list.

"Roy Higgins." Victoria pulled out her vape stick and took a drag as if to wash out a sour taste. "Asshole thought I'd be easy because I was a cheerleader." Then she looked up at me and gave a tiny grimace. "Sorry, I bet you like talking about High School even less than I do."

I looked down at the scar on my hand. Seeing the foul tattoo that I had cut off with a knife. "Yeah." I said.

"That's where it all started, you know." She continued, smiling sunnily. "After my parents died, I started hearing the dead. Whispers. Dreams. It was all fascinating. There was one spot in the house, in the kitchen, where I could hear Mom humming to herself if I turned off the lights."

"That's not creepy at all," I said, drifting out towards the hearse.

"Didn't think about it that way. Death suddenly became the most interesting thing about life," Victoria said. "You ever going to tell me what you saw in the Twilight? I mean all of it? We were there for three days."

I stared down at the discarded shotgun. Looking up, I saw Secret standing in my window, a girl again, watching me curiously. Who the hell was she? Why were these creatures after her? And where was this Queen I'd promised to bring her to? I had two days before my next 24-hour shift. Two days to get her there and get my world back to normal. Bending down, I picked up the weapon and pulled out a shell. Standard red and brass. Definitely not a slug. Probably steel. If the Evil Santa didn't like Cliff's wrench, he'd probably dislike this more.

"Fine, don't tell me," Victoria stood up and walked towards the car.

"It wasn't three days," I said with a sigh. "More like a few hours or so. You made Death itself angry. He didn't want you to leave. Wanted you to stay and be punished."

Victoria peered into the car's interior, "What a mess." Dusty fragments of bone lay on every flat surface, shot had cracked all the glass on the opposite side of the car and torn open the driver's headrest, exposing aged yellow foam. The leather was dotted with holes. "You've told me that part before. What did you see?"

The exact sequence of events had grown fuzzy over the

last few months. "You did die. Your heart stopped. Then you attacked us. Total code Z. We tackled you and shocked you back to life." Closing my eyes, I could almost see it again. The smell of rot, the sensation of everything falling apart around me, within me. Each breath hastening the process. Luna's bite started itching.

"And then? How'd we get out?" Victoria pressed.

"We ran, or drove, from a pack of zombie things. A knight nearly got us but we made it to Charon's ferry where I paid one dollar and seventy-five cents in coins to ferry us back to the living. He was amused and warned me that the age of iron was ending. Oh yeah. Almost forgot the other thing I promised him."

I fished around in my pocket and pulled out a small change purse. Shaking out two shiny pennies I gently shouldered Victoria out of the way of the driver side window. Lenny lay there, desiccated and headless, so I placed a coin on each shoulder blade. "Ferry fare for your ride back to wherever you're going this time, Lenny." The corpse made no reply, but a birdsong pierced the silence of the morning. Maybe that was a thank you?

Victoria sighed. "There's no need for that, Lenny only had a few pieces of his original soul, anyway. First one I found that remembered any skills at all. You know how rare that is?"

"No. Because I don't raise zombies," I said.

Victoria's pulled those red lips of hers inside her mouth as she bit something back. "Fine. Help me move Lenny into the back. Then I'll go get some supplies and come back."

10

When I entered my apartment Secret held a knife. Pointed at herself. My longest kitchen knife, stainless steel blade showing a few spots of orange tarnish. She clasped the handle with both hands, the tip of the blade an inch from her body.

"Secret!" I shouted with the universal bark of desperation that my mother used when she caught me sneaking out a window or touching her forbidden jewelry box. Her head swung towards me, slitted eyes wide. As I ran towards her, she turned back to her task, biting her elongated canine teeth down into her lower lip. The tip of the knife drew back in preparation for a thrust. In what had to be the parenting play of the year, I clubbed her little hands with the butt of the loaded shotgun. The knife hit the floor with a hollow thunk and stuck point-down in the threadbare carpet. She yowled like a cat with a stepped-on tail as I flung the gun away and crushed her to my chest.

"Lemme go!" She shrieked and pushed against me with a wave of something that tried to push my eyes off her. I fought it, focusing right on the space between her ears, and holding tight as her body rippled in my grasp. "Lemme go!" She punctuated the plea with a ragged hiss and her nails clawed at my jacket.

"It's okay. It's okay." I said again and again as she fought me. Hissing, scratching and biting at my jacket. Shifting tactics, I grabbed for her arms but she twisted away. Launching herself into a dead run towards the door. I tackled her, pinning her to the floor with my body.

"Mrrroowww!" she roared, bucking up against me. After a few heartbeats of useless thrashing, she went limp and panted. "You're mean, Abby. So mean!"

"If this is about getting a bath, then I think you're overreacting kiddo," I said too loudly, trying to hear myself over the blood thundering through my ears.

"Nooo! You're so stupid!" Secret cried out, her voice overfull with frustration.

Cautiously, I pushed myself up off her. She stayed sullenly put. She allowed me to pull her up into my arms, her limp body her only protest. "Why am I stupid?"

"Should have let me do it," she whispered.

Anger rose as I tasted bile. Whoever had driven her to this brink deserved to be disemboweled, and then fed the contents of their large intestines. "No I shouldn't have. You can survive this." I said, carefully pulling up the cuff of my sleeve. "Look, I know it's hard to see, but I've been there. See?" I twisted my wrist to show her the scars that mangled the skin on its underside. Most were what I had explained to my therapist at the time as guilty bleeding. When I couldn't think about anything other than the people Jimmy had killed, that I had both helped him with and failed to stop him, I cut myself. Focusing on a different pain and silently offering my blood as a salve for their hungry ghosts. The deeper scars were blood in the bathtub attempts. When the guilt mixed with anger and I wanted it to stop. It never worked. Aunt Sheryl always found me first.

Secret reached out and ran her fingers across them. "I don't wanna die." Then added very softly. "But I need to."

"No," I said, filling my voice with stern authority.

"I'm the halfling, Abby. I'm bad luck for everyone. The knight you watched twist away. A week ago, she killed the troll who carried me on his shoulders. I liked him. But he ate the pixies who tried to hide me in their trees. They tricked the goblin that tied me up in his hole into blowing himself up. I fell in the hole after my momma told me to run." She looked up at me. Her eyes only contained a small bit of white in the corners but they were bloodshot with fatigue. "And when I'm delivered to the Queens... They'll make me do bad things."

That was a long trail of bodies. Still, I swallowed and said, "I'm not going to die," with all the practiced confidence that I told my patients they weren't going to die. Usually it was true too. Usually.

She smiled, "That's not a promise you can keep. Can you fight off ten trolls, like the knight?"

I glanced over at the shotgun, "I'm human, Secret. I have weapons they don't."

The mirth quickly faded as she rubbed at her chest. "Momma said humans were dangerous food. If I were extra good, she'd bring home their hearts to share."

My sympathy faded a little bit. I decided I didn't want to know how literal she was being in terms of eating hearts. I pushed her from me and held her at arms' length. "Help me keep you safe. Tell me more about the things chasing you."

"I can't tell you about the Dreamlands." She grimaced in pain and clutched at the front of her dress, "I promised."

"The Dreamlands?" I echoed.

She gave a nod and said nothing more. With a sigh, I let go of her shoulders, understanding now. Damn the fairies and their promises. Secret drifted towards me and slumped against my torso. I held her, the wheels of my mind spinning. My own promise had included a clause to deliver her to The Queen. There had to be another way. Squirming drew my attention from my internal pondering. I found her licking the palms of her hands. Curious, I caught one. Across her palms streaked straight, angry red lines that had blistered; the right palm had several lines of recently healed pink flesh beneath the burns.

"Come on. Let's get these in cold water," I told her.

Instead, I heard the familiar rustle of fabric as I looked towards the sink.

"Merf!" Secret's kitten form zipped under the coach.

Groaning, I put my head to the floor to peer into the dark beneath it. Two little eyes glared at me. "I wasn't going to bathe you."

She hissed in response.

"Although if you hang out under there too long, I might have to. I don't clean under there, you know." I smirked.

"Mew?" She asked and then sneezed.

"Bit dusty?"

"Mrrf." The eyes disappeared, and she reappeared a moment later perched on the back of the sofa. Several small dust bunnies clinging to her black fur. She licked at one and grimaced at the taste.

I had to laugh. "Told you."

"Mrrf." She tossed her little nose into the air and yawned, showing me her needle-like teeth. Had she been oh, at least five times larger, it might have been intimidating instead of adorable. Even then, with her ever so slightly outsized eyes, and the more fluffy than sleek fur, it would be difficult.

"Look, Secret," I said, "Help me out here. Turn back and maybe we can find a way around your promise."

Saying nothing, she bounced down onto the floor, trotted over to my scarred entertainment center, little tail held high.

A knock sounded at the door.

She looked back at me as if asking if I was going to get that. With a groan, I collected both the gun and the knife before answering the door. Trying to keep Secret in my line of sight as I did so. She jumped on top of the lower unit that had held my TV. The entertainment center was three separate units, a low center table flanked by two tall cabinets that once held my dad's bewildering collection of ancient game consoles and games, which now sat in storage. In my care, they had held my aging Xbox, a few knickknacks, and lots of dust.

I cracked open the door to find a smiling and dead Mrs. Weatherby standing in the hallway. "Hello Abby! How are you today?"

"It's..." I stumbled, trying to keep one eye on her and another on Secret as she prepared for a leap up to the top of the taller cabinet; it loomed at least four feet over her little head as her butt wiggled with determination. "You know what? I've been better, Mrs. Weatherby. How are you?" I struggled to keep my face straight as I caught a whiff of a bile-inducing scent.

"Aww, That's too bad, dearie. You have such a stressful job. You should really relax more," she said as Secret scooted back for more runway. "As for me, I'm having the time of my... life." Her face split into a cheeky grin.

I heard a thump and the entertainment center wobbled

as if it had been hit by something heavier than a kitten. Secret scrabbled herself on top of it, tail straight and proud. Sitting back on her haunches, she puffed out her fuzzy chest.

"Great. Do you know how to get down now?" I couldn't help but comment.

"They're so cute at that age," Mrs. Weatherby commented, even though there was no way she could see Secret with the angle I held the door.

"So what have you been up to?" I asked, turning back to her.

"Finishing unfinished business as you do. I had a lovely conversation with our landlord Mr. McRobinson after I strangled him."

"You what?!" My jaw dropped, goddammit. Dr. Wiggins had been right.

She didn't bat an eye, "Oh trust me dear, it was his time. You'd understand if you ever were short on the rent. Never mind, though. I was wondering if I could bother you for the ferry fare. I'm afraid I don't have anyone left to pay it."

I blinked, mind spinning even as I groped for my little change purse. "Don't you go to church?" She held out her hand and I dropped two shiny pennies into her palm.

"I'd rather take a ride with Charon than go looking for pearly gates," she laughed, and pocketed the coins. "Thank you, dearie. Oh! And your mother told me to tell you to look in the bottom of your cupboard. She's sorry for not getting around to teaching you how to use it."

The change purse tumbled from my hand. My mind, bruised from the emotional whiplash from Mrs. Weatherby going from admitting murder to talking to my ten-years-murdered mother, stuttered to a standstill.

"You take care now, Abby. I have an appointment to visit

the bastard who raped me in high school. He's in memory care, but I bet I can jog his memory. Ta-ta!" With that, she turned and walked down the hallway faster than I'd ever seen her move in life.

I slammed the door closed and twisted the bolt closed.

"Murf?" Secret asked, peering at me from her perch.

"My mother told her?" I mumbled, stumbling towards the kitchen as if I were suddenly the building's resident doddering granny. Most of my parents' possessions lived in a massive storage unit outside of town. The rent for it rivaled some apartments I'd lived in. But I'd brought one thing from each of my parents here. The entertainment center had been dad's, and mom's I had buried in the kitchen. I had to excavate most of the stainless steel set Aunt Sheryl had gifted me to get to it, but there it was. Waiting for me. Mom's cast iron wok.

Guilt flared as I brought it into the light and saw the spots of rust dotting its once-smooth inner surface. Mom never spoke a word of Chinese to me, and actively discouraged me from asking my grandma about life before she met grandpa. But mom cooked with this iron monstrosity almost every day. A foot wide, with a threadbare red potholder wrapped around the handle with yellowed string. Secret, who had crept onto the counter, hissed at it as I tested its weight. Mother had rarely let me touch it. I still remember the sting of my slapped hands when I once attempted to fit it into the dishwasher. I made attempts to cook with it a couple of times under her supervision, but she shoved me out of the way each time, and finished the meal herself. I hated that. I hated this wok. I decided I didn't need it.

And yet it was the one thing I had grabbed from the storage unit. Mom in all her frustrating contradictions. I laughed; even the message was mom. Instead of saying I love you or maybe forgiving me for dating the child who murdered her, she sent, hey you should use my pan to clock this murderous gnome. That felt very her.

Brandishing the wok like a baseball bat I smiled at Secret. "What do you think? Our Santa friend might be a little wary of this?" I swung it experimentally and felt a twinge in my wrist.

Secret dove off the counter and retreated to the couch, where she peeked over the top at me with a concerned expression.

"I'll take that as a yes." I put the wok on the stove and shook out my wrist. How the heck did mom toss that thing around like it was nothing? The handle was a short hollow round of cast iron. Could I mount it on a longer handle? Or would it be better to hang it over the door?

Setting it down, I sniffed at myself. Definitely time to shower. Ignoring the wok for the moment, I went into my post-work routine. The hot shower felt heavenly; the world always seemed to settle a little as I breathed in steam. No matter how hard the shift, scrubbing myself helped me walk away from it. Today I exfoliated until my skin screamed for mercy. Little yellow eyes greeted me as I pulled back the curtain. Secret sat on the seat of my toilet. Cats...

I dressed in my civvies, skinny jeans, t-shirt and an ancient Red Cross hoodie, and fell onto the couch with a bowl of Cheerios and my phone. Phone balanced on the arm rest, I started looking up how to defend myself from fairies.

As I did so, it launched into Snap, Snap, they're creepy and they're kooky... Victoria had come back.

11

Victoria looked like she'd looted a greenhouse. Before I even had the door open all the way, she shoved a plastic pot holding a small tree into my hands. Strapped to her back she had a heavy duty backpack that was bursting with green from every pocket. Her black, red, and pale all over look was marred by the brown leather gardening gloves she pulled off as she entered the apartment. With a heavy sigh, she shrugged out of the backpack, leaned it against my entertainment center, and flopped down on my couch, which creaked in a threatening manner.

"Well, hello to you, too," I said, putting down the tree and closing the door.

She held up a finger tipped with a long shiny black nail, "Sorry, but I need a moment." Leaning back into the cushions, she closed her eyes and breathed.

I gave her a moment while I studied the tree. It had fernlike leaves and a few clusters of bright red berries. A rowan tree. She actually went and got one. Although the internet had said to plant it; I hoped she brought a shovel.

Victoria slowly drew herself into a lotus position and spent several minutes meditating; all that was missing were the Oooohms. Secret returned to the top of the entertainment center to stare at our guest, although this time she climbed up the shelving. "Okay!" Victoria animated suddenly. "Sorry. I went to a witch friend of mine for advice, but her energy is totally perpendicular to mine. I have to do a serious recentering of myself after any encounter with her."

"Perpendicular energy?" I probed.

Her eyes rolled, "She talks. A lot." Victoria took a breath, "A conversation with her is like laying down on the tracks and feeling every car run you over. Then you have a split second to switch the course of the conversation before you get hit by another train." She smiled, clearly proud of the metaphor she'd spun.

"Second question. Witch? Like a real one?" I asked.

Victoria shrugged. "She owns a shop and knows her lore. Sells crystals, herbs, and various MLM health remedies. Told her to give me everything that might ward off an angry fairy." She unzipped the top of her backpack and pulled out several hardcover books with bits of paper struck among their pages. "Got some recipes for herbal incense, and I hope you like licorice in your tea."

My disbelief must have been showing on my face because she smirked, "Something you want to say to me, Abigail?"

"Vicky, you're an actual, real, necromancer, and the best you can do is go down to the local new age shop and ask for anti-fairy woo?" I shook my head. "Don't you have ancient tomes to consult with or something? Anything more authoritative than Wiccan Instagram influencers?"

She sighed, "Yes, I have a few dozen rare occult books in my library. You know that talent I told you about? It doesn't work for fairy stuff. Some of those books probably have scraps of the truth scattered through them. And guess what they don't have? Indexes. Other than we know they don't like iron, we have zero idea about what works and what doesn't. I'd rather pull 40 things from the collective occult culture than five things from my books." Victoria said. "So let's get started." She reached into her bag and pulled out a horseshoe the size of my head. "First thing, hang this over the door."

I picked up the horseshoe, felt its heft in my hand. It was either this or shoving Secret in the car and driving away. But can you run from a creature like Little Nick, though? No matter how far we'd flee, he'd show up the moment the sun dipped over the horizon, ringing that perverted bell of his.

We set to work. I hung the horseshoe up over the door. Victoria had arranged a list of defense projects, first by the ones that included iron, and then by the ones that weren't likely to kill us, and then by ease. I placed an iron nail by each windowsill; poured salt along the walls; disabled my smoke alarm as we lit bundles of choking incense; carved a dozen protective symbols into the walls; tossed herbs and sprinkled holy water in the four cardinal directions, invoking the winds, the elements, and finally the archangels to protect us from evil. Secret watched us with professional feline skepticism. If any of the spells we attempted affected her, she gave no sign. She only reacted when one of us held iron. If it were me, she'd tense and puff. When Victoria held her ancient cold iron crowbar, Secret would hide.

As sundown reached us, I sipped a bitter tea supposed to fortify against evil spirits. Secret quietly slipped into my lap.

The iron wok sat on the coffee table within arm's reach, and the shotgun sat beside me. Victoria paced, holding her crowbar, and a four-foot length of iron that she shouldn't be swinging with her stomach injury, rested beside the door.

My ears strained, but no clatter of Little Nick's bell came out from the growing darkness. A minute passed, then two. I let myself relax and stroked Secret's fur. She let out a calming purr.

Victoria slowly settled on the other side of the couch. "Don't say anything," she whispered.

I nodded. We sat there, the room getting darker as the skyline went from blue to purple to the black of night. Finally, I allowed myself a breath and stood, planning to go to the bathroom. No sooner had I stood than my phone rang with a muffled weedoo weedoo. Mister Gifford's personal line and yes, almost everyone in my phone has a personalized ringtone. I hoped he was simply going to ask if I wanted more overtime, and was calling me in.

Victoria arched a sculpted eyebrow.

"Boss." My heart dived for my intestines as I flicked the green button and held the phone to my ear. "Hello?"

A mad, shrill cackle answered. "Merry Christ-mas! Peace and Goo-d will is over!"

Dread conquered my neck and rushed over my scalp, making every follicle prickle. How did he have Mister Gifford's phone? I tried to say something but my words had dried up.

"Kitten got your tongue puppy girl?" Little Nick taunted. "Bad girl you are. Forcing Little Nick to ask for directions."

"What did you do?" My voice didn't sound like mine, full of gravel and threat.

"Would you like to say hi to the nice man who told me of the hole you hide in?" A sound followed, a soggy rip.

"Abby," a hoarse whisper dripped from the phone. Mister Gifford's voice, "Stay away. Call..."

Little Nick's resumed, "Hee, hee, hee! He's bleeding again and my cap is already so bright tonight. Pretty he will be, pretty, pretty when they see."

"You monster. Leave him alone!" I was already moving towards the door. Victoria stood and blocked my way, shaking her head. I wheeled away from her and nearly shouted into the phone. "He has nothing to do with this."

"Ho, ho, ho! If only that was so!" He chortled, "Everyone who knows your name is fair game."

Victoria had her own phone to her ear, "I need to report an emergency. There's a maniac with a knife at the Hillsdale firehouse." She whispered into it, then to me she mouthed, "Keep him on the phone."

I swallowed, "This is between you and me. No one else."

"If you give me the girl, it can be," he allowed.

"I can't do that. I've promised to keep her safe. You are not safe," I said.

"I will swear oaths three that not a hair of harm will come to her while she is with me," he said.

"And then what? Who would you give her to and what happens then?"

A pause, another manic giggle. "Hee, hee, hee! Did you sic the cops on me?"

That had been awfully fast. Maybe somebody in the building had hit an alarm? I tried to keep his attention. "Little Nick, if..." Something around my heart gave a warning squeeze. "If I gave her up, I'd have to know precisely what would happen to her."

Secret gave a long piteous yowl of protest from her perch on the couch. I muted my mic. "I'm just stalling for time.

That's all." I pleaded at her hunched misery. She jumped behind the couch.

"The time for talk is done. Will you run? Will you fight? Or will you give me the girl and live another night?" The line died.

"Shit!" I swore. "I think he killed my boss!" I looked up at Vicky who still stood in the way of the door, cupping her hand over her mouth and phone. My mind reached for who else would be on duty now. "And he's on his way here!"

She hung up. "Good. We've got defenses here. Let him come. Then we'll call the cops on him. A hail of gunfire ought to give him a pause or two." She grinned uneasily. "Might be better than my backup plan."

"What's your backup plan?" I asked, suddenly worried even more.

"He'd said he'd be after you for three nights, right. Let's save some surprises for night two." She paused before adding, "Too bad the full moon's weeks away."

An inarticulate grumble of frustration rolled out of my throat. I turned away from her and caught the glimmer of eyes beneath the couch. With a huff I laid down to get a better view as Secret retreated deeper into its depths. "Secret, I was trying to keep him talking, I'm never going to give you to him." I reached out to the shadowy lump that was vaguely kitten sized. It hissed and moved farther back.

"Secret..." I pleaded, "There must be a way for you to tell us more, indicate which of this stuff might work."

Again she backed away towards the end of the couch. The light shifted there and a pale hand shot in from the nearest edge and seized Secret by the scruff of her neck. She yowled as Victoria dragged her out into the light. "Gotcha!"

"Careful!" I exclaimed as I shot up, not entirely sure who was in more danger, Victoria or Secret. The world wobbled from the speed of my standing. Victoria stood up much slower, holding Secret out at arm's length, who hissed and kicked at her with all four limbs with such ferocity that the air probably felt pain. Victoria stared hard at Secret and with a precise motion flicked the cat's nose hard with a fingernail.

"Mew!" Secret squeaked at the impact, clapping her paws over her nose.

"Vicky!" I shouted, horrified. "She's a kid!"

Victoria held a hand up, "She looks like a kid but how old is she, really. We're having a chat." Secret had stopped struggling and watched her captor with wide, terrified eyes. Victoria raised her so their eyes were level. "You might have Abby wrapped around your little paws, but not me. Stop playing cute and cuddly. Somebody just died for you. Turn back and start talking."

A possessive growl rolled up my throat as I snatched Secret from Victoria's hand. She turned her eyes on me, cold and angry. "That wasn't necessary," I scolded, cradling Secret to my chest, she trembled in my arms.

"She's not human, Abby. Remember she's the same thing as what's chasing her. She's entrapped you and me in this. Don't forget that," Victoria said, gaze shifting to Secret. "Now are you going to help, or is Little Nick going to take you?"

A pulse, that rippling sound, and Victoria averted her eyes. My hands rested on small shoulders. "You're a meanie and you hurt my nose." Secret's voice was a layered cake of sulk. "And I'm eight years old."

Victoria's lips stretched into a patronizing smirk. "Yes, I am mean sometimes, because I'd like to live. Start talking."

"I already tried to save you both. Abby wouldn't let me," Secret said sourly.

Kneeling down to Secret's level I ignored Victoria's incredulous look. "I know you promised not to tell us, but we need your help. Anything you can do. Could you nod your head yes or no if Victoria asks you a question?"

"That's still telling, Abby," she said. "But maybe... Maybe I can point."

12

Little Nick knew he should be running in the direction the little magic window pointed. Every second he waited the more dangerous the puppy girl grew. Yet Little Nick found he couldn't bring himself to leave the scene of his newest artistry. The first one in so long, he had to see it... appreciate it first. Rolling boxes screamed up to the entrance of the building, with their red and blue lights stabbing through the dark of the winter evening. They would do. Pity the room that contained it had no good hiding places. A window dominated the wall of the office that looked over the three sliding walls for the rolling boxes. Two desks sat butted together in the center of the room. Nick had done his art there, after clearing them of larger magic panels. Yet with his cap newly dyed, and giddy from the timbre of the man's screams, it was a simple thing to walk up the wall and lie against the ceiling. Waiting.

Eight more still slept in the bunks down the hallway, each in the depth of nightmares brought by a mixture of powdered pixie wing and mushroom spores. They did not respond to the repeated shouts of the assembling army outside.

The army took their sweet time. Stealing it from Nick. He had taken one step down the wall, when a huge black metal box exploded through the center sliding wall, scattering shrapnel through the air. Men bristling with weapons and strange armor came streaming through the blown-through wall. With a shriek of glee, Little Nick pressed himself against the ceiling. Lights shone into the room below.

"Holy fuck!"

They focused on his art and stopped. Little Nick inhaled that intoxicating mix of shock and fear. How long had it been since he had savored this flavor of dread? Not that it mattered, any length of time was too long.

"Room by room! Find the psycho! Move!" A calmer head barked. Boots echoed. Nick's task tugged at his soul. His leash, his collar, grew more insistent with each passing second but he dug his fingers into the plaster ceiling and resisted.

Shrieks of terror sounded as men and women woke from one nightmare to another of weapons and rough hands. "GET ON THE GROUND! HANDS BEHIND YOUR HEADS NOW! NOW! NOW!"

Little Nick wished he was in that room too; here he could only nibble at the edge of their unfocused terror. Had his brothers been with him, they could sample all the fears here and trade flavors. Too bad Nick had eaten them all during the long dark. Too bad entirely.

"Clear!" Reports echoed around the building as Nick heard boot steps outside the door. He drew his knife from the spaces between his fingers as the door banged open. Two men rushed through it, the lights at the ends of their weapons swinging wildly around the room. One lingered on Nick's art as the other checked beneath the desks.

Nick breathed deeply of their fear and waited as the first man shone his light back and forth across the carefully exposed rib cage, the surgical stabs that severed the tendons of each limb, reducing the man to a wiggling torso weighed down by useless meat.

And then as the light focused on the delicate flower of flesh Nick had arranged around the bloody bone of the skull, Nick tasted what he had been waiting for. The revulsion, the woozy twisting of the guts, and from the one whose beam had not left the corpse, the awe of artistry.

"Henderson!" Someone called.

"Clear!" One of the men shouted over his shoulder.

Nick could no longer restrain himself. "Are you sure? Hee, hee, hee."

Their weapons swung up towards Nick almost as fast as their eyes, but he was already falling towards them. He plunged his blade into the shoulder of one and tore it out the long way. His other hand ripped the goggles from the face of his admirer, the strap pulling him down to his knees, eyes level with Nick's grinning face. The blade slashed across one eye, perfectly bisecting its iris. He screamed in pain as Nick turned and launched himself towards the door. Flavors of fear leapt at him as the alarm spread through the men. Little Nick plotted his course through it and sprang, ducking under the barrel of one weapon as it spat fire at the place his head had been. Rolling past, a flick of his knife and the man crumpled on his useless leg, weapon thundering all the way down. Nick tumbled, jumped, and slashed through a line of the men, licking at their terror as the blade found their flesh. He dove through a red door and into the cold dampness of winter's night.

But it was not the darkness that greeted him but light.

"Stop or we'll-"

Nick did not stop, he did not slow. He leapt, springy legs propelling him into the air. The guns thundered, their bullets whistling through his wake. He landed on the neighboring roof and spun into a cartwheel, giggling with glee. In olden days when the wall between worlds was but a gossamer curtain, he would have already slipped back into the dark land of home. Barred from that escape, he ran to the far side of the building, and capered away into the night. The boxes on wheels screamed in frustration as he vaulted across roofs and scrambled through yards, his path too fast for any man to follow.

Judging himself far enough from the boxes' angry wails he crouched behind a chimney and inhaled, appreciating the vapors of his mayhem. The sirens had stirred the mortal morsels below his feet. Perhaps... he pondered, his knife dancing around his fingers. But the task tugged and twisted on his insides.

No time for fun. Work to be done.

He took out a magic panel and did the ritual of the buttons that his art piece had taught him.

Uncaring, the panel showed him the way. It wasn't even far.

"Merry Christmas!" He stepped off the roof. He heard a gasp and turned his head. A woman holding a child stared through a large window, their faces mirrors of dread. Little Nick tipped his hat and clattered his bell, then walked off to cause more hell.

13

"Merry Christmas!" Screeched from outside, carrying a promise of menace that no greeting card ever had. Secret had gone cat after pointing at the iron implements and one symbol. She now resided in the pocket of my hoodie. I picked up the shotgun. The click of the safety turning off echoed around the apartment. Was I really planning to use this thing inside?

Victoria stood up, hefted her long crowbar and took a position by the door.

A flicker of movement and Little Nick's grin loomed through the glass of the nearest window, baring his human-like but far too large teeth in his oversized mouth. "Oh, there you are, Puppy Girl! Won't you come out and play?"

I leveled the gun at him and pulled the trigger. Answering my own question.

With a shriek of laughter he dropped away as the gun kicked against my shoulder. The cloud of shot disintegrated the windowpane with a crash. I pumped the shotgun, Ker-chunk.

"Hee, hee, hee! So close!" Little Nick called out.

Something moved in the kitchen window. I swiveled, aimed and pulled the trigger. The shot tore off my kitchen faucet en route through the window. A spray of water fountained up and arced onto the kitchen floor. Swearing, I pumped another round and listened to his cackling laughter.

"Any brilliant ideas Vicky?" I asked.

She glanced at her silver watch. "Thirteen hours until sun up."

Nick's ugly grin popped up from the sill of the last window "Merry-"

Boom! The gun moved before I even realized it.

A blur of red and exploding glass. Did I get him?

He answered with a peal of laughter. "Ho, ho, ho! There's a hole in my hat. It lets in the breeze, a few more and it will be just like swiss cheese."

I ejected the shell and called out, "I can fix that!"

"Give me the girl and I leave you alone," he sang, and then his voice changed to a strained growl, "Deny me and through your halls I shall roam."

"Abby." Victoria whispered. She pointed at the horseshoe over the door. The very center of its bend glowed a dull red. It was working. It was keeping him out. Maybe in combination with something else we'd done, or maybe all by itself. "Stop wasting ammo." She said.

"You can't come in!" I shouted towards the windows, "You're stuck out there!"

"But where is there? Hee, hee, hee," Little Nick cackled, and I heard glass shatter outside.

I risked looking out the window I had just shot the bottom out of. Nick stood on the back of a pickup truck, illuminated by the parking lot lights, a red gas canister dangling from two fingers. Swearing, I aimed, but he jumped down behind the truck. At this range all I'd accomplish would be to pepper all my neighbor's cars with buckshot.

The sirens seemed to be coming closer at least. Neighbors had called the cops; surely he couldn't take them all on. Apparently, he made the same calculation. His red cap popped up two cars over and he flung something. The single light exploded as I fired. Car alarms screeched in response as I pumped the gun and fired at a blur racing for the door.

A crash of glass. He'd gotten inside with a canister of gas. I ejected the shell, but the pump offered no resistance on the return stroke. I checked it. No more shells.

I looked over my ruined apartment, the night breeze blowing in through my ruined windows. Vicky stood at the door holding the crowbar like a spear. "He's going to light the building on fire. What do we do?" I asked her.

Her mouth pursed and her icy eyes looked towards me. "We hold tight, cops will be here in a couple minutes."

A scream stabbed up through the floor, followed by a piercing giggle. Secret shivered in my pocket. I picked up my mother's wok. "We should have put the shoe over the main entrance!"

"It's a little late now," Victoria snapped back. "Fey are not supposed to be creative!"

"He's not a zombie." I snapped, hefting my wok. "We have to go help. We're the only ones who can."

Victoria barred my progress with her crowbar. "He dodged bullets, Abby! We both watched him. You go out there and he'll kill us both." Her eyes flicked down towards the shivering bulge in my pocket. "Going out there won't be keeping your promise."

A muffled rapid pop pop pop of a handgun sounded. Each shot jarred my heart and the following cry of pain a stab. The fingers of the promise squeezed, but I still found myself stepping forward, teeth bared at the door. Victoria strained to hold me back with her crowbar.

"Hee, Hee, Hee! Ho, Ho, Ho!" Little Nick's demonic laugh shook the walls. "This is so much fun! Oh Abby-Gale! Won't you come out and play? The night is red and you cannot run away." I could hear him stomping up the stairs.

"Abby, stop it! Stop growling!" Victoria pulled the bar back an inch before slamming it into my tits. With a yelp I stumbled back, dropping the wok with a clang.

"Ow." I blinked as my breasts rang with very real pain. Thoughts started moving again. What had I been doing? Victoria's eyes were wide; fear had finally cracked through her façade, but directed at me, not the monster outside the door.

"Knock, knock, Puppy Girl!" Little Nick's booming laugh tore Victoria's eyes from mine; it enveloped us, heedless of the walls. "I piss upon your barrier! I piss upon your floor! So I place my mark upon what was once yours."

"Oh gross." Victoria stepped back from the door as fluid creeped beneath it. I watched it in horror, feeling as if foul excrement were being poured down my back.

Every muscle twisted, my very bones seemed to strain against my skin as I bent to retrieve the wok. A little piece of me registered that the feral, sawing growl that filled the room flowed from my own throat. Anger filled me to the brim. He had desecrated my house, my home, my Den! And that two-bit Santa impostor was going to pay in blood.

"Abby! Snap out of it!" Victoria protested as I grabbed hold of her shoulder and tried to pull her out of the way, but she latched onto my arm, "That's not helping, he's goading you!"

I didn't care. He had to die, right now. I tried to reach for the deadbolt, but she had a firm grip on my free hand and I couldn't drop my weapon. So we stood there, struggling back and forth. I tried to shake her off, but she had both arms locked around my elbow and used every ounce of weight in her skinny body to pull me down.

"Hee, hee, hee!" Little Nick chortled. "Is it getting hairy in there?"

I gave up trying to tug out of Victoria's grip and tried to hold the rim of the wok in my teeth. Too slick, too heavy. It fell with a metallic clang. I reached for the deadbolt and two small hands intercepted mine.

"Don't let him in," Secret pleaded softly, adding a desperate, "Please."

The small hands that gripped mine were human but mine no longer fit that description, thick black claws protruded from each fingertip and a few dozen pale hairs decorated its back. "The hell?" Escaped my lips and the claws, like children suddenly caught out after bedtime, withdrew back into my fingers. The hairs fell away, unanchored to my skin. My entire body untwisted, bones relaxing, as both Victoria and Secret pulled me back into the center of the room.

A frustrated groan sounded from the hallway. "Well, if you won't come out to play, then I'll come in. A door is only a door when it's a door. If it's ash it cannot protect you anymore." He laughed softly as flames flickered over the surface of the growing puddle. It hadn't been piss at all, it had been gas. We all stared at the flickering flames as the wood that separated us from him caught.

"I should have... should have told you to come to my place." Victoria grimaced as she backed away from the door. "Please say the sprinkler system works."

"We have the pipes for one in the hallway." I recalled,

but I didn't hear the hiss of water, or even the call of the fire alarm.

He called to us from the other side of the door, "Will you jump and break your bones? Or will you watch the flames consume your home?" Seemingly untroubled by the flames that had to be worse on his side.

But he was wrong. We had other options. Staying put hadn't worked out; time to try running. "Vicky, there's a fire extinguisher in the kitchen." I ran to my bedroom and flung open my closet. One odd perk of working in emergency services is that you collect a lot of safety gear for free as training swag. I grabbed a cardboard box from the top shelf of my closet and heaved. The sweaters stacked on top of it fell down around me as the box's contents jangled.

From the living room, the roar of the fire extinguisher filled my ears as I rushed the box to the bedroom window and opened it. Shiny chrome greeted me, an emergency chain ladder. Sliding the window open I punched out the screen that never stayed put anyway.

The cops should have been here by now. The sirens seemed to have paused their progress towards us. Flashlights shone in the corner of the parking lot. Residents were gathering down there. I wanted to shout at them to run. I knew generally where my car lay, but I had a sudden worry that buckshot might have pierced my tires. Didn't matter, so long as they turned. But where to go? Where would there be a horseshoe hung over the doorway? Who would have a horseshoe to hang on the doorway? Aunt Betty would; she was about an hour out of the city. Either that or Victoria's place.

I placed the ladder in the window but didn't push the bundle of rungs out yet. It would be loud. The fire extinguisher roared again. We needed a distraction, something to keep him occupied while we got to the car. I went back to the living room. Victoria stood guarding the door against flames, but thick smoke billowed beneath and crept over the top. Already Victoria hunched her body as she stifled the coughing. The smoke coated the ceiling. The doorknob glowed as the fire alarm finally kicked in, its harsh beeping adding to the cacophony of Little Nick's gleeful singing to the flames.

I held up my phone to Victoria. "Use the spell! We have to use the spell."

She looked at me in confusion as I switched to my recording app. "Recite the spell!" I repeated while I pointed at the windows and mimed going down a ladder.

"Right!" She nodded, "Say it with me!" And she shouted in a loud, clear voice. "Elements of the Sun! Elements of the Day. Please come this way! Powers of Night and Day, I summon thee. I call upon thee to protect me! So mote it be." She bent with a cough.

A laugh came, "Oh, no, I am smote, my inferno quenched," Nick said. "Open the door and see your power over me."

I hit the play button, turned up the volume and tossed the phone on the coffee table. Victoria's voice filled the smokey air. We ran for the bedroom. Secret saw us coming, unfurled the ladder, and practically leapt out the window. I followed; the ladder swung as I climbed down. My boots threatened to slip on the smooth rungs but I hung on. Victoria tossed the crowbar and the wok out the living room window before clambering after me. The crowbar hit the sidewalk and rang. Secret stood by my car, a pointy-eared silhouette as the flashlights shone my way. I fumbled with the keys in my pocket, unlocking the car with a soft clunk. "Get in the car," I said, hurrying towards her.

She paused with her hand on the handle. "The iron. Grab it."

I detoured to scoop up the wok and crowbar, throwing them through the broken back door window. Someone in the huddle called my name, but I had no time to respond. Behind me, Victoria swore as she dropped down the last three feet to the ground. I swung open the driver's side door. "Come on, come on!" I gestured frantically as Victoria hobble-skipped towards us. In the shadow of the unlit entrance, I caught movement. I ducked into the car and slammed a knuckle into the start engine button.

"Fucking Damn," Victoria swore from the back seat, "I thought redcaps were supposed to be small."

Unhurriedly, grinning with malice, Little Nick walked into the glare of a half-dozen flashlight beams. No longer skinny, the demon had not grown but inflated. He more floated than walked, taking a step towards us like an astronaut on the moon.

14

"There he is!" One person shouted.

"Light the bastard up!" screeched the voice of... Mrs. Weatherby?

The grin only widened as gunfire filled the air. Little Nick opened his arms as if accepting a hug as the bullets impacted his body. I ducked down into my seat once a stray shot whizzed by my ear.

The gunfire died away and I slid back up into my seat. Little Nick still stood there, having not yielded a single step. His face was a mess of puckered holes, like dozens of assholes had been transplanted onto his face. The grin had only lost a single tooth.

With a wet *schlorp*, a single bullet squeezed out a hole in his forehead, as a blackhead might, and tumbled from his face, bouncing off his nose and hitting the concrete walk with a high pitched ting. He laughed, a low ho, ho, ho. Bullets continued to *schlorp* out and rain upon the ground as I threw the car into reverse. The tires squealed as we hooked out of the parking space.

"Go!" I heard Victoria urge from behind me, but I didn't

need any encouragement. Shifting into drive, I floored the accelerator, still unable to wrench my eyes off that grin.

"Stay and play!" The bastard jumped. I saw his feet leave the ground as the ceiling cut off my view of him.

The rear of the car swung back and forth, fishtailing, as the car shot out towards the road. Metal scraped across asphalt as the car bottomed out on the ramp. A thump above. Red rolled down into my rear view before thick fingers punched through the cracked glass of the back window. They caught the edge and Little Nick pulled himself up, leering. "This is but night one of the fun!"

Victoria shifted, tossing my mother's wok at him. His head jerked out of its path, but it hit his shoulder with a searing hiss. Nick fell away with a scream, his body bouncing on the road behind us like a water balloon that refused to rupture.

"Thanks, Mom." I muttered as I turned back to the road, focusing on putting distance between us and the murderous Santa. As the streetlights flashed by, I realized I didn't recognize the road. My heart fluttered with sudden terror. *Wrong way!* It shouted, screamed, through my everything with the same helpless panic of injecting a patient the opposite drug.

"Wrong way!" Victoria's voice echoed my mind.

I slammed on the brakes.

"No!" Secret cried beside me. "Don't stop! Go faster!"

"But it's the wrong way!" I protested, the thought slamming through my mind and out my lips.

Her eyes flashed gold and my head rang like a gong. "It's not! Step on it!"

While my mind reeled, caught between a hammer and an anvil, my foot obeyed Secret, lifting from the brake and lightly pressing on the accelerator. We lurched forward.

"Faster!" She urged.

My heart pounded into my ears, beating too fast, we were going too fast! I eased up on the gas.

"No!" With a strangled, half-animal sound, Secret leapt up from her seat and slammed both hands down on my knee, little nails biting through my jeans. The strobe of the streetlights above increased.

"We're going to crash!" I cried out as images of mangled car wrecks screeched through my head.

"Faster!" Her voice deepening to a tiger's, "Faster! Go faster! Or he'll catch us!" The nails became sharp claws, promising pain if I did not obey. Huge golden eyes bored up into my skull. Had to obey, had to protect. The car engine whined as the speedometer climbed, the pressure inside me rising with it. It hurt. My voice joined Victoria's in a scream of fear and pain as Secret's eyes pushed me on toward the wall I knew had to be there. Because we were still going the wrong way.

There, I could see it. A brick monstrosity stretching into the sky. "Secret!" I cried out. "Let me stop! Please let me stop." As we barreled onward towards certain death, the speedometer pushed into the red.

Her form flowed, no child held my foot to the accelerator, but a black pitiless panther pressed her claws into my leg. "Faster," she snarled while her eyes commanded.

"Secret, please!" I reached for the emergency brake and she bit my hand. A howl climbed from my throat, throwing back my head as the wall rushed towards us. I didn't want to die. My eyes closed, waiting for the terrible sharp crunch and the pain that would come.

Instead the pressure in my head broke like an egg crushed in a fist. The fear tore away from my heart like a wet napkin. Opening my eyes, I found no wall, no damage other than a listing to the left side of the road, which I quickly corrected. Beside me Secret clutched her head and chanted, "Owwie, owwie, owwie," over and over.

"What just happened?" Victoria asked in a hoarse whisper.

"I dunno." I reached over and stroked Secret's shoulder. "Are you okay?" We were barely going 30 miles an hour.

She uncurled and looked up at me, a stream of blood leaked from each nostril and met at her upper lip. "It hurts to do that."

"What did you do?" I asked. My brain ached. Deep circles were under Secret's eyes and when she wiped at the blood, she spread it across her cheek, making it look even more like the child had been in a fight. She had; my brain had been the battlefield.

"I..." she sighed, "Can't say. But I'll bring you to someone who can. Take us to a big park." With that, she slumped against the door and closed her eyes.

Here in the Hillsboro neighborhood, a big park wasn't far; this side of the river was half forest once you were out of downtown. A cop car screamed past, not slowing at the sight of my blasted out windows. Probably going too fast to see, after all, I still had both headlights on. Behind me, the cop slowed and turned down another street, rather than barrel on towards my building.

"Secret? Is that wall..." I paused, trying to wrap my head around it. The wall had seemed so real, but it hadn't actually existed. "Is it keeping the cops away?"

Victoria, who sat in the backseat, one hand clutching at her heart, said, "Has to be. I texted 911 that he was here while you played 'pop goes the bastard'."

Nodding, my mind simply felt numb. I tried not to think about all the people we'd left behind.

Within ten minutes of driving we made it to the edge of

Marquam Nature Park, a forested hill spiderwebbed by hiking and running trails. In drier months, those trails were highways for joggers and old ladies with their hiking poles. Try that now, and you'd find knee-deep mud patches that had landed more than a few people in the back of my ambulance, angrily muttering at themselves. Now, in the murky night, the dark forest loomed up over the houses at the end of the suburban lane as if it were consuming the neighborhood, house by house, compressing the asphalt before it into a dirt path that led into its depths. I parked at the curb of a large two-story house that threatened to overflow the borders of it's narrow lot. No lights shone anywhere on the street. It wasn't that late, but the air smelled like midnight.

"This work?" I asked Secret.

"Yeah." Her eyes scarcely opened as she fumbled at the latch and tumbled out of the car. Victoria and I followed.

"Where are we going?" Victoria asked.

"You can't come. You're of the dark," Secret said, facing the forest.

"Excuse me?" Victoria's voice trilled with offense. "I'm not a vampire. I don't burn in sunlight." I circled around the car and stepped up onto the sidewalk. Secret groped for me and latched onto my belt.

Steadying herself she faced Victoria giving a small breathless laugh. "No. It's not nice there, but your dark is dead, and the dark there is worse."

Victoria made a frustrated sound. "What does that mean?"

"It means you get to go home for a bit." I jangled my keys as I separated my civilian key chain from my work ring and tossed them at her. She caught it. "I'll let you know when we get back. Try not to scratch the paint."

Victoria's head shook, but the darkness hid her facial

expression. "I'll be lucky if I get it back to my place without a ticket." A pause, "Don't die, Abby."

"She won't die there. If we're caught, it will be much worse than that," Secret said.

"You are a little ray of sunshine, kid," Victoria carefully leaned against the car and pulled on her vape stick. "Good luck."

Secret took my hand and led me into the forest. As we stepped off the sidewalk, drops of cold began to fall on my head. The murk of the night grew as the trees closed in. My ears filled with the song of the rain drumming on the fallen leaves of the forest. Secret gripped two fingers of my hand tightly, pulling me along. Every fifty steps or so she stopped; my eyes strained to make out the outlines of her ears moving back and forth, scanning for something I couldn't hear. A moment would pass before they'd focus on a single direction and we'd walk forward. It seemed random; sometimes we'd walk back in the precise direction we'd come. I felt we couldn't have moved more than 30 yards out of sight of the car. Yet, the terrain changed beneath my feet, roots grasped at my ankles, and branches scratched at my face and arms.

And then... I noticed a subtle blueish glow that illuminated the gnarled trees, their limbs draped with thick strands of moss, their trunks decorated with gardens of fungus. It was from among these that the blue glow shone. A single mushroom reached out from each trunk, blue motes swirling into the air from their open gills. Secret hurried onward, tracing a wandering path between the trees. We came to a ring of seven trees, even more gnarled than the rest, their naked branches twisted together so tightly that not a single drop of rain swirled the cloud of blue spores that hung overhead. On the ground, a fairy ring of those glowing mushrooms grew among the tangle of roots.

Secret paused at the circle's edge and stared up at the twisted branches. In their bends and spirals were suggestions of human figures, but just as I isolated one, my mind found another overlapping it. My eyes flowed aimlessly, searching for the story hidden there but not quite making it out. A gentle tug on my hand, and we stepped into the circle together.

Turning, the predatory gleam of Secret's yellow eyes outshone the blue light. "I can tell you the Rules," she whispered with a stern little growl. "Do not eat. Do not drink. Give no one your name, for they shall take it. To make a promise is to gamble your soul. Do you understand?"

"Yes," I breathed. A little voice in the back of my head babbled in disbelief, but it was a little late.

Secret made a happy mew and hugged herself to my leg, rubbing her nose against my hip. "Mine."

The single word shivered up my spine, but before I could ask what the hell she had done, a glint caught my eye. She had let me go and turned to face the edge of the circle. She clasped a triangular shard of glass in her furry fingers and held it up as if the tree would bend to inspect it. "I am the halfling," Secret declared. "Daughter of Fey, Daughter of mortal man. A paw in the riverbed and a boot on the shore." She cut across her left hand with the glass and made a fist. Blood dripped down, drenching the mushroom beneath it. Secret stepped both right and left, splitting in twain; a tiny cat wearing a dress went clockwise around the circle and a naked girl went counterclockwise. "We blood this circle, open the gate. Crack the Seal of the Sun. Let Dream travel through the Crossroad. We shall roam wherever, our both sing of home." The girl said as the cat mewed along. They shimmered through each other as they met on the other side and merged back into one where they'd begun.

The blood on the mushrooms dripped into their gills, and the spores that poured out of them became a glowing red cloud. Dizziness hit me like a blow; I fell to my knees, the hard roots jarring my kneecaps. Secret stayed on her feet a moment longer, as the world beyond the circle melted like wax into a smear of muted colors. She fell against me and I crushed her to my chest as the spinning sensation grew.

"Close your eyes!" she said.

I obeyed, as the very ground tore away beneath me. Semisolid fingers tore at my clothing and hair. My boots were sucked from my feet as I clung to Secret as the only solid object in the middle of this tornado.

15

"Welcome to the Dream Abby." Something whispered through the wind.

The whirlwind died as suddenly as it came, dropping me hard onto solid ground. A knobby root slammed into the underside of my kneecap, stabbing pain up through my body. I let go of Secret to clutch at my knee, and opened my eyes. The same grove we had left greeted my eyes, but for the many winged figures that lounged among the twisted roots beyond the circle's edge.

"Hello?!" Secret crouched at the edge of the circle, nose nearly touching one of the gray wings nearest to the circle.

The spinning had stopped but my stomach remained twisted up. Looking out over the wings, none of them moved. All remained unstirred without even a breeze.

Secret sat up abruptly, her sudden movement pulling my eyes, her tail puffy and straight with alarm, "Mrowl!?! Anyone?" Her eyes scanned the still grove. I crawled over to her and peered at the nearest pair of wings. Thin flakes of stone protruding from the back of a tiny statue depicting a man struggling to stand. Beyond him lay dozens of others, some clinging to the roots as if bracing against a savage wind, others with their heads on their arms as if they had lain down to sleep.

There were hundreds of them. Secret remained sitting, lapping at her wounded palm as she stared at the tiny statues, ears wilted, eyes lost. I couldn't even do anything about the wound: no car keys, no cellphone, and no first aid kit. A little laugh tumbled out of me because I was as naked as you could get while wearing clothes.

"It's not funny. They-" Her mouth closed with a click of teeth. And without a whisper of sound, she rose to her feet. "Follow," she said before picking her way towards the trees. Not having much choice in the matter, I started after her, wincing as my stocking feet seemed to find jabby bits every time I set them down. Try as I might to follow in Secret's footsteps, the roots conspired against me, and my wind-milling arms snapped off several sets of wings. Secret turned to glare reproachfully at me. "They'll remember that."

"Sorry." I mumbled as I stepped between the trees.

"Don't say that, either. Here there are no accidents. Even if it is," Secret explained.

"Who taught you all this?" I wondered out loud at her.

"Mother taught me some, but sometimes I dream. My dreams are always true."

We walked out of the forest, no hidden path or zig zagging this time; we emerged out onto a lane that resembled the one we had left. All the straight lines of the houses had gained subtle curves and their windows hung at angles, like picture frames that had been bumped. And there was my car. But... the night was different. Gone were the murky shadows and drizzle of the Portland midnight; the moon loomed large in the company of stars. Nearly as bright as day, the pale moonlight felt cool on my skin in the same way that sunshine feels warm. Her surface shone with the gleam of a blade. A lump rose in my throat as the spark she gave me roared to life, scorching my heart.

The mark on my arm burned. *Touch me*, whispered a voice in the shining light as it caressed me. *In the Twilight you tasted my rage, but here you may know my strength. Leave the day, come to me and be the first of my new children.*

A tug on my hand brought me back to the present, and I swallowed the lump back down. "Don't stare at her! She'll notice you. You're mine! Not hers!" Gripping my hand with both of hers, she pulled me towards one house. My body followed, but my thoughts acted like a combination of tar and banana pudding. That spark clawed at the inside of my sternum. Burning to run, to hunt, to tear apart anything that sought to contain it. It promised that if I took that touch my apartment would no longer contain its madness when the Moon was full. I'd wake with the taste of sweet meat in my mouth.

Had it been only me I would have lost, but Secret kept pulling, dragging me after her. Anxiety shone in her eyes as she glanced back at me. Only when I stumbled up the porch steps and into the shadow did I lose the urge to reach up towards the sky. My legs crumbled like load-bearing noodles and dumped me onto the white-painted planks. "What the-" I gasped as pins and needles radiated out from every bone in my body. Like I had sat wrong but my entire body had gone to sleep instead of my foot. Secret shook her head like a disappointed parent. "Why did she notice you? No one can know I brought a mortal back."

"Did you miss the claws earlier?" I grunted, because I hadn't. "We kinda know each other."

"Knows you?" Secret squeaked. "You've been to the lunar court?"

"No," I pulled up my sleeve to show her the circular scar that Luna had given me. "She guided me and Cindy out of the Twilight. In exchange for... making me destroy my apartment once a month."

From Secret's face, the rounding of her eyes, and the folding of her ears, I got the notion that this wasn't a good thing. "No matter the sky, Luna is the night, humans are of the day. Momma said only madness waits for those who touch the Moon's court. And she'll never let you go." She glanced up at the porch roof that shielded us from the moonlight. "We'll have to take the dark road now."

"Where-" I started.

"I can't tell you!" she snapped, showing me fangs. "Stop asking!"

I flinched; my head banged against the house.

Secret let out a sigh and slumped down on top of me, curling herself onto my lap and claiming my left boob as a pillow. As the tingles faded, I carefully stroked one of her ears; when she didn't object I scratched along its base. She purred and snuggled deeper. "Has anyone told you that you run a bit hot and cold, kiddo?" I asked.

She pushed my hand away, fixing me with a sullen glare. "I'm tired. I wanna go home but I don't have one." Rolling off me, she remained on her hands and knees, facing an open cat carrier at the end of the porch. It had no door, and several blankets inside formed a nest of bedding. "Maybe the court will be safe enough for a nap."

The W word formed on my tongue, but I bit it to hold it in. Instead I watched in silence as she crawled towards the carrier. Did she expect to fit through that little door? "Hold on to my tail," she said.

Skeptical, I pulled myself up into a crouch and grabbed

her tail. It immediately slipped from my fingers into an angry lash.

"Not with your hand! With your mouth." Her tone suggested this was entirely obvious to anyone who wasn't stupid.

Feeling supremely silly and a little nauseated, I mimicked her posture then stuck the tip of her fuzzy tail in my mouth. My cheeks ran so hot they probably emitted X-rays as we crawled towards the cat carrier. It wasn't that we shrank, or the world got bigger, it was more like my perspective had been off. We crawled along the length of the porch for several minutes, and by the time we reached the entrance to the carrier, it loomed above use like a cavern and its insides had grown pitch dark. Ahead of me Secret heaved for breath with every step as if the kid were running a marathon.

Once inside the mouth of the carrier, Secret paused, "Don't let go, don't fall off." Her words sounded addressed more to herself than me.

The first bit didn't surprise me, heading into a dark place, but the second bit worried me. It was one thing to walk through a cave in the dark. Edging along a cliff would be quite another. We continued and the darkness swallowed us both. The tug of her tail tip in my mouth and her labored exhalations became my only awareness of her. The soft fleece beneath my hand gave way, first to the smooth hardness of plastic, then to the warm roughness of unfinished wood. My fingers wrapped around an edge. As the path narrowed to the width of my waist, sweat slid down my forehead. It continued to narrow, forcing me up onto my hands and feet so I could swing one foot in front of the other. I had to clamp my teeth down on her now sodden tail tip to prevent myself from breathing through my mouth.

She slowed a little, and I wobbled, my spine bent, compensating. Slowly, it waved in the opposite direction and I realized its weight extending beyond my hips.

I tried not to think about it, grateful for any help in navigating the path. It narrowed down even further, to barely the width of my knee as it undulated up and down, first smoothly and then sharply until I was crawling along the points of teeth. Teeth... like a fence. A path for cats. This was a fence. We were walking on the top of a fence as cats do. A fence for what?

As if to answer, a point of light appeared in the dark far ahead of us. As if a porch light had suddenly flicked on. But it revealed nothing but the light itself.

"Shit." Secret cursed ahead of me. Our pace redoubled and I had to push myself hard to keep up. The tail, my tail lashed back and forth to maintain my balance, my arms stretched longer, leveling my spine towards our travel. The fence changed beneath us, a wide vinyl plank with posts we had to scramble over. A crescent moon came out above, but its light revealed nothing.

This moon wasn't the moon at all. It had teeth.

"Why, heeeello there, little Princess." It spoke with a lazy drawl, swinging downward, revealing itself to be a grin floating above us.

"Go away Cheshire! I'm not talking to you. You're banished." Secret's voice trembled, but she kept moving; we traded the plastic beneath us for cold curved metal, the twisted peaks of wire to my left side trying to snag my elbows and knees.

"You could unbanish me," The moon suggested. "Hrrrm?"

"No." Secret huffed as we continued, the path becoming cold and curved. Closing in on the light ahead, a single feline eye, its iris purple and pale moonlight glowing within its slit pupil. The moon lowered itself from the sky, orbited around the eye once before settling below it. A second eye opened beside the first, completing the grinning feline face. It did not contain the malice of Little Nick, but a predatory amusement with its own sort of danger. "I'm sure momma had a good reason."

"Oh she did, I suppose. But that was so long ago. Now I could help you," said the grin. "Won't you stay and talk? We can share the mouse you've brought."

All of a sudden, Secret's tail felt larger. The curve of the metal lessened beneath all four of my paws.

"Stop! She's mine, Cheshire!" Secret cried, "She's my protector!"

"Oh, but she must be a mouse, to run from the Lunar Mistress when she already bears her mark from the twilight," Cheshire growled.

Secret's tail tugged at my teeth, trying to lash. "She's big! Strong! My protector is not free to roam until she guides me home."

A sharp tug jerked me upward. Secret's tail tip shrank again to a fraction of what it had been, clenched between interlocking fangs. My tail lashed as I fought to stay on the narrow pipe I stood on. Wire bit at one side of my ankles, a chain-link fence. My ears moved to focus on Cheshire's laugh.

"I smell the mark of your claim but I see no collar that bears her name." Cheshire purred, "Only a lunar mark." The luminescent eyes and mouth closed, disappearing into the dark.

"You're a meanie. A big meanie." Secret whined in the dark. "Don't let go, Abby. Please."

"Mrryah." Cheshire grin open inches away from my

nose. "Abby, is it? Hello." The grin became asymmetric, sly and sultry. "A mortal in this dark quickly forgets what they are." He moved against me, sliding his unseen body against mine, fur against fur. The warmth of him penetrated my skin, defining inhuman muscle. So close, so warm, my heart fluttered, parts of me I'd left for dead stirred. "But it's not a bad thing. Life can be good in the dark." He pushed along my other side, sweeping away any doubt as to what Secret had done to me. I inhaled through alien nostrils. And he smelled... inviting.

"Stop twisting her!" Secret hissed. She started forward again, and I struggled to follow with my clumsy size. Cheshire's shoulder steadied me.

"Oh. but it's so fun," Cheshire answered her before purring at me, "In this dark, you could let go. Even the promise wouldn't know."

I growled in answer, threaded my paw more firmly around the wire and shoved against him. He backed off suddenly, leaving me to heave against empty air. Off balance, I missed a step and jerked hard on Secret's tail. She cried out as a soft crack resonated through my teeth. "Owies!" She cried out into the dark.

"Pity, being forced to be a knight is so no fun." As he spoke, heavy armor clamped around my body, its weight staggering, my claws slipped from my fingers and hooked around the metal wire of the fence, straining against the force of my body.

The weight of the armor nearly tipped me over the other side of the fence. With a muffled yowl, I grabbed hold of the pole beneath me with all four limbs. The armor clattered against the metal, but I hung on.

"Ooooh," Cheshire sighed with disappointment, face

floating above us. "I guess you keep her, Princess. But do bring me a morsel next time you visit the dark."

Secret said nothing, but I didn't need my huge ears to hear her hold back sobs as we continued on.

It wasn't far; the fence changed to a wide stone wall with metal spikes we threaded ourselves between. Light appeared, real light shining out of a passage.

Secret sniffed hard as we approached, "Close your eyes. Don't look at yourself by the light."

I closed my eyes and walked through the gateway with her. Searing pain marked the threshold.

16

My body suddenly remembered what it was supposed to be, and violently snapped into its proper positions and sizes. My tail retracted into my hips, each bone impacting like the blow of a jackhammer up my spine. Baggy flesh followed suit, squeezing and retracting around the bones. My eyes popped open, but the pain rendered me blind.

"Stop screaming! Please stop screaming. Quiet!" Secret urged.

I fell back against something; a metallic clang hit me from all angles. I opened my eyes to find myself looking out over a nose that intruded into the bottom of my field of vision. My hands rushed up to my face and ran into something hard, the impact sounded with a clang. Bringing them into my view, I found them encased in metal. Armored gauntlets. Human fingers. Oh thank god. I wore the bastard's armor! A full suit of plate mail encased my body. Frantic, I pulled off the helmet and threw it to the ground. It bounced and rolled away, stopping when it hit a pile of multicolored cushions. The silver helmet styled in the shape of a cat's head with a grin across the mouth, like a metallic mascot costume. In a fury I stripped off every piece of the armor, my mind burning with the memory of the way he had slid across my body. Alien and intimate. My innards rippled with violation, as I recalled the manipulative want. Ick, ick!

It took a while; there were latches to spring and snaps to undo. Then layers of padding to strip off. Secret hovered nearby, saying nothing, or perhaps I was so focused on getting it off me I couldn't hear her. Finally, beneath it all I found my jeans, shirt and sodden socks. Everything human. I checked beneath my shirt to make sure. Just my hoodie, my layabout favorite hoodie had disappeared. I breathed a sigh of relief and looked up to find Secret standing sullenly watching me. Both hands gripped the end of her tail, the tip of which hung limply.

I bared my teeth at her in my anger, a feral growl in my throat. She had twisted my body without warning and silenced me. My bones still rang with the pain of snapping back to human, but looking at her, I felt echoes of the body she had forced on me in the dark. Claws sliding in and out of digits, my mind tried to lash a heavy tail that had never been there.

Yet the anger boiled away as she stood there, clutching her broken tail. She had done her best. She was still trying her hardest.

And I'm a total pushover.

Warily, I offered her an arm. Without a word she shuffled over, knelt in my lap and fell against me. Pressing her face against me, she sobbed. Quietly at first, but it quickly progressed to a full out bawl which she attempted to muffle by grabbing fistfuls of my shirt and stuffing them into her mouth.

I don't know kids. Other than remembering far too well

how stupid I was in my teens. So I didn't know why she cried so hard. Whether she was sorry for what she'd put me through, or whether her tail hurt, or if she was simply so exhausted she couldn't see straight. The fact that surrounding us, lounging on pillows, in a bookcase, and on a sofa were dozens of stone cats might have also had something to do with it.

What I do know is that I held onto her as tightly as she clung to me. Blinking back my own tears as Secret's sobs slowly faded to sniffles, and finally to the rhythmic breath of sleep. I kissed the top of her head and immediately felt guilty. She wasn't mine. They had forced me into this against my will. Hadn't they? It had been maybe a day? Her slumbering against my chest felt too right to be wrong.

Pushing off the heavy thoughts, I forced myself to take stock of the room that surrounded me. There was a cat-sized pillow beneath my butt; the place had the sensation of a cat cafe where Cindy and I would occasionally stop for lunch if we worked a day shift. Their cats were more animated than these stone tabbies that lounged on every surface though. A human door seemed to wait for me, although it had a cat flap at its bottom. Were we safe here? I considered trying to transfer Secret to the couch, but I found myself unwilling to risk waking her. More magic? The joke of being pinned beneath a sleeping cat made real? Either way I nodded off for a bit.

I woke to the sound of her yawn. Her eyes shone brighter, but bore deep bruises beneath them, her tail still limp at the end as it waved behind her. She said nothing about it as she stood and stretched. "Feel better?" I asked, trying to massage some feeling back into my legs.

"Have to get up," was her only answer as she walked

towards the door, dragging her feet as if there were great weights attached to them.

Beyond the door lay a space that couldn't decide if it was inside or outside. Trees with long, twisting branches grew alongside numerous cat towers wrapped in plush carpeting. Beyond them cathedral-like walls stretched up and disappeared into a blue sky. Great shafts of sunlight streamed through the stained glass windows as if two suns competed on either side of the court. Human furniture was scattered about willy-nilly, beds, couches, lazy boy recliners, and on every surface there were stone cats. Mostly house cats. They curled around each other, some sprawled out along one sunbeam, others squaring off, tails puffed. Others were cats not acting like cats, several read books, a pair played chess, a lion and a tiger dueled with rapiers. Secret drifted through them all, carefully stepping over those in her way, her feline ears deflated.

We came to a semicircle of cushions and cats gathered round a grand piano, its surface a mess of scratches and teeth marks. On its seat stood a cat that wore two small boots over its hind paws and had its mouth opened as if speaking to the assembled crowd. The Puss in Boots. Secret stood before her and bowed her head. "Hi Momma. I'm back. This is my fault, momma. I should have listened to you. Shoulda been good."

The statue did not move but a wet shimmer danced in her gray eyes.

"The Queen put you back. Let me fix it." Secret reached out and grabbed the air, it bent like a piece of cloth in her fist. With a jerk of her arm, the image of the Puss in Boots came off as if it were a painted bedsheet, revealing the statue of a smiling woman sitting cross legged on the bench. Her long boots came up to her thighs, and her top was clad in a low-cut shirt: a hybrid between a corset and a blouse. Pawlike gloves covered her hands and large cat ears poked out from her long hair. Were she flesh, she'd be a cosplay version of the Puss in Boots with very realistic cat bits. Despite the cute appearance, something about her made my scalp prickle. Frozen in rock, still I felt her gaze on me.

Secret looked at me, "Momma, this is my guardian. Not part of the courts." She turned to her mother with a tight smile, "But she knows nothing of us. Even if you released me from my promise to you, the knight made me swear it again. I need someone who is not bound to keep the secrets of the fey to tell her the ways."

Nothing moved, but I felt a thrum of something in my chest, a single note of bass from a concert spoke through the room. The sharp crack of glass echoed through the court of the cats. I turned to see shards of glass falling from a base-ball-sized hole in one of the impossibly tall windows. Secret jumped up onto the bench and threw her arms around the statue's neck. "Thank you, Momma." And licked her cheek with her pink tongue. The statue moved ever so slightly, flexing, straining momentary against the stiffness of their composition before giving up. "I'll be back. I promise."

A tear leaked down that frozen cheek. Secret caught it with a fingertip and plunged it into her mouth. She sucked on her finger, closing her eyes as if the tear had a flavor to savor, and it was as if a sun beam struck her and her alone. The ragged dress she wore gained a satin sheen, her face's weary lines did not ease, but her jaw had a determined set to it and her eyes shone. "I am the halfling" She announced to her audience of stone. "My name is Secret. I... I will live to see this undone. With my name I pledge this oath." A distance thunder rumbled above, as if a distant god had blasted the little girl's promise into the side of a mountain.

Nothing moved in the room. Secret hopped down from the piano bench with a spring in her step, and I found her hugging my leg. "Thank you for giving me a name to pledge by." She beamed up at me.

"Don't you have a name? Surely your mother gave you one?" I blinked back my own tears.

"She gave me a name that can never be spoken. It belongs to the heavens and the earth. You gave me a name that is my own. A name from which stories can be grown." She rubbed her nose against my hip and sprang away, skipping towards the broken window. I followed after her like a dog on a leash, no direction without her tug. What was all this? I felt perched on the edge of a shooting scene, police tape blocking me off from going inside to assess the injured. She had just done something important, but what?

The windows were stained glass without the color. I squinted to make out the figures. Rounded characters, chibi-style. Secret tore away another hidden cloth, and color sprang into existence. I blinked; it was a manga! The entire stained glass window depicted pages of manga. Showing people wandering rows of vendors, characters with cat ears and brightly colored hair posing for pictures. An anime convention. Farther up, the style changed, a bit more realistic, the cat costumes became far more elaborate full body-suits. The hole in the window was midway between the transition. It sat in the middle of a large group scene and was flanked by two figures. One I recognized from my father's game collection: a fox standing on two legs in a flight suit, Star Fox. The other was a thin woman who wore little, and had a peacock's fan of blue foxtails behind her.

"What does this mean?" I asked.

"You should put that armor back on" Secret responded.

"I'd rather peel off my skin." My words were sharp on

my tongue. If I wore that armor then every movement would remind me of the way Cheshire... smelled. Then Jimmy would be on my mind like a leaden weight. "I'm a paramedic, not a knight in armor."

Secret stared back up at the hole, her ears panning different directions. "They're coming. No time."

"Who's coming?" I asked, straining my ears, but hearing nothing but Secret as she hurried back the way we came.

"Knights! I shouldn't have napped." Her voice rose with panic as we hurried back through the court, towards the cat café door we had come through. She stopped short of it, tail hooking with anxiety. After a blink I saw that there was not just a single door but many, arranged in a long hallway. Not only tall rectangular things but anything a cat might slip through, cracked windows, doggie doors, holes in tree trunks, gaps in fences; the more I looked the more I saw. "The fox will be in the temple. Need something near the temple." Secret muttered to herself, breaking into a brisk walk, led by her sniffing nose.

Outside I heard the rhythmic strikes of hooves on pavement.

"Here!" Secret exclaimed, throwing herself to her knees in front of a green dumpster. "Follow me!" She declared, flattening herself against the floor and crawling beneath it.

"Open in the name of Queen Titania!" A voice boomed from outside, and I felt the promise flutter around my heart.

No! Not yet, I told it as I followed Secret's lead. I had to turn my head to fit. Rough asphalt kissed one cheek while cold metal greeted the other.

A more genteel but no less loud commanding voice sounded, "You shall halt in the name of Queen Mab. The true Queen." A door banged open as I used my toes to push myself forward, wiggling my body through the compressed space.

"There!"

I swore as I forced my hips through the opening, felt the thin denim of my jeans rip and give way as one of my useless back pockets caught. Buttocks bruisingly compressed, I slid the rest of the way with relative ease. Two hands grabbed one of mine and pulled me out into the night.

"Don't look at the moon this time," Secret warned as I gathered myself and savored the cool night air. We were in a parking lot, a Portland municipal parking lot, by the shadowy shapes of dozens of heavy trucks and equipment. Above, sparse electric lamps flickered, suspended from the bottom of the on-ramp that stretched overhead. Fingering the holes in the butt of my jeans where my pocket had torn away I turned to look at what we had just escaped through. The front of the green dumpster squatted there behind us, just enough space beneath it for a cat to slip beneath.

"There it is. The Temple." Secret whispered, "I've never seen it from this side before."

I followed her gaze, expecting a structure with golden pillars that invoked a divine chorus to sing in one's head as you beheld it. Instead, it bore twin pillars of glass shaped like narrow tents of fabric. A sight I beheld every day that my ambulance roamed the highways. Beneath them sat the rectangular, squat shape of the Oregon Convention Center.

17

The convention center looked little different here in the Dream than it did in reality at first. Only as we slipped through the gate and began walking did I appreciate the differences. The other buildings around us had a muted quality to them, there but not entirely. The realness of the center shone as bright as the moon. Other people and creatures occupied the sidewalks, going towards or away from it while almost no traffic crossed the intersections perpendicular to it.

Luna's cool light did not speak, but made the mark prickle and itch. Whether this was what everyone felt beneath her gaze in this place, or she was letting me know she saw me there, I didn't know.

As we approached the entrance, we started attracting the attention of other things. Misshapen beings clustered around the entrance, their bodies cobbled together from corporate-branded castoffs. A shambling pile of sneakers shifted to keep its pink baby shoe eyes on me, another constructed of Starbucks coffee cups and sleeves held out bits of itself as if expecting me to toss coins into it as I passed. The largest one bore teeth of martini glasses with their bases broken off, horns constructed of crushed soda cans, and eyes of donut holes. It grumbled aggressively.

"Don't talk to the Forgotten," Secret warned as we walked by them and stepped up to the sliding automatic doors, which opened smoothly without sound.

I stepped through the doors, expecting to see the familiar cavernous hallways that I had visited dozens of times on various calls and occasional EMT conferences. It was cavernous, but the familiarity stopped there. The walls that separated the hallway from the exhibit halls did not exist. A palisade of wildly different scenes clustered together on the floor. A stone pyramid with a golden keystone stood next to a fortress constructed solely of books, and next to that, a storm of sparks raced around the rectangular borders of their territory. Watching them, I heard the siren of my bus echo through the night, and felt the push of the acceleration, the whooping thrill as we hurtled through an intersection and barreled on towards trouble. The sparks expanded in my vision; looming up, they were racing each other at mind boggling speeds. Faster, faster, faster. They chanted invitingly to me to come play, come race.

A sharp tug on my hand pulled me back. I looked around and found myself several steps from where I had been. "Careful. Don't look so close." Secret warned.

"Secret, what is that?" I gasped before I could strangle back the question.

To my surprise she didn't rebuke me. "I don't know." She answered. "I've never seen it from this side. Momma told us we have to find Reynard the Fox and the sky road brought us here."

Trying not to look too closely at the "booths," I directed my gaze upwards. The ceiling of gridded lights shone like stars in the sky far above, making space for the titanic but distant throne. Its occupant drew my gaze as the sparks did, but his thousand-gigawatt animatronic smile ignited my rage. Framed in a long, almost cylinder-shaped head. Above it green text circled in a thick halo declaring "IF I DID IT, SO CAN YOU!" The halo did not float, but was held in place by a pair of red, branching horns that blended with the red velvet of his throne's cushioning. The horns were completely obvious if you knew they were there. Taking Secret's hand, I strode towards it. Memories replayed against a red haze. Jimmy and I lying together, eyes glued to that brilliant and vapid smile as it spun a vision of a broken world in need of heroes to clean out the filth. We dreamed of being those heroes. We wanted to trump over THEM all.

"Abby!" Secret hissed and pulled in my grip. "Don't let it see you!"

I didn't let her stop me. That was the smile that had drowned any good that had been in Jimmy, and if he hadn't tattooed a fucking swastika on my hand, I might still breathe the shit it sprayed. All of that made incarnate. "It needs to die," I snarled under my breath.

"It's huge!" Secret whined as she dug in her heels, "You can't fight it! It will stomp us!"

Fingers wrapped around my heart and squeezed, forcing me to stop in my tracks and grip my chest. Jimmy and I had wanted an understandable world, a reason everything was so fucked up and unfair. Internet gurus had given us that, and I had spent literal years relearning how to think. Viewing myself as lower than scum in a drain pipe as I reexamined every assumption I held. I redirected every ounce of hate in my body towards the legions of morons on YouTube. Violent fantasy about their type would be pointless, but here sat the distillation of men who sell you lies. My own dragon there for the slaying.

And the promise would kill me if I tried.

"Wow, that's some powerful stuff you have there. It smells so fresh. Can I make you an offer?" a voice crackled.

I blinked to find a creature standing below my line of sight to the Guru's smile. Hunched with the weight of a huge pack, her head that of an aged hound, gray creeping up her muzzle, one eye sighted me through spectacles perched at the end of her nose. Her other eye was frozen in stone.

"Uuh, you are?" I asked.

She grinned doggily. "Pheme is best gossip hound. The best gurl, 7 out of 5." A husky laugh rolled out of her, "It an old one but I likes it."

I looked around. We were on a crowded path; on one side loomed tall stacks of server racks crackling with electricity, the other held a display of bloody daggers. Inhuman figures flowed around us in either direction, most wore business attire, regardless of how many heads or arms they had. Secret hid behind me and peeked out at Pheme.

"We're looking for someone." I told her, and after a final squeeze, the hand in my chest let go of my heart.

The hound face grinned, displaying a silver and gold canine. "Outsiders always think that but Pheme get you better price. Even after finder's fee. You got rage," she sniffed, "Anger... pain."

"Betrayal?" A new voice drifted out from the knife display, a hooded figure with a cloak that might have been white once beneath all the blood spatters, peered at me eagerly.

Pheme flashed her teeth at him. "Pheme's commission! Back off!"

"I haven't committed to anything yet! We're looking for

Reynard the Fox. Do you know where he is?" I said in my I-am-being-very-polite-here tone.

Both stopped, before bursting into laughter. Pheme snort-sneezed. "Reynard? Did you just get unstoned? From what Court do you come?"

"Just tell me where we can find the Fox." I asked.

"Anger, rage, not for Fox." The gossip hound snorted. "Pheme get you much better price." She sniffed the air. "You have annoyance too? Quick. Heel. Follow."

"The Fox is in meme alley," the Betrayal vendor moaned and pointed behind him. "That way."

Secret and I quickly walked around Pheme as she berated the Betrayal vendor. "Pheme throw soap on you. Is my mark!"

"You blocking traffic." I heard the Betrayal vendor's whispered voice as we turned the corner.

We wandered down the aisle, my eyes on the concrete which wasn't always; the realities of wares on the display bled into it. Sometimes we walked on lush grass, hopped across a stream of lava, or stomped over a carpet as plush as snow. Every now and then, I'd glance up to look for anything vaguely fox-related. But nothing appeared to me.

Secret, sniffing the air, took the lead, pulling me off the main floor. The booths were closer together here, more specific. The surrounding occupants slowed their gait to more of a shuffle than a walk, many dragging a foot or paw along the ground. I ignored the glare of a small gray man sitting at a spinning wheel and dodged around a giant pink draft horse that argued with him. Secret pointed down the row, and there, nestled between a massive recreation of Snoopy's dog house and a hole that blew out a swirl of snow, sat a tall cardboard box with a neon sign that read: "The Fox

Box," with an animated arrow that pointed to the door cut into the side.

Gingerly, I pulled open the door and stepped through into the opaque white light. A sharp scent stabbed at my nostrils as my eyes adjusted. A cozy bar glowed with warmth; rusty fur was everywhere. Stuffed animals lay on every surface, all foxes; some beloved tattered children toys others official merch of characters, like Tails the two-tailed fox, Disney's various fox characters, and many others I didn't recognize. Over the bar was a huge mural of the fox Robin Hood dancing with a slender human woman with a peacock's fan of fox tails.

At the bar, a hulking man in a blue suit argued with a sparsely clothed woman with large fox ears and three white tails that shook with her agitation.

"I know you have it, Rey! Give it to me! I'm hungry." His wild mane of hair shook as he spoke.

The fox woman smirked and crossed her arms. "Beast-ie…" she drawled softly, "I can't simply give it to you, that's not how this works. My prices haven't changed, for you it might even go down a little because you're such a good customer, but nothing's free, love." She pouted prettily. "You don't want me to waste away, do you?"

The man growled, "You're flush!" His hand swept over the bar's decorations.

One ear twitched, although her coy expression didn't waver, "I haven't had a good movie in nearly a decade, Beast! Maybe you shouldn't glut yourself, it would last longer."

"I'm hungry, Rey," the man snarled, drool dripping from bared tusks. While he wore clothing, ripped almost directly from Disney's envisioning of Beast, his face had a more human cast, except that his lower jaw pulled out to accommodate the tusks that jutted from it.

"You want to owe me a favor instead?" the small fox-woman growled right back.

The beast flinched. "I ain't giving you no favors, Rey. I know what happened to Brom."

"Then get out." Her large tails reared up behind her, like snakes about to strike. Beast stepped back as if the fluff might hurt him somehow. Grumbling an oath, he turned and thumped out of the bar, slamming the door behind him.

Rey's eyes glided to Secret and her demeanor softened with pity. "Oh, honey, you've hit the catgirl so hard I don't even recognize you anymore. Unless you want to share in the fate of the Cat's court, you'd best find a new flavor to appreciate. I think I have some wolf girl fan fic, and there's still some werewolf left over from Halloween, if you can stomach that. Who were you?"

Secret sniffed and held the end of her tail with both hands. "Are you Reynard the Fox?" She asked.

The fox woman blinked. "Part of me once answered to that name." One elegant hand slipped behind the bar. "Are you from Summer? I am still neutral."

"My mother called you that. We need your help," Secret said, approaching her.

"We?" Rey's red brows furrowed before her gaze snapped up to mine. A breeze brushed through my hair and I heard a whisper of breaking glass. "Pierce me with iron!" She swore, eyes going wide, bright and hungry. "A mortal in the flesh."

She flowed over the bar in a blur of rusty red, moving so fast that her human skin trailed in her wake, momentarily exposing the animal beneath. Then she had fistfuls of my T-shirt, black lips inches from mine. "Five minutes," she panted, "You can have everything for five minutes of her devotion." Her golden slitted eyes broke into pixels and in them images flashed, each more erotic than the last, some mostly human, others very much not. As if every naughty image on the internet were flooding through her eyes. "You haven't had sex in years? Let me be your first!"

My breath echoed her panting as a fire wormed its way through me, ignited by her sheer want. "Male?" she asked. The gender in the torrent of images flipped and I felt a flash of revulsion. "Oh, no. Something bad happened there." The images shifted again, as innocent as the previous ones were dirty, foxes snuggling one another, nestled in loving arms. "How 'bout a cuddle? I can be very soft," her voice was a desperate whimper.

Her tails curled around my body, one sliding across the back of my neck. Warm, impossibly plush, I could sink into it forever.

"Let her go!"

18

"Yip!" Rey fell back from me, arms pinwheeling through the air, and landed on her fluffy-tailed ass with a loud clunk.

Secret stood in front of me. Hands on her hips. "Abby is mine. She's my knight!"

I shivered and then shook myself. My entire skull felt stuffed with fluff. Squeezing my eyes shut didn't help, all the images waiting in the dark for me. We were going to have to find a place that served brain bleach.

Rey pouted and rubbed her hip, "I wouldn't have done anything without permission."

"I think downloading half the internet's store of fox porn into my head counts as something that should require consent." I growled, smacking the side of my head with a palm in a futile effort to knock the images out of my head like water from my ear.

She maintained the pout as the corner of her lip curled into a tiny smirk. "I was... advertising." She made no effort to get up. While she only wore a woven metal bra on her top, a long red skirt covered her legs. Her expression soured as her gaze drifted back down to Secret. "Yippy dottle day." she said in the tone of a curse, "You're Puss's daughter."

"And you owe my mother a favor." Secret stated.

Rey winced. "I'm no help to you now. See?" Grabbing a fold of her skirt she pulled it up, revealing dainty human legs but one was stone to her thigh. "Look at me. Do I look like an ancient trickster at the top of my game to you? I'm a combination of scraps. Anything fox. I drink. I'm a mishmash of horny hopes, imported stories, and video game characters. You don't want me. I'll only slow you down. Even if you give me all of your mortal, I will still hobble." She regarded me with hunger.

"Moved pretty fast when you were trying to eat me." I observed. Now that we had stopped moving, exhaustion yawned, and my legs felt hollow and weak.

She smiled, "I didn't move. I moved you, mortal."

"Abby needs a teacher." Secret said.

"Free history lesson then, mortal. Puss in Boots is stone because she slipped into the Crossroads, that would be your world, before either Queen could do the deed. Summer forcibly annexed the entire court of cats and ordered them to retrieve Puss. They refused and turned to stone. Then she caught the Puss in Boots. It's very sad. But I can't repay the favor until Puss lives again." Her tails pushed her up into a standing position.

Secret thrust out a finger at her, the tear she had taken from her mother wobbled on it like a jewel of gelatin. "Even the Queen of Summer could not take all of Momma."

"No." Rey wheezed the word as if someone had punched her in the gut. "That's not fair. The seal is finally weakening. I'm so close to surviving its closure. If you make me help you, I'll be unraveled or worse."

"Reynard has to." Secret said, "And he's part you."

Her upper lip trembled even as she started to sniff at the tear, as if it were a piece of meat in a trap. "I want more. You have a mortal here, so you can open the circles; you take me with you. And the mortal gives me a moment of her."

"You owe my momma everything." Secret said in an imperious tone, tail lashing against my legs.

"Part of me does. The rest of me doesn't." Rey plucked the tear from Secret's finger and held it between them. "This will compel my service but everyone knows how that works out with foxes." Rey grinned toothily, "You need my loyalty. A moment will give me the strength to follow you, and I want to see the mundane world with my eyes, instead of listening at the cracks."

I knelt beside Secret and whispered into her fuzzy ear. "Is she safe to let loose in the city?" Rey hardly had half the menace of Little Nick but she had her own brand of unhinged danger.

"No," Secret whispered back, and giggled softly, "But she'll be our monster. I will bring you through Rey."

"What?" I swallowed as Rey grinned at me.

"Nothing she needs." Secret instructed. "And she needs a lot."

Rey gave a soft undulating yip, an inhuman laugh. "The smallest nibble, I promise." The tear went into her mouth and she swallowed it like a dry pill before dragging herself closer.

"I didn't say yes to being nibbled." I protested, but I found my hand entwined with hers

"Mortal, I can't walk unless you do. If you have to haul me everywhere, then your education will be very short." Her smile turned sly.

"Tell me why I need to give you anything. How does that help your leg?" I insisted.

She stayed silent a moment, "I was forced to break an oath some time ago. Scraps can keep me fed, but to heal I need a powerful prayer directly to me. A sacrifice."

"I thought you couldn't break an oath, period?" I asked.

"Sometimes promises cannot be kept. That is how Titania culls her court. Orders them against their very natures." Rey shifted and her slitted eyes glittered, "Now, have a little faith in me, and think of a moment where you were a fox."

"What?" I asked.

"Have you ever dressed up like a fox for a party?" She asked.

"No. I was more of a fairy princess type for Halloween." I said. I'd been a cat one year, but I'd never been bold enough to declare myself a fox to anyone. Foxes seemed far more confident than I had been as a kid.

"Second best then. A time when you were foxlike, proudly clever, deviously sneaky, or sexy as hell; any of that works." She squeezed my hands tight, amber eyes staring into mine as if they were screens that displayed my soul. I looked down to Secret; she watched me back, ears tense and focused. Did she know what I was getting into? Or was she as in the dark, too?

Under the weight of my misgivings, I searched my memories for times when I had not only been clever but felt clever. That would be far less painful than looking for pretty moments. Pretty me had gotten sarcastically cut down, either by my mother or Jimmy. Clever, though... The first time I'd skipped school floated into my mind. I licked my lips and nodded.

Rey stepped up to me, leaning her hips into mine. Reaching up, she placed a hand on either side of my face. Fingers soft and warm on my cheeks as she tilted my head down to stare into the pixels of her pupils that expanded to swallow my vision. "Now tell me the story when you were like me."

I heard myself speak, "Once I was as clever as Rey, the three tailed fox..." And there I was at the kitchen counter, 3-ring binder open to math homework, calculator off to the side. My mother's iPad was across from me, totally unguarded. All as I remembered, but I wasn't me. My tongue slid along poultry-menacing teeth and I held a pencil in a hand clad with black fur. My ear turned to listen to Mom snoring away on the couch in the living room. With the barest guilty glance in her direction, I snatched the iPad and pulled a printout of mom's face mounted on a popsicle stick from beneath my binder. Holding it up to the camera, I thumbed the on button. The iPad pondered the image for a long second and opened to the home screen. I swiftly navigated to my school's website, the iPad helpfully supplying the password. My three glorious tails wagged as I dug through the menus to mother's contact information, and changed the phone number to mine. I gave a little yip of victory as mom let loose a sawing snore. Carefully placing the pad back where it had lain, I finished my homework. For two years afterwards, if I cut class, the school called me instead of her. I had been Rey, the three tailed fox, that day.

A blink and Rey's warm lips parted from mine, shaping into a victorious smirk. Tentatively I touched the memory of that day, and again remembered the weight of tails on my spine. In my room later, bragging to Jimmy, I saw my human black painted thumbnails slide across the surface of my phone. Back when I changed the number, I had physically been a fox girl.

All I could do is blink, paging back and forth between that moment when I had been inhuman and everything else. Scratching at it, as if this sensation of fur and tails would fall away. But the more I looked at it, the more details I remembered, toe claws tapping on the metal rim of the stool, idly smoothing my whiskers as I waited for mom to sleep. More real instead of less.

"Don't look so shocked. It's my moment now. My piece of your life. I'll never let it go," Rey displayed her predatory teeth, "Abigail Samantha Night." Something about the way she said it tugged on me.

Secret hissed.

Rey let me go. "Peace, child. All part of the lessons. Here's the first one. Your name blazes on every piece of you, give a moment, you give your name on that moment. A mortal's name isn't their soul, but it is a thread I can pull or follow. Until it changes, I will know whether you live or die."

I stood there dumbstruck and awestruck, trying to test the integrity of my mind itself. Giving up on digging up the original scene, I turned to other clever moments in my life: switching the paperwork on behalf of a rider to make sure her insurance covered something, or a prank me and Cindy played on Cliff last year. They all spiderwebbed back to that moment where I had been Rey, as if all the cleverness had been added to my personality while I had been her. "You're.... Everywhere in my head."

"You gave me a foundational moment. Be more careful next time." She smiled, proudly, totally unapologetic. Her entire being brighter, more saturated, more real. "You'll get used to it. Or you could give me all of yourself and become part of me. Sacrifice yourself to me. Wouldn't that be fun? What do you say to that, Abby Night?"

"How about no way in fucking hell, Rey," I growled. "You're supposed to help us!"

She shrugged with her hands. "Can't blame a fox for

trying to get the whole pie." Bending over, she grabbed the ankle of her frozen leg and wrenched it upwards. With a resounding crack of breaking masonry the leg bent at the knee. "Much better," she sighed before standing back up and taking a few limping steps away from me. With a flourish, she bowed to Secret and then to me. "And so anchored by our pact, I will serve as your mentor until your death or my unmaking."

"Your attention, please." An intercom hissed to life from everywhere and nowhere. "We have been informed that there is a renegade cat in the building. Collect her and bring her to one of the Knights at entrance D for a court position."

Rey laughed grimly, "For however long that is."

19

"We need to get out of here." I looked around the bar. "Is there another exit?"

"I wouldn't be very clever if there wasn't." Rey's tails fanned out. "Hide behind me," she told Secret, "And put your glamour back on Lady Abby."

Secret's eyes shone momentarily, and then she wiped a dark drip from beneath her nose with a small sniff. Worry panged in my chest; she'd gotten a boost from her mother, but she still looked haggard, with deep circles beneath her eyes. Reminding me I wasn't the only one pressing against limits. She nodded to herself and then stood behind Rey. The tails fell on top of her, draping across her back and sides, nearly concealing her entirely.

Rey waved and the entire room slid away, replaced by a white stone path. Two marble statues guarded a downward stairway. One depicted a fox the size of a man, with a sword at his hip, and a triangular cap. The other depicted a maiden with a thin lipped smirk, bearing nine fox tails fanning out behind her. The positions and poses mirrored the stained glass window back at the Court of Cats. "Take my arm," Rey whispered from within the shadow of the deep hood of a tattered brown robe. Rounded spectacles covered her eyes, their lenses black.

I took her offered arm, and she leaned her weight against me. Together we walked forward. "So, were these your parents?" I heard myself ask in the silence.

She laughed, "Inari and Reynard. One ate the other, but who can tell which wound up in the belly? Rey is the result, who has no legends of her own but the one now in your head. A fox god without a story to call her own. So she claims every prayer to a fox. It's a strain to be all the foxes. To constantly twist to fit whatever stories I gather."

"I don't really understand," I said truthfully as I stepped down into the stairway. Lit by the glowing eyes of abstract fox masks that hung on the walls.

"You are from the Crossing. Where chaos gives birth to order, which yields to decay, to birth chaos once again. Here in the Dream, there is no death, only chaos and order in a constant back and forth. To become stone is to be locked in order, while to be undone is to devolve back to chaos. Limitless possibility and comforting patterns. Once we traded the Crossings for what we lack. This place was a bright reflection of your world. Humans could visit us with but a knock and name. We bled into each other, fostering children and sheltering our favorites from the decay and corruption that sup at your souls and body. A foxhole like this could lead anywhere in my world or yours. Then the Seal came."

"The Seal?" I asked. That seemed familiar somehow.

"The Seal of the Nine. Four Fey, Four from the Decay. Together they chose Sol as their leader and sealed away the invasion of the corruption. But in choosing Sol they shunned Luna, and she cursed the Seal. It rose in power year by year, cutting off both the Decay and the Fey. Now this land is not a reflection but a shadow," Rey whispered as if this were a deep secret.

"Luna cursed the Seal?" I asked, "Why?"

A small shrug. "The Night, The Day, and Earth. They exist in all realms but rarely in harmony. Luna is the night; by favoring Sol's children with Gaia, hers were sacrificed," she said, "I do not remember it well."

We came to a heavy-looking but unremarkable metal door with a long, polished handle. Rey grabbed it and paused. "This will bring us to the second floor. The knights will expect us at the rear of the building. We'll escape from the roof. Follow me." She opened the door into a heavily populated thruway. Yet they weren't moving; instead myriad creatures, from goblins to elves in business suits, sat or lounged on the red carpet at regular intervals. A tension strung like wires between them. "Iron chains and spikes." Rey swore softly. "Guru junkies; there must be a late-night session. Keep moving and don't stop." Suddenly, Rey put almost all of her weight on my arm, walking stiff-legged, as if her knee had not been unfrozen.

The signs read Oregon Ballrooms, A through D. The crowd increased in density around the doors A and B, which were guarded by large, burly creatures which look like the Beast's ugly cousins. Eyes and other things narrowed in warning as we navigated a path between the fey. "Happy hunting, just passing through." Rey called sunnily at them as we moved by, her limp heavy and obvious.

"What are they doing?" I couldn't help myself from asking through clenched teeth as we made it through the majority and their density decreased.

"Hunting prayers," she said, nodding towards a creature who sat along the wall, a spindly thing with a nose like an ice pick; his hands had reached out to encircle a shimmer that floated in the air. His fellows nearby glared with eyes green with greed. Rey gave a short, pitying shake of her head and we continued on. "Once you gave us blood and sacrifices and we gave you true dreams in return. As the Seal tightened, and only hidden places welcomed us, we became your warnings, a way to frighten your children into behaving. The Courts thrived on stolen children who wandered into our places. But as iron poisoned your world against us and the Seal shut us out entirely, you stopped fearing us, stopped mentioning us. Only those who could live on through stories you told about one another could get anything to eat, like the Guru who thrives on tales of power from nothing. Even the grand courts grown fat on captive mortals waned. Summer petrified while Winter cannibalized their ranks. Those in the middle did a bit of both or consumed whatever passions they could scavenge, forgetting themselves entirely. Yet at the height of the Seal's power, as nearly everyone stood on the cusp of stasis or unraveling, a hilarious thing happened. Do you know what that is?"

"I don't," I admitted. We were on the very edge of the crowd now.

She smiled happily. "You missed us! Stories about us flowed across the world, the lucky few were remembered verbatim, like the Puss in Boots, but most had our stories remixed and adapted. Small little snippets of discussion at first. The barest taste of passion and worship. But we hung on, and soon places that had only hosted the Guru or Mercury's offspring gathered in these temples."

A dog's bay cut through the air.

"Ach-chu!" Came from underneath Rey's tails and my nose itched fiercely.

Heads swung towards us.

Rey made a sort of wibbling whine and picked up her

pace. "Why does a gossip hound have your scent?" she asked as we reached a nondescript door.

The itch broke and reflex tossed my head back as another howl reached us. Rey's hand shot out and pinched my nose, stopping me mid-sneeze. "Ah," I tried to sniff, "met her trying to find you."

Panic lit up her face. "And she knows you're looking for me?"

I gave a little head shake to indicate yes. She let go of my nose and I sneezed with a quiet "-chu".

Rey pushed open the door. She took one step into the stairway beyond, and something huge crashed down on the platform. A huge Forgotten, its head a pizza box lined with pineapple wedge teeth yawned open in a forceful roar. Rey squeaked as one of the teeth flew from the mouth and smacked her cheek, "Hi, Brom! Bye, Brom!" She grabbed the handle and pulled the door closed with a bang. It shook with an impact. She jabbed her finger towards the end of the hall. "We'll take the elevator instead," Rey said, flashing me a toothy grin rimmed with panic.

We rushed down towards the bank of chrome doors; Rey dropped her straight leg act and pulled me along. No sooner had Rey slapped the call button then I heard a crackling voice, "There, there! See Pheme good! Show you. Cat bad! Fox bad!"

I glanced back to see Pheme grinning at us. Two knights on huge mounts, their beasts clopping after the gossip hound. The knights and their steeds were the inverse of each other. The knight on the white stallion had shoulders as broad as my arm is long, swathed in brilliant golden mail that clung to his muscular form. His opposite rode a creature the color of coal, horns of ice curling up from its brow. The black-armored knight was less impressive than his steed, tall and so painfully thin that his limbs resembled heavily armored broom handles.

The elevator dinged, but before the doors fully parted, a massive fist shot out between the silvery metal doors and seized Rey by her neck. "Going up?" Beast smiled as he jerked her inside, her tails dragging Secret in with her.

Swearing under my breath, I stepped in after them, and the doors slammed behind me faster than I've ever seen any elevator move. He held Rey up from the floor, two fingers and a thumb wrapped around her neck.

"Hello Beast," Rey gasped, "Fancy running into you. I'm so glad to run into someone who's very kind."

"Kind," He spat the word and stabbed the up button without looking at it. Growling, he brought Rey close enough to his face that flecks of spittle hit her in the face as he spoke. "This is my new bridge, Rey. How 'bout you pay me a toll for two?" He grabbed for Rey's tails and extracted a struggling Secret, holding her by the scuff of her neck. He whistled between his teeth, "Well... There really is a cat."

I couldn't stop my shout, "Hands off her!" And I swung my foot into the back of his knee. It had the same effect as chopping at a tree with a rubber mallet. He grunted with surprise, but not pain, and looked at me.

His eyes went round. "A mortal!" He boomed, grabbed me by both arms and laughed before breaking into song "Crack her skull! Suck the Marrooooow from her boooooones."

"No! She's mine!" Secret leapt onto his arm, biting into his wrist.

The barest flinch at the corner of his overjoyed grin was the only register of pain on his face. I tried to kick him but his long arms held me out of range. For the first time I regretted leaving the Cheshire's armor behind.

"I don't need your permission, if this is my bridge!" He hissed out.

"Beast, you don't have a bridge; you have a castle now." Rey said, grin renewed.

Secret hissed, kicked, and tried to claw at the arm like a feline Scrappy-Doo, with about as much effect. I dangled helplessly in his arms watching him salivate, a long drip of drool extending down from the corner of his mouth. The nostrils flaring on either side of his massive nose. And it slowly dawned on me that they were coming no closer.

Kind. Rey had reminded me of that. He dressed as Beast as in "Beauty and the Beast". A little laugh came out of my chest, and Secret paused her attacks to look at me. "Would you please put me down, Kind Sir? I would appreciate it."

His hands shook with strain. The lips pressed together and sucked inwards, fighting to hold in something.

The fox gave a little nod, urging me onwards, "Sir, you are frightening me." I said.

He let out a fetid breath, "I-I-I'm terribly sssssssorrry f-for frightening," each word ground past his lips, "y-you, Lady." My feet touched the floor and he withdrew his trembling hands, staring at them as if they were traitors. "What did you do to me, Rey?"

Rey giggled, "You did it to yourself! Been eating nothing but Beauty and the Beast excitement for decades. You can't revert back to being a troll simply because you feel like it. That's not your story anymore."

His massive hands cradled his head as if they were holding together his skull, a groan of pain filled the elevator as he sank to his knees.

A bright ding sounded and the doors opened. "This is our stop!" Rey called and tossed a glimmering something at the former troll. "For your troubles, dear Beast. A panel on writing B & B fan fic. Enjoy being a giant teddy bear."

Secret rose and dusted herself off as Beast sullenly sucked on the glimmer as if it were a hard candy. She wiped her lips and spat. "He still tastes bad," she said before looking up at me. "Are you okay, Abby?"

"I--- am," I forced a smile. Truthfully, I felt the strain. As if my body didn't quite fit right, as if something inside me hadn't quite popped back into place after the dark. "I need to get home."

Too bad I no longer had one.

20

Luna said nothing, waiting, watching as I followed Rey, her light cool and patient as a predator. On the roof was a corral of sorts, a trio of pegasi watched Rey warily. A pair of horses: one black as a moonless night, one shining pale white, yoked to a silver chariot, they snorted with suspicion and pawed at the concrete. "Who wants to be stolen tonight?"

The pegasi shied back and whinnied. The horses merely tossed their heads contemptuously.

"Thanks for volunteering!" Rey untied the reins from the thin exhaust pipe that held them and hopped up into the chariot. "Come on. Tell them where to go."

The light on my skin rippled, tickling like laughter, as Secret and I approached the chariot. My legs wobbled and her grip on my hand tightened. "The nearest circle. A forest that mortals can get lost in," she instructed.

"Then we need to cross the river, head for Washington park." I said, pushing Secret up on top of the platform.

Rey shook her head. "Crossing the river is dangerous with a mortal. Trolls rule the bridges and harpies nest in their heights."

I pulled myself up and thought. My ambulance usually kept to west Portland, but other jobs frequented the more densely packed east side. "Then Laurel Hearst Park might work. It's about three miles." My mind grasped for a GPS map, I knew it was near Burnside Street. Immediately, Jimmy flared through my mind. I wondered: if I saw the Burnside bridge, would I see a mark of Jimmy's final rage on this world? If there were fey who fed on stories, then there were fey who had to feed on rage too. The chariot creaked slightly beneath our weight. The texture of the railing I clutched had the warmth of wood and smoothness of metal. Secret grabbed hold of my leg as the horses started with a reluctant walk.

"Ha!" Rey cried and snapped the reigns, sending a wave rippling along the silver leather. The two horses looked at each other, and I had an impression that they were both holding back a laugh.

"Come on! I have your reins! Run." The fox girl's tails shook, buffeting me and Secret in their agitation.

"Halt in the name of Titania! The one true Queen!" A voice boomed from behind us.

"No! If you halt, do it in the name of Queen Mab! Queen of Winter, Who shall be Queen of all!" The second voice did not boom, but carried all the same authority.

I turned to see the knights, still astride their beasts, stepping out of the elevator, which jutted from the gray surface of the concrete roof.

"Do we stop for Summer, Brother?" asked the pale horse.

"Neigh," responded the night horse. "Do we stop for Winter, Sister?

"Neigh." The pale horse smiled with teeth that were too sharp to belong in a horse's mouth. The chariot lurched forward as the horses burst into a run. Their hooves thundered against the concrete as we raced for the edge of the roof.

"Cease!" Cried the knight with the armor that shone gold, but still the paired mounts stepped after us with that same unhurried pace. His armored helm swiveled to his black armored companion. I lost the rest of his words beneath the staccato rhythm of the hooves as the edge drew closer.

My heart surged up into my throat. They could fly, right? They were on the roof so that had to mean they flew up here. I had seen too many wonders so far to believe that these talking horses were suicidal, but doubt hammered at me as I gripped both the chariot and Secret in equal measure. No more than ten feet from the edge, the horses swerved, jerking the chariot hard. The wheels skidded across the pavement as we fishtailed across the roof, one wheel dropping off the roof before slamming back on. Everyone shrieked as the chariot bucked beneath us.

"What the hell are you doing?!" I found myself shouting at the horses. "Aren't you supposed to fly?"

The horses giggled like two schoolchildren as they galloped along within inches of a sheer drop off the building. "Now they want us to fly as the moon does through the sky!" The pale horse shouted.

The night horse glanced backwards. "A fey knight does come, sister. With murder in his eyes." And indeed the golden-clad knight had broken away from his partner and charged across the roof directly at us, the stallion's hooves making cracking sounds as they cut across the ocean of solar panels that reflected Luna's silver light.

"Do you want to be stone?!" Rey cracked the reigns. "Run!"

The horses leaned into their speed, and the expected

clatter of their hooves ceased as they lifted into the air, pulling the chariot up onto an invisible road. This time as the edge neared, they did not turn, but carried us over the edge, running on over the tops of the tallest trees.

But the knight didn't slow at the edge, either, multicolor hues shone beneath his steed as it over ran the roof, chasing us on a rainbow. "Know that Ser Gabelleri pursues you, mortal! And there is nowhere you can run that I cannot find." He hollered at us. "You will yield the halfling to me!"

The horses laughed. "We have outrun the wolf who would eat the moon for centuries. He will never catch us."

True to their word, while the knight galloped after us on his rainbow road, he did not loom closer, but neither did he recede. I watched roads below pass by; we were roughly following Burnside Street out into east Portland. There, ahead of us, I spotted a dark rectangle of forest, a block south of Burnside. It had to be the park, or at least one like it. "There it is!" I pointed, "Take us down there." Then added, "Please."

The horses bent their necks to regard us with a single glossy eye each. "But we have just begun to run. Let us circle the earth and come on back. Maybe we'll stop on a future pass," the dark horse said.

"Besides," the pale horse said, "if we stop now, he will catch you. Overrun. Stay safe with us, and let us run from the day."

"Rey? Is this the moon's chariot?" I asked softly before looking back at the knight, claspinga shimmering sword in one hand and the reins of his white stallion in the other. He flipped his visor up, revealing eyes that burned with the same light that I had watched fade away.

"I would have thought that would have been obvious,

even to a mortal," Rey huffed. "Should have taken the pegasi though, they'd be faster."

"Secret, once we get through the circle, can you close it?" I asked.

"No," Secret whispered, "if I could, then none of this would have happened. No one would have followed me back."

I watched the knight, he stared back with his blazing eyes. Horse not slowing, tireless, every hoofbeat broadcasting a terrible strength. All this to get away from Little Nick. To understand what he was. I'd run from my flaming apartment, run from the moon's offered power, bent into the shape of a cat, run from the Cheshire's armor, and given a piece of myself to a gleefully untrustworthy fox. I wanted nothing more than a bed and a long sleep. This journey had to end soon, or there wouldn't be enough of me to hold myself into a coherent whole. I had run out of fucks. I had run out of fear. "Okay, Luna. You've made your point," I whispered softly as Secret hugged my leg possessively.

The horses said nothing but abruptly made a sharp turn. They pounded down towards the rectangle of woods. The knight copied our turn, not cutting the corner, but seemingly bound to the same path the horses took. A grin of victory split his lips as his stallion's hooves sparked on the pavement. The moon crept low in the sky, appearing to follow Ser Gabelleri as he chased after us.

While our chariot swerved around the shadows of cars, the knight sliced through them with a sweep of his sword. What had the Cheshire said? One for darkness, one more for power. And the third touch... what would that do?

The chariot slowed as we crossed into the park. I pried off Secret's grip. "Abby, no," she protested but didn't fight. I stepped off the chariot and onto the paved path. My feet stumbled before I caught myself and stood up with my arms stretched out to the side. "Stop!" I shouted at the Knight.

The beast he rode skidded to a stop, and he dismounted with a disturbing smoothness for a body so large. "So sense finally prevailed. Quickly now, pass the girl to me before the usurper's dog catches up. I can spirit her to the arms of the Queen before Winter closes on us."

"No," I said. "I will deliver her to a Queen when I'm ready."

"You must, my sister's geas requires you. Hand her over. Or you will share the fate of her other protectors." The thick blade glinted as she twirled it in her hand.

"Never said which Queen. Maybe I'll bring her to the Queen of England." I smiled tightly as I reached up until the moon floated between my thumb and forefingers.

"So be it." He took a step forward as my fingers closed around Luna's cool light.

"Finally. You have touched me in the Twilight and now in the Dream. No human that breathes can say the same. The orbits shift, and you have made yourself a fulcrum." A soft voice spoke in my head, and her light flooded down around me.

"You set me up." I growled as her form poured down from the sky. A woman, clad in armor and pale feathers, hands clasping spear, bow, and gun stood before me. Then a beast, swathed in white fur, with a muzzle of gleaming silver, curled around my back. And again she shifted, unable to contain herself to a single form for more than a moment, and in between, as she flickered and flowed I felt the sheer vastness of her existence pressed against my infinitesimally small spark.

I crystallize your choices, Abby Night. My chariot would have let you run until my brother grows cold. Even a fey grows tired. But you chose to answer the destiny I offer. She grasped my left arm, holding me with a pale, three fingered hand, a paw baring wicked claws, a silver hoof.

"Shove your destiny," I snarled. "I'm a medic, not a farm boy with a sword. I just want your help once more."

In response she sank those silver teeth into the flesh of my left arm. Her gentle laughter rolled through me as I cried out from the pain. *Who else will give you what you need? I will take no price for this touch, but do not reach for me with an empty hand again.* Her teeth burrowed into my arm as she spoke, slithering like snakes up my arm and into my very mind, their sharp tips piercing through the barriers I had built to wall off the past. They wrapped around the countless closets labeled "later," where the memories of bad runs rotted, dialed the combination to the safe that bore Jimmy's name, and overturned the pot of my bubbling resentment.

"Stop!" I called out, pleading.

She answered with a stern growl. *If you do not give me your love, then I will reforge your pain.* With a merciless strength, she pulled and twisted, spilling every single hurt I had ever sustained, deserved or not, external or self-inflicted, it didn't matter, I relived it all in a cacophony of agony. The sharp-edged memories cut into my heart and shredded my flesh as I howled. The snap of a girl's ribs as I pumped her chest at the side of a mangled car, the twin caskets of my parents lying before me, the gleaming blade that carved the clumsy swastika off my flesh, the way Jimmy leered up into my vision every time a man smiled at me with a flirtatious sparkle in his eye, life in my bare apartment, my lonely routine outside work. Empty as the rest of my life. So Unfair! This life. I wasn't supposed to live this life. Watching children die on the way to the hospital? Not on my watch! No one could die on my shift!

The world shifted form; shifted from silver to red, strewn with the wreckage of my life. Center stage, Jimmy grinned as he held up the black assemblage of plastic and metal, the gun that I had purchased for him. I slammed a fist into his grin. He staggered back and charged at me, swinging his gun as a club. Catching it with my teeth, I ripped it from his hands and raked my fingers across his belly with the same motion. The screech of metal echoed as the blow spun him into the air.

A horn blared. I turned to find a pickup truck weaving drunkenly towards me. It struck me head on, driving into my stomach. Caught on its grill, I tore off the hood and ripped out the engine. Gas fountained in my face and I tumbled, rolling back onto all fours. A buzzing of wings drew my gaze up in time to see a swarm of Mister Gifford's stupid checklists before they dove on me in a whirling torrent of paper. Rearing up, my mighty talons slashed them to ribbons. Behind them I found Jimmy's snide smirk flying at me. His gleaming pistols popped feebly. I crushed his wrists and pulled him into my maw, sinking my teeth into his shoulder. He bled blue and tasted of sour apples as I shook him side to side, reveling in the way his flesh tore around my teeth. A knife slashed at my arm and I threw him away like the trash he was. A hospital administrator came running at me with a hatchet made of "cover my ass" and lawsuits. I kicked her with the flat of my foot and sent her sprawling. Minor annoyances.

Turning, I focused on the Jimmy thing. The bastard had killed himself, leaving me to suffer for his sins.

He lay on the ground, a gaping hole where one of his arms had been. His mouth spouting filth, "The war's coming Abs! It's us or them, and it's gonna be them! The Jews, the damn brownies. Shoot first!"

I roared, burying his voice. How could I love that thing? Dead or not, I'd make him hurt now. Stalking forward, I hauled him upright and drove my knee between his legs.

Blood poured from his mouth as he parroted his first words to me, "Hey, you're kinda pretty."

It earned him a slam dunk into the pavement and a kick in the stomach.

"Pretty for a chink!" he spat.

Maybe being dead had made him extra thick. I brought up my foot to shatter his femur.

Something latched onto my ankle. "That's enough! You win!" it cried, a strange blur in my vision. But it was wrong. Jimmy was dead, but still breathing. Still taunting me. He had to suffer, he had to understand what he did. How he shattered me. I reached after the blurry thing and it sprang, grabbing hold of my wrist instead. I felt small hands grabbing fistfuls of my fur as it climbed up to my elbow and clung to my forearm. Legs wrapped around my wrist. No matter how I swung my arm it held on. It remained blurry, shapeless, as if it didn't fit in the world correctly. It smelled familiar. I brought it to my chest and gently stroked its soft length. It purred, and silver light burned through the red.

Secret. I had to protect Secret. I remembered. Jimmy was dead, he'd been dead for ten years now. He couldn't hurt anyone. I had to focus on the now, not the past. I gave a small laugh, how many therapists have told me that one? The now was Secret. Not Jimmy.

I breathed out, and a heaviness left with it. Looking down, I found Secret nestled against my breasts, purring as hard as her small feline body could. The moonlight, pale and cool, bathed my skin, all my skin, save my hands, covered in an inky blue ichor. I stood butt naked in the moonlight. Scattered around me lay mangled bodies, the

Knight and his horse, along with a scattering of curled insect wings, vines crawling out from beneath the armor, flowers blooming from the blue blood.

Turning, I found Rey clutching her stomach, a dark substance marring the corner of her mouth. Rey's golden eyes were round and wide, reaching anime-like proportions. Meanwhile, the horses watched me with studied animal neutrality.

"Berserker." Rey finally broke the silence. "I'm chained to a berserker."

"Did... I hurt you?" I asked. My voice felt rough, my innards hollow.

She nodded. "I am sorry, Mistress," she said with stiff formality as I smelled her fear. "The knight surrendered, and you didn't hear him. I foolishly attempted to get in your way. Thank you for not ending me for my presumption." She bowed.

"He... surrendered?" I looked back at the fairy corpses. "I didn't hear that."

"Mew," Secret pawed at me, and I looked down to watch her feline eyes give a slow blink and then rub her nose against me. The fear that clutched at my heart didn't reflect in her at all. With another, more urgent meow, she leapt down from my arms and ran for the trees. Pausing at the cusp of the forest to look back at Rey and me with tail-lashing impatience.

I allowed myself one glance back, not at the bodies, which were now melting into other things, but the moon. She sat in the sky, patient and serene as my own guts roiled. There had to be another way. There had to be.

21

"Blind in one eye." Sergeant Joffrey Lambert lay in his hospital bed, those words echoing through his head. The drugs had dulled the pain that throbbed from his cotton covered eye, leaving the constant beep of the machines by his bedside. He had only been awake for half a dozen hours, since the drugs had withdrawn from his system. A team of doctors had put his eye together and they hoped for the best. The doctor's face had told him not to hope for much.

Mom had offered to fly to see him, but they were discharging him tomorrow. He had only lost an eye. Compared to Henderson, who might lose an entire arm, one eye was nothing; he'd get a glass one, retire with disability pay, and move on to something else. The Captain had been by, promised to catch the bastard who did this. That the PPD would not rest until this Santa lay bleeding in the dirt.

Joffrey supposed that made him feel better. But other than the smiling nurses who assured him that he was so brave, checking on him once an hour at their appointed times he felt adrift. He tried to watch TV with his one good eye, but in the dark of the other, he kept seeing the door in that firehouse open. The man there laid out on the desks. Flesh carved away from bone into delicate flowers that framed the white. Channels carved in the still-living bone that filled with blood to create the outline of a rose on the skull's forehead. The jaw wrenched open to display a tongue cut into six petals of flesh. The center holding up the roots of pulled teeth like stamens waiting for a bee.

A horrific work of art. Still, it sat there in the dark of his mind, indifferent to his nausea, which subsided in time. Joffrey had remembered nothing as vividly as that man whom he didn't know the name of.

He made sure to focus on the people who came to visit him, but once they left, it was only him and the exquisite corpse in his mind. Better to look at that than his own mangled future. The questions of why dimmed, and he turned more to the how. How do you cut muscle like that? What sorts of tools did you need to chisel such a line into the skull? Had that malicious gnome been hiding an entire set of tools beneath his suit? Or had the shiny mirror of a knife been his only tool? At what point in the process had the victim died?

Such was the state of his mind as the sun set once again, and night cloaked the early evening. Perhaps with time and therapy, Joffrey's newly manifested morbid curiosity would have faded, or perhaps he may have embarked on a successful career as a medical examiner, occasionally finding the time and opportunity to practice folding flesh.

But a radically different fate rode up the elevator for Joffrey Lambert an hour after sundown. So wide and bloated that its form clipped both sides of the elevator door. A bell clattered as it giggled down the hall. Patients drugged into comas pulled the bedsheets up over their heads. Every nurse on the floor took a bathroom break, and were shocked to find colleagues crowded in with them. They did not voice this surprise, lest they be heard. They did not hear the clattering bell, but each felt the cold skeletal hands of dread wrapping around their spine.

Joffrey heard it, though. As sweat started leaking from every pore, the crystalized image in his head shimmered into a grin with oversized teeth. Then the image split apart and collapsed into pain.

"Merry Christmas." The high-pitched squeal sent Joffrey's heart into overdrive, and yet he found himself unable to move.

The manic grin reached to the edges of the doorframe. The creature stepped through the doorway, that was much too small for it, its flesh stretching and straining like a partially deflated balloon being pushed through a hole. With a snap, his body lurched through, jiggling and rippling as Jell-O might. He filled almost the entirety of the end of the shoebox-shaped room. Cap pressed flat against the ceiling, it left a red trail as Little Nick stepped closer to Joffrey.

'He's come for my other eye!' Was the whimpered thought that ran through Joffrey's mind, but there was no knife twirling in Little Nick's giant swollen hand. Instead a long cap drippled its crimson dye onto the floor.

Joffrey's hands drifted up to ward off a blow, mouth working up and down as he dredged the very depths of his soul for the courage to scream.

"Ho, ho, ho!" Little Nick laughed, his flesh undulating with the force of it. Through his splayed fingers, Joffrey saw that face had a constellation of angry welts across it. "Are you a good little boy? Because I brought you a present." He held up the cap and let it fall from his fingers. It dropped into Joffrey's lap with the wet slap of a slab of raw meat.

The hat radiated heat into Joffrey as the red crawled into

the white of his bedsheets. "Wha-wha-what?" He managed to force the word out between the stiff flesh that his lips had become.

"Christmas comes early for boys that appreciate my art," Little Nick said, sweeping the chair and end table beside Joffrey's bed away with a massive hand and sitting down beside him in a companionable manner.

"What- No! I-I-I didn't." Joffrey sputtered. He couldn't know that, it was impossible for him to know his thoughts. Nobody should ever know that.

"Little Nick knows when you've been naughty," he whispered. "He saw your eyes linger over the beauty. Hee, hee, hee." And with that, he jabbed a fat finger in Joffrey's wounded eye.

The pain made him cry out, clutching at the wounded socket. As he did, the scene replayed in his head of entering that room, of seeing the display in slow motion, every tiny detail magnified, things that he couldn't have possibly have noticed became obvious. How the very veins and arteries had been arrayed as flowers, the scrimshaw on the ribs, the cuts that severed the nerves. "B-b-beautiful" He choked out the word, tears squeezing out from his good eye.

"The why is on your mind. Turn on your magic panel, and let's watch the show," Little Nick said, taking one of Joffrey's hands within his.

Shaking, Joffrey lifted the remote from his side and clicked on the TV that hung from the ceiling at the foot of his bed.

A well-coiffed news anchor appeared on the screen with a strained smile. "As we continue our top story tonight, images of the first victim of the Savage Santa killer, George Gifford, have leaked online. They are gruesome in the extreme and the Portland Police Chief has denounced the leak, saying it is a hindrance to the investigation but did not deny their validity. They are available online on our website, but viewer discretion is highly advised."

"That's right. Go take a peek," Little Nick said to the room.

They sat for a minute, Joffrey's heart thundering as a sharp coldness pushed into it. Each beat pulling it deeper inside like a barbed quill.

Little Nick exhaled suddenly, the breath flowed up Joffrey's arm and inflated his own chest. The coldness ignited in a hail of fiery sparks. Voices jolted through Joffrey's being, *Ohgods!Whowoulddothat?Heoutthere!* And hundreds more in a symphony of fear and shock, the sheer force of it barreling through him.

Then gone, as quick as it had come. Joffrey slumped down against the bed, jaw slack, remaining eye dilated to the barest rim of brown. A euphoric chill spreading through his chest. The sensation of wind whistling through the holes in his soul. "Again," he breathed.

The ancient redcap grinned wide as a proud father. "Put on your cap, One-eyed Joffrey, and I will show you how it's done."

Joffrey picked up the sodden cap and slid it over his skull. A small "hee, hee, hee," crept from his lips as his grin widened beyond the confines of his face.

22

Cold slapped across my tits with the sting of a sopping wet towel wielded as a rattail by a bratty cousin. That's how I knew we'd finally made it back to Portland through the swirling forest circle. Breathing out a frosty "Fuuuuu-" I wrapped my arms around myself and shivered in the gray light of morning. The sudden loss of my clothing hadn't seemed like a big deal in the Dream. That night had been cool, but not the least bit uncomfortable.

'Welcome back', reality seemed to say in the most bitchy way possible.

I wasn't the only one looking uncomfortable, either. Beside me, Rey wrinkled her nose as if she'd opened up the break room fridge after a long power outage. Of the three of us, only Secret appeared to be remotely comfortable, lapping at her bloody hand. We again stood in a circle, this time of 13 flat stones that bore droplets of reflective mirrors on their surface. I had been a bit worried that the fairies had mistaken magic for mercury. No stone pixies had guarded this circle, instead a pair of them watched us make our way. Now in... Crossroads? My brain tossed around terms in a bid to ward off the chill. The dead ruled Twilight and the Fey lived in the Dream. Those had been Luna's terms.

"It's all the iron that smells bad," Secret told Rey, "Momma said you get used to it."

Rey frowned, clearly dubious.

Meanwhile, my body started to shiver rather violently. "I don't suppose either of you could l-l-lend me some clothing? Or magic up a robe or something?" I looked at Rey.

She opened her mouth to reply when something clattered behind me.

"Careful!" Someone shouted, a male voice.

I spun and simultaneously heard the rustle of fabric on either side of me. Oh some help you two are, I thought bitterly. Turning back to run, I spotted both a small cat and a fox breaking for the trees. It had been a long time since I had last attempted barefoot running, since I was five and slipped on dog doo. I'd been a fan of shoes since. I ran, hating every moment. This grove was not nearly as impressive as the primordial forest Secret had led me to for our entry into the Dream. The trees here were not even as thick as me. Still, their twigs scratched at my skin as I ran by them.

"Hey! There goes something!" Another man called out as I slipped and slid on the leaf litter. Falling down to my hands and knees twice and scrambling back to my feet. No surge of rage or transformation, just me frantically trying to find a place to hide. The forest thinned out quickly, trees became sparse, and I nearly tripped over a paved running path, my ankle rolling as I crossed it. The side of my foot tasted the sharpness of the craggy asphalt for the duration of that step. Pain lanced up my leg as the shout of a shocked jogger rocked my head. I stumbled on, my ankle screaming. There was nowhere to hide; the park had no underbrush to dive into, just trees, muddy ground, and paths.

A thick redwood stood not five feet off the path, a solitary survivor of the olden days. I made like a squirrel, well, a squirrel would have climbed it, I put it between myself and my pursuers, at least.

"I got her!" The second man called out.

"Leave me the fuck alone!" I shouted back, a hysterical squeak to my voice. It'd be just my luck for it to be the cops, and if I was lucky, I'd be arrested for public indecency. I covered myself the best I could and waited. The footsteps stopped and I could hear heavy breathing. Not a cop. Cop wouldn't have stopped. I peeked around the tree and recognized the beard that hung over the Ghost Hunter T-shirt instantly.

Slade Higgins, of all the luck. He held some black contraption in his hands that had several extendable antennae protruding from it. And behind him, Nigel Higgins stood holding his camera. Worse than cops? No, neither of them had guns out, at least. I pulled myself back behind the tree, "I do not consent to be fucking filmed!" I shouted, proud that I managed to sound more angry than desperate.

"Nuts. Holy goddammit." Slade sputtered. "You're that chick from the apartment building yesterday! The one with the crazy goth friend who pulled a pistol on us!"

No denying it. "That's me," I said, then thought a half-second. Either I have to walk a mile ass-naked or... I took a deep breath. "You two have a blanket I can borrow?"

"Where's my gun?" Slade answered with a huff.

"Probably burned to a cinder along with the rest of my worldly possessions." I snarled, although my teeth had suddenly remembered the chill and started to clatter together.

"Burned?" He said with a note of incredulity.

"It's been a hell of a n-n-night alright?" I said unable to prevent my teeth from chattering any longer.

"I'll get ya something." Nigel said, "Be right back."

"Nige!" Slade barked.

"She definitely isn't a fairy or a ghost, bro." Nigel said. "Not gonna film it."

"Maybe she's a witch!" Slade countered.

"I'm not going to cross a witch in Portland. They've practically got a union," Nigel half-shouted, "Stay there, I'll be right back."

I chuckled beneath my breath. Nigel had this long-suffering quality to him that I couldn't help but like.

Slade grunted. "So how'd you get out here naked?" he asked after a moment of brooding silence.

"I r-r-rode my broomstick, but I ran out of nightshade and crashed into the park," I said.

"That's not funny." Slade said. "Burning apartment... You somehow mixed up in this Santa killer shit?"

My smile died and the cold air redoubled its efforts to bite off my fingers and toes. "What killer Santa?" I asked.

"Killed like nine folks and slashed up a whole mess of cops. Burned down an apartment building. They've got checkpoints all over the west side, going house to house to find him. News channels saying he's gotta be some sort of asylum escapee or something, but I know he ain't even human." He said.

"Why do you say that?" I asked.

"Tell me how you appeared in the middle of this park. We were two blocks away trying to contact a ghost when then my EMF reader went nuts. Tracked the signal all the way here. You lit up the infrared too. Column of heat climbed right into the sky. What the hell did you do?" Slade asked.

Dang, apparently Secret's crossings weren't subtle at all if you knew what you were looking for. Thinking of the girl, there she was, not a girl through, still a cat. Both Secret and Rey were peering at me from either side of a tree a little further from the path. "I survived." I said.

Slade didn't press as I heard Nigel returning. "I got a blanket and a spare pair of boots." He set the blanket on the roots of the tree. Camo patterned of course. I guess Slade's zombie-hunting channel wasn't so popular that he had sprung for branded blankets yet. I grabbed it, threw it around my shoulders, and immediately felt better surrounded by the thick fleece. The boots were comically oversized, but the real world didn't seem to care that I'd been walking around all night in socks. My stumble on the path had claimed a fair bit of skin as a toll.

"Can we bring you somewhere?" Nigel asked as I stepped around the tree. I considered walking to Cindy's like this but a blanket was only marginally better than naked and I could see the cops getting interested. My hair wasn't quite matted enough to look homeless and uninteresting yet.

"Yeah," I said. "Let me get my pets. Come on, you two." I gestured at the fox and the cat.

Secret hesitated a moment before running directly for me. I opened the blanket and she leapt right up into my arms. Rey took a half step from the safety of the tree and nodded. With Secret against my chest I immediately felt warmer.

"Familiars!" Slade declared. "You really are a witch!"

I ignored him, pulling the blanket tighter around my body. Instead I looked at Nigel; he examined me coolly through his gold-rimmed glasses. When our eyes met, he quickly looked away, a slight color to his cheeks. "Alright. Thanks for the ride." I wouldn't trust Slade but his brother definitely had a core of something I liked. Too bad he seemed saddled with a man-child like Slade.

"Truck's this way." He moved his head in the direction of the parking lot, and we all set off. The oversized boots flopped around my feet, but I managed not to trip. Rey kept pace with us, trotting quickly tree to tree with a three legged gait. Slade walked beside me, strangely silent, sucking on a strand of his bushy beard. The jacked-up zombie ghost hunter truck waited for us. Nigel opened the passenger door as Slade tossed a bunch of debris into the back of the cab, clearing the middle for me.

I was about to be sandwiched between two men whom the last time we'd met, guns were drawn. Before climbing up, I searched Nigel's face for any sign of malice or snideness. He looked back at me with a nervous smile; he had warm blue eyes.

"Come on," Slade patted the seat, "We won't bite, promise."

"You try anything, I do." I snapped.

He showed me the palms of his hands, huffed indignantly, and placed them on the steering wheel. "Just tell me where to go, crazy."

Clutching Secret with one arm, I pulled myself up into the seat and slid to the middle. As soon I settled, I caught a red streak of motion in the corner of my eye. "Woah," Nigel exclaimed as Rey landed in my lap.

She looked like a very natural fox, if you discounted the three tails and the stony gray fur that covered her left hind leg. Slade stared at her for a moment. "Shite," and started the engine. "You ever..." he paused uncertainly, "Heard of something called the Seal of the Nine?"

I considered. Rey had mentioned the Seal in her little lesson. That Slade would know anything about it was curious and worrying. "Maybe," I said in a noncommittal tone, and I gave him Cindy's address. I regretted it immediately, last thing Cindy needed were these two yahoos harassing her. Slade nodded as the truck started to move. "If I said that something's happened to it, would you know how to fix it?"

"No," I said, "I wouldn't have a clue."

"Nine," he stared off through the wind shield. "There have to be nine to close it again."

"Bro, don't start this." Nigel crossed his arms.

"What if she's one of the Nine?" Slade pulled on his beard and cast me a side-eyed glance. "If the Seal isn't renewed soon by a pact of nine, it will fall. Then night will rule. That's real bad. Like 'end of the world' bad."

"Sorry, he gets this way sometimes." Nigel grinned at his brother, eyes pleading with him to shut up.

"She's a witch, Nige, she's got a black cat and a three-tailed fox. It's real." He looked at me, his eyes; the brothers had the same warm blue eyes, but Slade's had a sharp glint in them that made me uneasy. "It is real. Isn't it? The Seals failing, faster than they're supposed too. This killer Santa thing is just the first creature creeping through the damn crack."

"Slade, she's had a rough night," Nigel said. "Don't give her the crazy. Sorry, Slade gets dreams sometime."

Someone behind honked and Slade jumped through the green light he had almost missed.

"I'm not crazy," Slade muttered. "The world's gonna end if we don't do something."

I laughed a bit nervously. "I would have thought you'd think that would be a good thing. Don't all you Higgins go to Reverend Tony's church?" I inquired.

Both Nigel and Slade looked at me with an identical sharpness. The same expression on two very different faces. "How the hell do you know our name?" Slade demanded.

23

Shit. "I looked you up on your channel." I said, feeling suddenly flushed.

"It's not on the channel," Nigel said, staring hard at me, "I'm very careful about that."

Slade pulled over and cocked his head. Recognition sparked in his eyes. "I knew it! I knew you from somewhere. You're that creep Jimmy Lipple's girlfriend! The maniac that shot up the Burnside bridge!"

"Was!" I snapped back and growled. He didn't even know my fucking name, just Jimmy's. That hurt like claws twisting in an open wound.

Slade flinched, slamming his head against the window. "Jesus!" He swore. "What the hell are you?"

"My name's Abby. Not Jimmy's girlfriend. In case you've forgotten, Jimmy killed both my parents. Do not mention his name to me! Got it?" My voice had gone low with the threat, and the growl rolled up from beneath my words. I looked up at the road. We were only a block away from Cindy's. Taking a deep breath, I forced myself to let go of the growl.

"Your name doesn't explain those eyes." he said.

"Nothing's wrong with my eyes." I turned to Nigel, who watched us both with wariness. "I'd like to get out now. Thank you for the ride."

Nigel watched me, his eyes going to his brother before he popped open the door and slid out of the cab. If something had happened to my eyes, he made no comment.

"Dude you saw that! Nige, she's part of this! She has to be," Slade pleaded as I made my way out of the vehicle and onto the sidewalk.

I offered my hand to Nigel. "Gimmie one of your cards. I'll mail you this stuff back.

With a nod he pulled a business card from the breast pocket of his flannel. "Sorry. About my brother and for your loss and all." Eyes not quite meeting mine. I glanced at the card: Slade the Ghost Hunter Inc. The address had a PO box.

"Nige!" Slade shouted, I had no idea what he meant for Nigel to do. I took the card and started walking. Nigel got back in the truck.

The truck caught up, and Slade yelled at me through the passenger window. "How are you involved?! Are you bringing the Seal down? Do you know of the Nine?"

"I have no idea what you're talking about, Shove off!" I flashed him the finger.

"Dammit!" The truck roared off, leaving me in a very odd position. Secret purred lightly against my chest, while Rey ventured, exploring the unfenced yards of the houses we passed.

Cindy's house was easy to spot among a neighborhood of brightly colored, or at least clean, two-story houses of various architectural schools. It stood the tallest on the block, while simultaneously looking like it'd fall over if the wind managed more than a gentle breeze. It had been in Cindy's family for three generations, and passed to her two years ago after her mother died. Her mother had run it as an Airbnb for two decades, but the plagues destroyed the business. It had been a hair's width from being condemned when Cindy inherited it. She'd been making what repairs she could afford since, but the roof had nearly collapsed two months ago. So the cracked and peeling paint was vastly outshone by the bright blue tarp that covered about a fourth of the roof.

The house had originally been a Craftsman, but had expanded in the days before modern building codes, so it looked as if a small square manor had grown from the back of the original house, like some sort of elegant tumor. My boots clomped up the stairs of the porch. I hoped she was home, or the neighbors would probably call the firebugs on me for being a vagrant. The bell hadn't worked in a decade, so I reached for the heavy iron door knocker.

"Ahem! Might I have a word?" The voice from the roof of the convention center, the Black Knight. I gave the door a single bang and turned around. There on the sidewalk, he sat astride his dark beast. His helmet stretched tall and narrowed in the middle. He bore no weapon, only a golden pocket watch rested in his absurdly long fingers. Its face was open, and I heard its soft ticking.

"The answer is no. You cannot have her," I said, my eyes searching Cindy's front yard for weapons; the path up from the sidewalk had a black chain railing along one side. Probably steel, but if I could knock him into it...

"Pity, that," he said. "Let me introduce myself, at least." He swung down from his beast and bowed. "I am Sir Damocles, Knight of Winter, Duke of Inevitable. In the name of

Queen Mab I am here to formally request that which you will not do, but will happen."

"Piss off," I said, hugging Secret close. "You'll wind up like Ser Gabelleri if you try." I'm sure that sounded very intimidating coming from a woman huddled under a blanket.

"I will make no attempt on you now. Ser Gabelleri was desperate, I released him from our agreement to reach you together, knowing your favor with the Lunar Court. The outcome was... Inevitable." The helmet he wore betrayed no expression, but I heard the smile in the way he savored that word. "A Knight of Summer this close to the Winter Solstice is at a whisper of their true strength."

"Then why bother me at all?" I asked.

"I obey my Queen. And she seeks to remind you that a cat can thrive in darkness, and offers the withdrawal of the Redcap should you oblige her wishes. Otherwise the blood he spills is on your hands. And even if you survive him, the Queen herself will ride on the Solstice. Not even iron will save you from her." A cold, clinical part of me kicked in: the part you call on when a disaster struck, when there were too many victims and not enough hands. Triage, a time when you have to decide who to treat based on who's likely to live and who's likely to die. I could trade Secret for an unknown number of innocent lives in exchange for her innocent life. But in this Queen of Winter's hands, Secret would be some sort of terrible tool.

No. I wouldn't be giving her to that Queen.

Fingers tightened around my heart. I'm protecting her, you fuckhead promise. Okay, look, Portland had a Rose Festival in the spring which crowned a Rose Queen. I can present her to that Queen. She'd give her back. The promise let go. "You can't have her. I'm... I'm adopting her."

"Mew?" asked from beneath the blanket.

"Unlikely." Damocles shook his helmeted head before spinning on his spindly heel, grabbed hold of one of his beast's horns and vaulted up onto the saddle. Exhibiting that same bone-bending flexibility that Little Nick had when he attacked Cliff. "My offer remains open until my Queen rides the skies, mortal protector of the Halfling," he called at me. "Say my name. Till then. Tick-Tock." A hollow laugh filled the air as he spurred his mount. It whirled and galloped down the street. Within three long strides, he disappeared into a fog that rose suddenly on the street.

I let out a breath and leaned back against the door.

Somebody opened it.

"Abby! You're alive!"

Secret mewed in alarm as two arms tried to crush us. I managed to protect the cat at the cost of Cindy squeezing my midsection so hard she picked me up from the ground.

"Hi, Cindy," I wheezed.

She let go with a quiet "Sorry."

Turning, I found her blinking away tears. A long blond wig was pulled into a ponytail, and she had a bare minimum of makeup, just lipstick. A pale blue house dress that reached her calves contrasted with the leather tool belt around her waist. I knew two Cindys at work, dressed always presented as an effeminate man with her shiny nails. Then the occasional times we hung out after hours, she'd shown up in a fancy dress that shouted to the world, *this is me!* Seeing her in this sort of casual state jarred me.

"Yeah, yeah," she said, "I know I'm a wreck. Come on in."

I hissed at myself, realizing I'd been staring her up and down, "Sorry Cindy. I didn't mean..."

"Forget it. Get in here." She moved out of the way, and I stepped inside. She'd told me lots about the house and her adventures in repairing her mother's neglect of the place. It smelled faintly of mildew, and the hardwood floor looked chipped and rough. The atrium bore white walls with fresh paint, and had portraits of Link and Zelda framed on the wall. Both wore wedding dresses, beneath a triforce colored white, pink, and blue. The same piece had been Cindy's lock screen for a year, until Cliff noticed it a few months ago.

"Looks better than the before pictures," I said.

"Yeah, I finished this right before the roof fell in. I needed to at least walk in and see something that felt homey." She closed the door, jumping back in surprise as Rey dashed through the crack before it closed. "Hey!" Cindy yelped.

Rey circled around me, eyes scanning the room.

"Three tails!" Cindy nearly squealed, "Did you make friends with a kitsune?" Cindy squatted down and extended her hand to the fox. "You are so pretty!"

Rey's attention snapped to Cindy, pausing her exploration. Dropping into an elegant pose, she sat with her thick tails wrapping around her body, concealing the grey leg. She watched Cindy back, her own head cocked with curiosity, but with a hunger plain in her slitted eyes.

"Cindy this is Rey," I gestured to the fox. "She's somewhat similar to Secret, but more hungry."

The fox shot an affronted glare at me, and turned away with an upturning of her nose. Cindy pulled her hand back. "Well, I think I have some chicken. And Secret is?" Her gaze turned back to my camo blanket fashion, and I let the blanket open a bit to show her the cat. Cindy smiled at the sight and shook her head. "I really thought you were both dead once I heard about the fire and Mr. Gifford."

I nodded. "It was close. Cindy, I have to make some calls. I lost my phone."

"Abby, looks like you lost more than your phone. Let me get you a robe first. Then coffee. Then maybe you can call someone if you don't put your nose in the mug." Cindy hurried up the stairway before I could protest. "Stay right there!"

As soon as Cindy disappeared around the bend of the upstairs landing, I heard the rustling of fabric and my eyes were driven away from Rey's position, but the sound continued, stretching out for several seconds. It ended with a soft thump and a yip. I looked down to find Rey in her human-like form sitting on the floor, her tails rumpled, one hand pressed flat against her chest. "That was hard!" She exclaimed, blinking rapidly as she struggled up to her feet. I set Secret down to help her up.

"Murf." Secret protested and yawned as Rey clung to my offered hand.

"Don't get any ideas about feeding from Cindy." I whispered as softly as I could.

She whined and looked at me with pleading eyes. "There's iron everywhere here. I will need to... refresh myself soon. Otherwise I'll be nothing but a pretty statue."

"Not Cindy," I told her very sternly. "She's my best friend, and she's got enough problems without you mucking with her head."

Her bottom lip pressed out into a sultry pout. "But she's perfect. She adores foxes already. If she gave herself to me-"

"No!" I hissed, "If you even take a moment from her like you did me, I'll impale you on an iron spike."

Fear shot through her eyes, mirrored by my own that flashed in my chest, but I had meant every word. Rey's ears fell and she looked away. "I will... not feed on your friend. But I remind you that I am not bound to obey you, merely educate. If you place another restriction like this on me, I will educate you on the ways of an angry fox."

A floorboard creaked above, and she jerked away before I could respond. Cindy appeared at the top of the stairs, a pink terry-cloth robe held in her hands, "Dun dun DA!" She exclaimed, hustling down towards us. "This will be better than that blanket."

"I'm not sure. Miss Night is more of a woodsy girl," Rey opined, leaning suggestively against the banister.

Cindy stopped mid step when she caught sight of her. "Oh. You're Rey... again."

"Of course," Rey answered.

Shaking herself, Cindy came down the rest of the stairs and handed me the robe. All without taking her eyes off Rey. "Would you like some coffee?"

I ground my teeth. I needed Rey to help us against Little Nick, but until this moment I hadn't really considered how dangerous the Fox Fey might be to my very few friends.

24

Secret seemed perfectly content to stay a cat until she spotted the large can of hot chocolate on Cindy's kitchen counter. Then we had a very excited child clinging to the counter, making moon eyes at me and begging, "Chocolate? Chocolate, pleeeease?" The sight momentarily pried Cindy's eyes off Rey, who, despite her limp, managed to walk towards the kitchen in a way that drew both our eyes: something about the way her tails swished behind her.

Cindy grabbed the can with a laugh. "I thought chocolate was bad for cats."

"I'm not a cat now!" Secret pleaded.

"Okay okay, keep your tail on. Let me heat the water. Coffee, Abby?" she asked as she patted Secret on her head.

"You know it," I responded as I looked around the kitchen. It, like the rest of the house, had seen better days. The countertop's colorful ceramic tiles depicted various Oregon wildflowers, but bore cracks and missing pieces. The walls were stripped bare of paint and wallpaper, while the hardwood floor had jagged pits waiting to insert splinters into bare feet. Despite that roughness, it had a warm, cheery feeling, a scent of baked bread, and the eclectic collection of colorful mugs that hung from hooks beneath the tired cabinetry. We gathered around a butcher block that served as a kitchen island. Secret perched up on a stool.

Cindy distributed mugs. Mine had a big ol' red cross, Rey's depicted the smiling muzzle of Disney's foxy Maid Marian, and Secret's sported a pair of big-eyed kittens in a snowball fight. Rey held up her mug and stared at the image with an almost religious reverence. She held it to her nose and inhaled, despite the mug being entirely empty. "Thank you! Oh that was a good·day." She beamed at Cindy. "You are very kind, Madam Cindy."

"I loved that movie when I was a kid." Cindy smiled.

Rey blushed and looked down into the mug as if she could see something at its bottom. "I know."

I coughed. "So Cindy. What day is it?"

"The twentieth. Two nights and a day since I saw you last." Cindy sighed. "That bastard was busy last night, too. The news said he carved up an entire family last night. Like he did... Mr. Gifford."

"What do you mean by that?" I asked, my mouth suddenly dry.

The kettle behind her on the stove began to whistle, and she turned to grab it. "Cliff will tell you, he saw it." She poured most of the water into a drip coffee apparatus before reaching for Secret's mug.

"Is it... alright if he comes here?" I asked.

She mixed up a mug of hot chocolate as the question rolled about in the air. The chocolate became very well stirred. "It's... Fine. With this new firehouse model thing, it's either come out to the company or quit, anyway."

"Chocolate?" Secret made grabby hands at the mug.

"Oh." Cindy placed the mug in front of Secret. "Sorry no

whipped-," but Secret had already grabbed the mug with both hands and gulped eagerly. "Cream?" Cindy finished and laughed.

"I could meet him somewhere else." I offered.

"No." Her voice firm. "My house is yours. I meant that, Abby. And if Cliff can't handle me, then after this is over, I'll find another ambulance company. That's assuming NLR exists post Mr. Gifford." She pulled her phone from a pocket in her dress, unlocked it and slid it across the table.

With a nod, I picked up the phone and found Cliff in her contacts. It rang twice. I heard a tired voice on the other end. "Colin? What up?"

"Not Colin, Cliff. It's Abby." I said.

"Abby!" His voice boomed. "Where the fuck are you? I thought you were dead. Nobody will fuckin' tell me anything. Goddamn cops nearly arrested me last night for what that red capped bastard did to Dad." I heard him take a deep breath and expel it with a rattle. "You okay? Did he get... the cat?"

Was I okay? My bones still felt like Jell-O and I sat down on one of Cindy's stools. I might fall off dead asleep. "I'm alive. And so is Secret. We've had a long night."

"Why'd you'd go home? I told you I'd help," he asked, his voice gruff.

I sighed, "Because I thought I could handle it. It didn't occur to me he'd... Go after your dad. I'm sorry."

Silence was heavy on the other end for a time as Cindy poured coffee. "Yeah..." Cliff said finally. "Well we're getting an education on how real this stuff is. I tried to warn him. Told me not to pick a fight with addicts."

"Well I could use your help now. Listen, I'm at Colin's. Could you come here?" I asked.

"Sure. Give me the address. Want me to grab a few of the

others? Everybody's worried about you, Abby. Everybody thinks he got you," he said.

"Not just yet." I gave him the address and we said good-bye. Victoria was next on the list. Her contact info was a bit more difficult to find. Took some Internet sleuthing to find her as a "Portland Mortality Consultant" on a page that seemed to sell creepy artifacts. I emailed with Cindy's number.

I took a swig of coffee and looked around the table. Secret stared forlornly at her now empty mug, while Rey sampled her coffee delicately; each sip made her left ear twitch. "Not a fan?" I asked.

"I have never actually tasted actual coffee. It does not seem worthy of the worship it receives," she said.

"Would you prefer hot chocolate?" Cindy asked with an amused laugh.

Rey cupped the mug protectively, "No, so long as it's in this mug I will drink anything."

"Keep it, then," Cindy said.

Rey smiled, her ears perking up some, their fur gaining a warmth to their redness I had not realized they had lost. "You don't know your kindness. I have nothing to offer but this." She pulled out a black leather wallet from the sleeve of her kimono and held it out to Cindy. It was mine.

"That looks familiar," Cindy smirked at me as she plucked it from Rey's hand.

I blinked and glared at Rey. Although more bewildered than angry. I hadn't even thought to look for it. "It's mine," I said in a more tired tone than anything else.

"Is it now?" Cindy grinned, making a show of peering into the billfold and tsked with disapproval, "Nothing but cobwebs and regrets in here." Before handing it off to me.

As soon as my hand closed around it I realized the

futility of reclaiming it now, while I wore boots four sizes too big and a similarly-sized robe.

The phone rang, the number I recognized as Victoria's on the screen. For once I was truly happy to hear Victoria's voice. I told her where I was and asked her to lend me some clothing. I didn't want to tell the whole story three times. We didn't have time for it.

The caffeine only made me further aware of how tired I was. After slugging back two cups, all the stimulant seemed to do was cut off the last bit of adrenalin in my system. We migrated to the living room, and I lost minutes at a time to each eye blink. A double-barreled bang bolted me awake and I managed to lever a leaden eyeball open. The living room was right beside the atrium, so I had a clear view of Cindy gripping the doorknob, taking a breath that lifted her shoulders, and flinging open the door.

"Hi Cliff," Cindy said in her falsetto.

"Colin? What the f..." I heard Cliff's voice trail off.

"It's Cindy, actually," she said, swallowing. "Here it's Cindy. Won't you come in."

"Oh. Oooooooooh. I got it, man." Cliff said then after a long pause. "Well you know... okay, let me try again." He sucked in a breath. "Hi, Cindy. Abby's here, right?"

With a nod, Cindy stepped out of the way. "Thank you, come in. For the record, I wanted to do this via an email, but you know. Time's a bastard."

"I apologize for my face right now." Cliff blustered. "Wooo, it's been a day, night, whatever." He stepped into the house and sighted in on me like a drowning man on a floatation device. "Abby! How you doing? If you got any other life-changing shit to hit me with, now's the time. I'm reeling so hard right now that I don't think I'll spin any faster. So lay it on me." His sunbeam smile had a definite frayed edge to it.

"Nothing like that, Cliff." I couldn't help but smile. "I'm a werewolf."

He shuddered as if I'd slapped him. "What now? Don't kid me, Abby"

"She's not kidding." Cindy said. "Too bad the moon's closer to new than full."

"I'm only saying it now because, if you're in charge of the NLR, I'm going to need full moon nights off," I said.

"Woah." He held up his hands to ward off danger. "Guys... GALS. You can stop dropping bombs now. When I said hit me, I was lying. Know the difference."

Both Cindy and I laughed as Cliff dumped himself into a recliner. He made a show of wiping his forehead with his sleeve and looked out the window. "Ah man, tell me your other friend isn't a G-Man."

My eyebrows went up. "She's definitely not." I stood to follow his gaze to an unmarked white van that struggled to parallel park between a blue Ford EV and Cliff's red pre-naughts Mustang. Cliff sucked in a breath when the van nearly kissed bumpers with his car. The driver's side opened and Vicky squeezed between the van and the Ford sideways.

She slapped the windowless sliding door of the van and shouted, "Settle down in there!" before taking a furtive glance down the street and hurrying up the walk to the house. Cindy opened it before she knocked, and Victoria stepped in with a breath of "Thanks." She had a backpack slung over one shoulder, and wore white beneath her black trenchcoat. Hardly sparing her a glance before spinning in my direction. "Abigail! You have no idea how happy I am to see you alive and well."

"Well is an arguable point. Cliff, meet Victoria Quentine, Portland's best, and hopefully only, necromancer," I said.

"What did I say about bombs?" Cliff muttered, standing up as Victoria walked into the room.

I introduced Cliff, and the pair nodded at each other before looking each other up and down.

"Victoria, you know the woman behind you as Colin Maverick. My partner on your call." I pointed.

Cindy offered her hand, and Victoria shook it with a simple, "Charmed."

A few more murmured pleasantries and Victoria claimed the second armchair in the room while Cindy sat on the couch with me.

"I had kinda hoped you would bring my car back." I said to Victoria.

"The only place that car is going is to a body shop." She pulled my keys from the pocket of her jacket with a jangle. "I got these. Not that you have much to fit them in anymore. I swung by your apartment, third floor's a total loss. I brought you some basics." She handed me the backpack and I nodded in thanks. Victoria had an inch or two on me but her hand-me-downs would be a much better fit than whatever was in Cindy's closet.

At least I had the storage locker waiting for me. If we survived this night and the next then I wouldn't have to rebuy everything. Victoria settled back and everyone in the room looked at each other before their gazes returned to me. I tried to sort out what to tell them. It all felt insane: the road, the moon biting me for a second time, the knights. We marinated in the silence. I stroked Secret, who slumbered in my lap.

"Sorry. It... was pretty weird, struggling with where to

start," I said, not entirely sure if I completely trusted Victoria with what I had learned about Secret.

"Maybe start with what you brought back?" Victoria offered.

"Yeah," Cliff echoed her, "Like did you get a magic sword or something that will help us kill the bastard? According to Twitter, they just found another house he hit last night. Although the police are saying it might have been a copycat. They got no clue."

Wood scraped on wood as the pocket door opposite the windows slid open, to reveal Rey slinking into the room with downcast eyes. "That's my cue, hello everyone." She'd discarded the brown robe for a silky red kimono that clung to her thin figure, the white sash accenting her hips. Her tails flowed behind her with an ethereal grace as she knelt down and bowed so deeply that her nose might have touched the floor. She rose with a coy smile that oozed with demure sensuality. "Forgive me for not being a weapon, Sir Cliff but I know of the Redcaps and how to trap them."

My brain's gears ground together as I attempted to reconcile this Rey with the one I had left in the kitchen drinking: same face, different clothes, but the way she moved... Then I saw Cliff's slack-jawed stare, awe plain in his eyes, and understood. Worship, I'd forbidden Cindy but that meant Cliff would be fair game. I swallowed, hoping that the moon eyes would be nourishing enough for the Fox Fey.

I cleared my throat. "Cliff!"

He startled. "What?" sputtered a little and blinking rapidly as he focused on me.

"This is Rey, a Fox Fey who is bound to help us. She is a little hungry at the moment. So be careful around her." I stared at Cliff, hoping I could punch the message through the center of his brown eyes.

Victoria, who'd also been staring, a single eyebrow raised in appreciation, shook herself. Cindy glanced at me with a concerned frown.

"Miss Abby..." Rey's soft voice had the hiss of a threat.

"I'm not forbidding you. I'm warning them." I said.

Rey gave the barest of nods, "Ahh, you are learning."

25

"Once upon a time," Rey began, "a fox named Reynard traveled north on an urgent mission for his king, a sack of gold slung over his shoulder. Rats and weasels dogged his steps, seeking to take what was his. They laid an ambush for him on the road ahead, and he knew if he set foot there, he'd wind up dead. So the fox took a hook, a fork in the road, traveling in a direction his destination did not lay in. This road went up, high into a craggy mountain with ledges so narrow that men feared to pass. Smashed bone and broken skulls littered the border where the gentle hills gave way to stone, an unsubtle warning for travelers to not come alone. For Redcaps, the Katboutermanns, called those sharp rocks their home."

"Reynard, the opposite of a fool, knew what to do. Into a farmer's barn he stole, taking a one-day-old ewe into his arms. In daylight he trudged up the mountain path, holding a cross of iron and ash. He did not look down, for in those days there was nothing the Redcaps loved more than the fear of hitting the ground. As night came and his pursuers drew near, he slit the ewe's neck, mixed her blood with wine, and poured it into a silver pan. On it he floated a raft of bread, slathered with honey and laced with lead."

"As day surrendered to night, Redcaps came, itching for a fight until they saw the gifts offered in Reynard's lantern light. They ate the leaden bread, and drank the bloody wine, then they fell down, almost but not quite dead. Reynard drew his sword and the Redcaps pleaded for their lives. He charged them with protecting his sack of gold from those who were too bold. The Redcaps agreed and swore oaths against the would-be thieves. Reynard smiled, flipped a coin so they would know its scent, and down the mountain he went. Those Rats and Weasels were soon no more, but Reynard found out later that the gold could not be spent, because as soon as a coin touched an outstretched hand, that's where the bloody Redcaps went."

The story ended and I found my mouth dry as I turned the story over in my head, as if it were a physical piece of stone.

"Newborn ewe," Victoria said out loud. "Blood of the innocent?"

"Leadened bread?" Cindy asked, "Is that literal?"

"We could bake a loaf of bread with lead shot," I thought out loud.

"So fluffy and soft." Cliff whispered. "Too soft."

"Cliff that's not-" The scene before my eyes finally broke through the cloud of her story and entered my mind. Cliff's eyes were pinholes as Rey reclined on his lap, one arm casually across his neck, her three tails wrapped possessively around his back. His chin was half-buried in the black tip of one tail, and one hand had disappeared into the fluff of another. "Rey!" I barked at her. "Let him go."

Her coy smile didn't waver as she pecked Cliff's cheek.

"Oh please, I'm not hurting him. And he touched my tails first. Now we're making a memory together."

I growled, "You promised loyalty, Rey. Doing that to my friends is being a traitorous bitch."

Rey's entire body spasmed as if the B word had been a bolt of lightning. Letting out a window-cracking scream of agony, she fell to the floor, convulsed once, and froze as if I had paused her with a magical remote.

"Jebus, Abby what did you just do!?" Cindy gasped as the color drained from Rey's fur towards gray.

"I don't know!" I said as Secret grew heavy in my lap.

"Forgive her!" Secret mewed, "Quickly, Abby."

I swallowed, wetting my mouth, and even as I did that, Rey's open lips roughened with the texture of stone. "I forgive you, Rey." I said, meaning it, no part of me had intended to kill her.

Instantly she reanimated, gasping for air. The fox fey yipped as she rolled onto her hands and knees. "Thank you for your mercy," she whimpered, crawling towards me, her entire body trembling. Grabbing hold of my ankle she pressed her head against my foot. "I will do better."

"You were being mean," Secret said, her tone thick with disapproval.

"I was." Rey wept. "I was testing the boundaries. What sort of fox would I be if I did not tug at my chains?"

"What the hell did you do to her, Abby?!" Cliff shouted, his face warring between rage and disgust as he watched Rey quiver.

"I-" I started to say, but Rey interrupted.

"She declared me in violation of my oath. Accidentally, but rightfully." Rey said, not moving to rise. Muted red crept back into her fur, but her skin remained the color of pale ash. "The favor my mistress holds over me is strong enough to make me cease entirely, as you saw."

"Wait, are you saying Abby owns you?" Cliff asked, lips fighting between a sneer and frown.

"In the same way that my Mistress is owned by Secret. Yes." Rey sighed. "If Abby willfully fails to protect Secret, her oath will kill her. I have pledged to be Abby's mentor to the rules of the Dream and its inhabitants. I also offered my loyalty and cannot act against her interests. By charming you, her ally, I crossed that line."

"Precisely what did you do to him, Rey?" I asked.

"It's... a very minor thing, mistress. He'll simply be unable to think about an attractive woman without thinking about me. It will last a few days," she said.

Cliff squeezed his eyes closed, face scrunching with effort; his left hand fluttered, the same one that had been buried in her tail.

"And then spiral into obsession?" Victoria huffed.

"No." Rey said, her voice souring. "I'm not a succubus. I'm a fox."

"That is... weird." Cliff shook himself.

My own thoughts strayed to that moment I gave Rey and I twinged in sympathy, but we needed to move on. Little Nick had to be the focus first. Then Rey and I needed to have a talk about her... dietary requirements. "Get up Rey."

She rose from her bent pose but stayed on her knees, eyes downcast. "Should I go?"

"No, stay here. We might have more questions."

With a meek nod, she turned herself around, settled against the couch, and leaned her cheek against my knee. Again my own memories of the times I had been clever cycled through my mind. There on the edge of it I felt her, not intruding like she had when she'd pressed her lips into mine, but basking in the thoughts like a lizard in the sun. Feeding on me? I wondered. I considered pushing her away, but I feared hurting her. Her presence against me opened, a trickle of emotion flowed, shining gratitude, with a slick of fear on the surface, and a dark current of loathing beneath. A plea bubbled in the flow not to shove her away, it snapped sharply to illustrate her hunger. Another image rose of her fox form curled on my lap, encircled with the fear that she was too weak to resume a human form if she did so.

Secret reached down and scratched behind her closest ear. The gratitude and loathing increased in equal measure as she grumbled softly, hugging my calf. A flicker of aware-ness flashed through my mind of how ridiculous this had to look. Secret sitting on my lap while Rey clung to my leg like a pulp priestess to a muscle-bound hero. Forcing myself to look with my eyes instead of the strange internal world she pulled me into, I found everyone in the room once again staring at the Fox fey. Cliff with naked want, Victoria with disapproval and Cindy with a shine to her eyes that I couldn't even begin to sort out.

"Rey," I warned her.

"A few more minutes please mistress. If you want me to be anything more than a pathetic pet tonight, then I need to recover my strength." She whispered.

"Later." I said and slapped my hands together with a crack of a clap. Everyone jumped. "Right!" I half shouted. "So what's the plan? We have to at least keep the evil Santa at bay for one more night. Hopefully, we can get him to eat the leaden bread, and then what? Club him over the head with cold iron?"

Cliff rubbed his eyes, "Yeah. As long as he can't move."

"Is that enough?" Victoria asked, her eyes hadn't moved

off Rey, "How deadly is cold iron to your kind, Rey? I winged him with cold iron but it clearly didn't kill him."

"It didn't?" Rey stiffened. "Cold iron is like being sliced with the fires of a volcano. The pain is blinding. To heal the wound takes immense effort and power."

"When he came after us, he had swollen up. Much larger than he had been when he first announced himself." I said.

"Redcaps were small, their nose no higher than a man's kneecap." Rey thought for a moment, "But... This is the last of the redcaps, the one who has eaten his brethren. When a race of Fey is reduced to one they, are no longer as tightly bound to what came before. While no resident of the Dream could shrug off the bite of iron, they could heal from it given enough fear."

"The entire city is terrified of him." Victoria said bitterly.

"Entire city?" Rey stiffened against my leg and her tails thickened.

Cliff, Cindy, and Victoria nodded.

"He's creating a new legend, then." Rey whispered, emerald jealousy flowing from her. "Then when he falls from the bread, you'd best not miss. It must work but it might not be for long."

"Then we'll not rely on it." I said, "We know warding entrances with iron will keep him out. Maybe we can wait him out, and then focus on surviving this Wyld hunt."

"No." Victoria and Cliff both said at once. They glanced at each other and shared a nervous smile.

Cliff went first, "We have to end this thing. Can't let him keep carving people up, Abby."

Victoria stood up. "And holing up didn't work at all in your apartment, Abby. And we're not doing it here, where you've got neighbors within a stone's throw. We're going to trap him at my place. And we're going to have a solid exit plan this time. No more dicking around with stuff that doesn't work. We've got her now." She pointed at Rey, "And we're going to make sure that any other fey gets the message that this isn't their world to play in."

She was right. Even if Secret opened no more circles, they were opening anyway. We had to teach the Fey that their hunger would destroy them. Nodding, I put Secret aside on the couch. "Then let's go bag us a Redcap" I said in my Auntie Brimstone Betty voice, forcing a smile onto my face.

26

I wish I had the personality for boosting spirits, like gathering everyone together for a group hug, or putting all our hands together in a circle and screaming "GO TEAM!", or something like that. As it was, everyone nodded grimly as Victoria took charge and gave out directions to her house. Apparently she'd been setting it up as a sort of bunker-slash-fortress against the supernatural since we left. The others made some lists, and Cindy, seeing me floating on a cushion of exhaustion, convinced me to take a nap while she took Rey out to hunt up lead shot. Or lead anything.

Three hours of sleep didn't banish my exhaustion, but made me feel a bit less stretched. It also let me finally realize that the four of us were all planning on confronting Little Nick again, willingly. Insanity had truly descended on my two friends and one... magically inclined comrade. Secret and I woke to an empty house which had no landline, so we raided the kitchen and made lunch before Cindy and Rey came back.

When Rey walked into the house, she made it ring with her laughter. Both Secret and I shared a worried glance at each other. Rey glowed, not quite literally, but her ears and tails were almost oversaturated. Her limp was almost unnoticeable as she leaned on Cindy. I almost didn't ask, but I had to know.

"Cindy is a treasure, Mistress! She took me to the house of books and had me read to children! I haven't felt this full in centuries!" Rey exclaimed.

Cindy set down some bags on the counter, giggling to herself. "I know one of the children's librarians, and I had her set Rey up to do a cosplay reading. By the time I came back, she had 50 of the little buggers hanging on her every word. Glorious."

"Oh, and the books!" Rey grinned. "So full of foxes! I read five and there were still more, Mistress!"

I worried for the mental health of those kids. "And how long will they be seeing foxes when they close their eyes?"

"I made her promise not to use any of her stuff." Cindy waved away my worry. "She's a very good performer!"

Rey blushed and batted at Cindy's shoulder, "They were all foxes; of course I can do their voices."

Very good performer who had been acting like she'd been at death's door a few hours ago, I noted. "Did you get what you needed?" I asked.

Cindy sobered immediately, reaching into a bag and pulling out a tin can about half the thickness of a tuna can. "Lead pellets for a BB gun. You have no idea how hard these were to find. Found them in an antique market. Now I have to figure out how to get them into bread without them falling out? Four hours till it starts getting dark. I hope they're okay with a quick bread."

"Well grab your stuff and let's head over to Victoria's," I said, wondering why she was bothering unpacking anything.

Something unreadable flickered across her face, and she looked towards her stove. "Shit. You're right. I should make it there, not here. Do you think she has gas or electric? She probably has a nicer kitchen, anyway. I wasn't thinking. Let me get my stuff."

"Cindy, you could just lend me your car and give me the stuff." I offered, "You could stay here."

She gave me a flat stare. "Have you baked anything in the last 2 years, Abby?"

"I... can follow a recipe?" Suddenly I sputtered. Try closer to ten, and we might be talking. I occasionally cook for myself, but the closest I'd gotten to baking anything came in cardboard cylinders.

Cindy drew herself up, towering over me, "Abby, I shouldn't let you take point as much as you do. We're both paramedics, and if I had taken point on the bridge call, then I'd be the one to make that promise. But I didn't and I let you leap on every damn grenade this city hucks at us. I always freeze, you don't. You move first, and that's when I remember to move."

"You-"

She cut me off with a slice of her hand, "Not done! Maybe I'm going to be just as useless tonight as I was when that gremlin came strolling into the garage. I've never touched a gun, or stabbed anyone with anything more than a needle. But I know I was seconds away from getting saddled with all the stuff we're dealing with. I'm glad it's you, Abby, and not me. You have instincts that move, not freeze. We're partners and I want to help. Maybe whenever there's some monster breathing in my face, I'll freak out, but I can bake you some goddamn bread." Cindy huffed, reached behind the counter, grabbed a large cloth sack and started shoving baking equipment into it. Cookie sheets, bowls and a flat stone.

Wisely, I didn't argue after that. I helped her grab her stuff, loaded it into her little car, and she drove the four of us to Victoria's. The cops had set up checkpoints going out of the west side but not going in. We pulled into Victoria's expansive property within twenty minutes, which usually you couldn't do even with ambulance lights on and sirens screaming.

Victoria had, well, a spooky Victorian mansion clipped right out of a horror film. When I had visited last, its scale-like siding had been black, but the noonday gloom revealed the actual color to be a deep purple. Three stories tall, it sprawled across the wooded lot like a stretching cat, the many peaks of its roof begging for lightning to play over the sky above it. A circular driveway guided us up to the front steps. The massive porch sported a bewildering array of what I first took to be wind chimes but as I stepped out of Cindy's car, I realized they were stylistically warped symbols: crosses, pentagrams, others, all carved from wood and blowing in the wind.

When I set my foot on the first step, the ornate door that sported a stained-glass rendition of a Day of the Dead multicolored skull, swung open to reveal a grinning Victoria. "Abby! Come on in." I shouldered a bag and hurried up the steps, Secret close on my heels.

"Wow!" Secret exclaimed as we crossed onto the plush white carpet of the palatial entryway of the mansion. "It's like the temple, but with no escalator." She spun, dress twirling outward as she took in the décor. Black display cases studded the walls bearing a wide array of artifacts, from ancient swords to vases that appeared to be carved of interlocking bone. Two full sets of medieval plate armor with blood-red plumes guarded the massive stairway.

I heard Rey sigh, and found her standing beyond the doorway smiling patronizingly at Victoria, who crossed her arms and frowned. Above the door frame, a very large horseshoe sat on the lip of the doorframe.

"So Secret can come in, but you can't. Why?" Victoria asked Rey.

"It's not polite to come inside a house uninvited," Rey said. "May I come in, Miss Victoria?"

"I invited in Abby, that doesn't extend to you?" Victoria asked.

"No. I'm not Miss Night." Rey moved aside to let Cindy by.

"Where's your kitchen?" Cindy asked and Victoria pointed without a word.

"Very well, please come in Rey, and be my guest," Victoria said, glancing up at the horseshoe.

With a nod Rey stepped off to the left and disappeared with the familiar rustle of fabric. Brow wrinkling, Victoria stuck her head outside and peered in the direction the fox fey had gone. "What the?"

Secret giggled.

"What a lovely house!" Rey's voice came from above, and I turned to find her leaning on the railing of the second-floor mezzanine. "Pity it reeks of the angry dead, but you can't have everything."

"Where did you get in?" Victoria demand. "Did I miss a window?"

Rey half shrugged, grabbed the ornamental ball of the railing at the top of the stairs, pivoted around it and twirled onto the railing. Grinning with mischief, she slid down the bannister and dismounted with a back flip, narrowly avoiding crashing into the armor at the foot of the stairway. "If you invite a fox into your house, but refuse to open the door, she'll make her own." Rey's tails fanned behind her as she blew Victoria a flirtatious kiss.

"Which window did I miss?" Victoria snapped.

Smirking viciously, Rey leaned on the armor, and Victoria hissed like a pearl-clutching snake. Rey looked at the empty helmet and asked, "should we tell her? She didn't say the magic word."

Reaching behind the armor, Rey puppeted it to make it shake its head.

"Don't touch that! It's four hundred years old!" Victoria exploded.

The armor toppled with a crash. "Heh. Oops!" Rey covered puckered lips with two fingers, and failed to look innocent.

Victoria whirled at me, her goat so beyond gotten that she'd been forced to swallow it, snarled, "Abigail! Control your pet!"

"I am no one's pet!" Rey crossed her arms and stared defiantly at me.

"What was all that simpering this morning, then?" Victoria blasted back.

Ears went back and a flicker of energy went down Rey's tails, face extending to a narrow muzzle that bore teeth.

"Rey, stop!" I stepped between the two of them. "That's enough. You played your trick in response to the insult. You're even now, and we're Victoria's guests. Vicky, if you have a question how something works, ask Rey. Don't use her as a guinea pig."

Victoria crossed her arms and settled for glaring at the Fox fey. "How can we trust what she says if I can't test it?"

"That would be the loyalty thing, Vicky," I sighed,

"You're both in the same boat. If we don't pull this off tonight, none of us will likely see another."

Rey's expression flipped from hostile to quizzical and Victoria visibly forced herself to relax. "Sorry," she said.

"Accepted," Rey gave a little bow.

"Let me run down the defenses." Victoria gestured at us to follow. "All the doors and windows are warded with iron. Although I missed one, apparently."

"The one in the orange bathroom," Rey volunteered.

"That doesn't open." Victoria frowned.

"Does now." Rey said.

Victoria typed a note into her phone and we went outside. "We'll put the offering here on the rim of the fountain. That's far enough away from the house that we can shoot at him from any of the upper windows." She pointed at the black-shuttered windows that loomed over the front of the house. "I couldn't find cold iron ammunition so it's all steel-jacketed or steel shot." Her finger swung over to a utility shed that stood against the line of sculpted trees that marked the edge of the property; a twin stood on the other side. "And this is the surprise for Little Nick. Let me show you."

Secret clung to my side as we approached it, and I noticed the stomach-churning smell of rot. With a flick of her finger on her phone, the shed's door slid open. I choked on the smell.

"Eww," Secret opined as a chorus of moans came from the dark.

"Hello, boys!" Victoria said as the light turned on, revealing four standing dead inside the shed. Unlike Lenny, these were bloated with decay and festered flesh, displaying savage knife wounds. Totally naked, their swollen hands gripped old farm implements, except for a larger man in front whose jaw was entirely missing. Victoria turned to us, "Meet the volunteers from the Morgue. All itching to take a bite out of our friend tonight. They'll face him without a lick of fear." Victoria grinned with pride. "The only thing on their minds is vengeance."

"He killed them all?" I asked, taking a step back, hand straying protectively to the top of Secret's head.

"Last night. Gus, show them your hands," Victoria said. The largest zombie held up his fists, displaying fingers and knuckles pierced with large iron nails. "He did that himself."

The zombie groaned and nodded.

"Is Cliff's dad here?" I asked.

Victoria winced. "No, anyone that was... worked over was unresponsive to my calls."

An engine roared from the road. Victoria quickly shut the shed's door as Big Red turned into the driveway. In the cab sat Cliff, and I'd never seen him smile so wide.

"Why the hell is that here?" I asked, my jaw falling open. He'd gotten it working! When? How?

"Remember I said we needed an exit plan this time?" Victoria stepped up beside me.

"Yeah," I heard myself say as Cliff carefully turned off the driveway and squeezed the huge hunk of metal around the side of the house.

"Cliff had a really good one."

27

"I have no idea if Irish soda bread is actually Irish, but it smells good," I commented as Cindy put a loaf of crusty but fairly flat bread on the plate.

"Yeah, don't breathe too deep, though, you'll get lead poisoning." Cindy warned, "I wish I'd thought to use a respirator. Third try was the charm at least."

I looked out the window of Victoria's expensive and clearly seldom-used kitchen at the deepening gloom outside. One day away from the darkest day of the year. We were all gathered here. Cliff, Secret, Rey, and I sat at a breakfast bar while Cindy and Victoria prepped the offering that had been in the story. We'd all busied ourselves with preparations. Every room in the House had some flingable cold iron object in it. Rey had worked with Victoria to seal every opening. As the afternoon passed, Rey's fur color had noticeably paled to a light orange and her boisterous attitude faded with it. Now she leaned against my shoulder, drawing strength as she had this morning. This was nothing compared to the clinginess of Secret. Once the last attic vent was sealed, she stopped talking and her ears remained wilted. Like a cat, she didn't complain of pain but I could tell she was well beyond her comfort level entrapped in all this iron.

"So what, we lather the thing with honey now?" Cliff asked from his perch as Cindy finished cutting the bread into thick slices. He'd hadn't smiled since he'd stepped off the truck.

"And blood," I added, as Cindy bent over the bread with tweezers picking out any visible pellets.

"Got that handled." Victoria took out a small blood bag from a drawer in her fridge. "Blood from an innocent. At least as innocent as you can be when you're eight years old. O neg. Universal donor." She shook the bag.

"Wait, is that legal?" Cliff asked. "Thought we were getting a lamb like in the story."

Both Cindy and I exchanged looks. The answer would be the same as the reason she had access to the hospital morgue and how she'd gotten the blood of 300 virgins to wake up the vampire who stabbed her. Andrew Millar.

"You want to kill a lamb?" Victoria asked so innocently.

Cliff shrugged, "Not really. I'd do it, though. Not like I've never eaten lamb."

Objections conquered, Victoria looked to Rey, "This is about 12 hours old. That fresh enough?"

Rey nodded, "He'll love it."

Victoria took a black lacquered TV tray and filled it a quarter inch deep with dark red wine, snipped open the blood bag and poured it in, mixing it in with a spatula. The blood disappeared into it. Cindy picked up the loaf of leaden bread and carefully placed it in the tray, angling the slices so as to display the hearty texture. Next, she poured an entire mason jar of honey over it. Then Victoria stepped forward, jabbed the side of her finger with a long needle and squeezed out a single drop of dark blood. It fell onto the honey and beaded up onto its surface, like dew on a blade of golden grass.

A hush fell on the room, and the hairs along the center-line of my scalp prickled. We all froze like mice who'd spotted the shadow of a hawk in an open field. Something watched us. Something massive. Something huge, like when Luna stepped down from the sky.

It moved on.

We took a collective breath.

Rey's ears flicked. "Tomorrow is the Solstice and it's not only Winter that stirs in the dark. And when mortals cast into waters that have been still for centuries, the ripples can be noticed."

"This really is a spell, then." Cindy whispered, carefully lifting the tray.

"Please don't spill that on my carpet," Victoria said in hushed prayer, and hurried to open the doors in her way. The rest of us drifted in her wake.

Cindy didn't spill a drop as she glided outside and set the tray on the lip of the fountain. "See, mom. Decade and a half waiting tables does count for something," Cindy said once she stepped back.

We all watched the entrance for the moment. Half-expecting to hear the clatter of that bell at that very moment.

"Can I say something?" Secret piped up beside me, stepped forward, and turned to face everyone. Her tail lashed behind her, thick and puffy as she gathered breath, a tight smile on her lips. All eyes settled on her, and Rey watched from the doorway, unable to breach the wards of iron. "Some of you are here because of bonds you swore." She looked at me. "Some of you are here because you're friends. Some because there's a score to settle." She looked down at her feet, "I'm not very good at this, momma," she muttered to herself before forcing herself to smile and lift her feline eyes. "I want to say, no matter your reason for being here, I thank you. 'Thank you' is a dangerous word in the Dream and I'm not supposed to say it, but you all deserve it tonight. Thank you, thank you, thank you. Three times."

With that she took a fast step towards me and jumped. I caught her as a cat and folded her into my arms. She purred hard. "That was a very nice speech," I told her.

"It wasn't a speech," Rey said from the door, I turned to find her shaking her head with disapproval. "She's unwisely granted us all a favor that she didn't have to."

"Remember that, when you seek to claim it, Rey, don't ask her to do anything that would hurt her," I warned, walking towards her.

She laughed weakly and bowed out of the way, "If I am not undone by the morning, I will ponder your words."

"I thought it was a great pep talk for a kid." Cliff said. "Now, as she said, let's settle this score."

"Battle stations, then," Victoria said. "Trap's set."

In the living room, or one of them, at least, laid a gun nut's Instagram waiting to happen. A shotgun, a rifle, and a stake of cold iron for each of the humans. Cindy gripped her guns firmly but wore an expression as if she were gripping two long sticks of shit. Everyone else wore solemn expressions as we checked them over and showed Cindy how to operate the weapons. Images of Jimmy and I spending hours on his backwoods range flowed, and his stupid cry of "bang, bang, baby!" when he nailed a good shot. I shook him away. I needed the skill, not his idiocy.

Cindy and Cliff went upstairs to the upper bedrooms we'd set up as sniper nests. Cliff faced front, and Cindy watched over Big Red in the backyard. Victoria sat in a chair by the door, occasionally puffing on her vape stick. Secret, Rey, and I stayed in that living room. It had a large window to look out of and we had a clear run to the back door.

I watched the road and strained my ears, worry twirling around my head. What if he came from the neighbors instead of the back or front?

The clouds had cleared, letting the moon's sliver of light draw my eye. So far away from full, so far away from being helpful. ...*do not reach for me with an empty hand again*. Her whisper rang out from my memories.

I looked at my hands, resting on the black metal surface of the hunting rifle across my lap. The iron spike heavy in the pocket of the black hoodie Victoria had lent me. These were human defenses against the night. I didn't need claws. We didn't need more monsters out there in the night. If I reached for Luna's outstretched hand and gave her what she wanted, then I might become something that drove others to huddle in their homes with guns across their laps. "She can stay a big rock in the sky." I said to myself.

Both Rey and Secret raised their heads at this. Secret had slipped into her cat form and lay in Rey's lap, both in a plush chair on the other side of the room, away from the iron.

I didn't answer their questioning eyes, but continued my vigil.

As the last of the daylight died away, a figure moved at the end of the driveway. As soon as it set foot on the property, dozens of battery-powered lights scattered through the lawn illuminated the entire front yard. They dazzled me, and the figure rocked back in surprise. Squinting at the figure's outline, I saw enough to breathe both a sigh of relief and disappointment. Whoever it was, it definitely wasn't Little Nick.

The figure walked with his nose thrust forward, dark blue clothes, wide-topped cap. A cop. A cop alone at night?

It wasn't Nick, but it wasn't right either. The cap sat oddly on his head.

I clicked the safety of my rifle off and went to stand beside the window. Victoria stood by the door, pistol hidden behind her back. He'd come about halfway around the fountain when she opened the door and hollered, "That's far enough, officer. What do you want?"

The cop stopped and the many lights reflected off his mirrored shades. "We're checking on the neighborhood, ma'am. Want to make sure everyone is safe with that killer on the loose." Even from this distance I saw the corner of his mouth twitch upwards. Something was wrong with it.

"We're fine here. Thanks for asking." Victoria said, the strain obvious in her voice.

"Sure you are. All snug as a bug in that big house of yours." He shook himself, "But you got something that smells grrrreat!" Rolling his shoulders back, he leaned backwards, but his head stayed put. Sniffing desperately, like a dog being restrained by an invisible leash. "What is that?" He gasped as the force that held him snapped, and he stumbled forward, nearly falling.

His hat tumbled off his head, revealing a red tapered cap he had hidden beneath it. A redcap, this was another redcap! Cold clutched at my heart at the thought of more of them. He ran forward a few steps towards the platter before catching himself again. Legs working with the rest of his body. "No! Daddy said wait! Wait for the wagon!"

That thread of control snapped, he flung himself at the platter, grabbing two fistfuls of bread, and shoving them into his mouth. Cheeks bulging out impossibly wide as he chewed on the poisoned offering. His throat bulged as he swallowed the mass with an audible gulp.

He issued a thunderous belch and toppled. His arm caught the edge of the platter and flipped the entire contents of it on top of him.

"Rey!" My shout was little more than a strangled whisper. "What is this?"

"He, he's been adopted." Rey's voice was a fearful flutter. "It hasn't happened in hundreds of years!"

The Redcap cop had been clutching at the air, unable to move as he stared up at the sky. His hand fell down to his shirt and grabbed a shiny black thing there. "Officer down!" He cried, "Officer down!" curling his head towards it.

A siren answered him, then another, and with it, the clattering of a broken bell.

"Heeee, heeeee, heeeee!" screeched the redcap, "Daddy's coming now!"

I raised the rifle, sighted down the barrel at his swelling nose and fired through the window screen.

The newborn monster's left eye popped. The horrible laughter stopped.

"Oh shit." Victoria gasped, "Abby we can't fight the cops. Not all of them."

"I know." I whispered as I lowered the rifle, numbness creeping over my body as the gun shook in my hands. "We'll-" I had intended to say, 'We'll surrender' but flashing red and blue through the trees stilled the words in my throat.

"Ho, ho, ho!" Little Nick's laugh boomed over the cacophony of screaming sirens and revving engines. A black SWAT van whipped onto the driveway, and holding onto its back, a massive body flew behind it like an evil parade balloon. Little Nick.

28

The armored van lights blinded me to everything but the silhouette of the fountain as it roared towards us. No screech of brakes, only the roar of the military-grade engine. Overhead, I heard a rapid popping. The lights swerved away, the armored van tried to steer around the fountain without brakes, popped the van up on two wheels. It tipped. Kept coming as its side screeched across the ground. The van hit the porch with a woody crunch and the impact rippled through the house. The shock wave beneath my feet jostled me into movement. I ran back away from the windows. "Everybody to the engine!" I heard myself scream as I scooped up a wide eyed Secret.

"Holy shit! Get down!" Vicky shrieked.

I tossed myself at the floor as the rapid chatter of gunfire tore through the building. The windows exploded as the walls above eye-level blew apart in a storm of whizzing bullets. Clutching Secret to my chest, I pushed myself out into the hallway and put another flimsy wall between us and the cops.

"Hee, hee, hee!" came the laugh as the guns clicked

empty. "What a merry night! Get me boyos! Get me good! I'm in there! Ho Ho Ho!"

"Get the bastard!"

"Make him pay for Henderson and the boys!"

"Sniper! Open fire!"

With an inarticulate scream, I lost the cops' voices in another bullet storm. They were all mad. Absolutely mad. I didn't like cops as a rule, but this... they were mad with fear. Little Nick was driving them mad, just like he'd almost forced me to turn around when we escaped the apartment. He was using them to flush us out.

"Get the ram!" one screamed.

"Cover me!" another answered as Little Nick's bell clattered. Secret mewled in my arms.

Rey huddled next to me, hugging her tails. "He's so powerful! I smell him through the iron."

Further down the hall, Victoria fumbled with her phone. "I'll keep them busy. You get out of here, Abby!"

A chorus of groaning battle cries flowed from the front of the house. She'd released the zombies.

"Get on the ground! Get on the ground!" Was all the warning the zombies got before the cops opened fire. Above I could hear Cindy and Cliff racing down the stairways.

"Everyone get to Big Red!" I shouted and ran towards the back door. I had no weapons, I'd dumped them all when the cops had opened fire. I grabbed the horseshoe from the doorframe, gripping it in one hand, carrying Secret in the other. Cliff's dark hand closed around the knob before I had a chance to. He had a shotgun and the top of one ear was just a bloody mess.

"I go first," he said in the same no-nonsense tone that his dad had used.

I scarcely had time to nod before he shouldered me out

of the way and pulled the door wide. Big Red stood shining in the dim moonlight along the wall of trees, positioned to rocket out around the house. Victoria's backyard framed a large, covered in-ground pool surrounded by a manicured garden of flowers, overlooked by statues of figures that I hadn't looked too closely at. The most direct shot without jumping hedges was out to the poolside and running down a path that cut straight through the garden's center. It hadn't struck me before that moment how exposed that route was to the sky. "The keys are in the ignition." Cliff whispered. "Ready? Go!"

Secret mewled in protest as I squeezed her close.

Cliff leaped out the door before a response even occurred to me. Even before he reached the pool, he spun around and brought his shotgun up to bear at something above us. The gun boomed, the flash illuminating the lines of rage in his face as I rushed out towards him. I didn't see what he fired at, but I could hear Nick laugh and see the shadows darken. Cliff's gun roared, almost in my ear as I ran past him, out to the edge of the pool.

"Going somewhere, puppy girl?" Little Nick crowed as I skidded into a turn. Silver flashed and pain lanced through my thigh. I looked down to see Nick's knife buried in my leg up to its black hilt. The limb crumpled, and I crashed down onto the pool cover.

Secret popped out of my grip, somersaulting once before catching herself. She turned and hissed.

I rolled over onto my back and saw Little Nick on the roof, grinning down at us, dancing from foot to foot. Cliff fired shot after shot at him, blasts ripping up the solar panels and roof tiles but the Redcap simply zipped a few feet right or left in the precise moment Cliff pulled the trigger. "Stop moving, you motherfucking bastard!"

"He's not there! You're firing at a glamor!" Rey shouted, from somewhere near Big Red.

"What?" Cliff paused in his barrage and a curtain of reality fell away next to him, revealing Little Nick. He'd been standing on the pool patio the entire time. He hadn't thrown the knife, he'd stabbed me as I ran past him.

Cliff swung to face him but the fey lashed out with a backhanded swat. The force of the blow spun Cliff around and the gun went flying, but the big man didn't go down. Catching himself, Cliff's huge body turned in a wild pirouette and lunged back at Little Nick, iron stake in hand. The redcap sprang backwards and rolled, crushing a few lounge chairs.

He really feared the cold iron.

"My knife, Puppy girl." He growled as he stood and thrust his hand towards me. The blade ripped from my leg in a spray of blood and flew to his hand. Blood turned from a splash to a stream arcing from the wound. I slammed my hand into the wound, driving fingers deep to find the sliced artery.

"Abby?" Cliff lowered himself behind his stake.

"Just kill him, Cliff! I've got it." I shouted back. Some protector I was.

Nick waved his blade in Cliff's direction. "Ho, ho, ho! Sir Knight, you stand in my way. Let us dance, but know if you lose, I will carve you as I did your father the other day."

"Shut up and pop, you fucking balloon." Cliff stepped forward with a slice at Nick's knee. Nick parried, wielding the blade half the width of his fist as if it were a sword. Cliff jabbed upward and Nick bent away.

But there was no time to watch. I had to get Secret out of here. Gripping the horseshoe as though my life depended on it, because it probably did, I pushed myself in the direction of the truck. I had only one arm and a leg to work with but I managed. I refused to look at the trail of wet shine I left in my wake. Little Nick and Cliff danced back and forth, swinging and stabbing with their ridiculously small blades. Framed in the doorway I saw Cindy, aiming down the barrel of a shaking rifle, but not firing. Where was Victoria? What happened to the cops?

My elbow slammed down on the stone lip of the pool. The fresh pain forced a "Fuck!" from my lips. "Cindy!" I called, "Throw iron shit at him."

But she didn't move. Fuuuck. And Victoria was probably in the house clutching at her own leg.

"Don't stop." Rey hissed behind me.

Releasing a torrent of curses that would make a comedian blush, I dragged myself onto the stone-tiled patio. Rey stood behind a marble statue of a hooded grim reaper and gestured frantically for me to hurry it up.

"Ha!"

I looked back to see Cindy hurl a long black something at Little Nick. It twirled end over end towards Little Nick's head. His knife flashed up, and with a heavy ting, the metals collided and the iron went spinning up into the air. Cliff took the opening and stabbed his spike deep into the Fey's knee. Little Nick screeched and seized hold of Cliff's arm with his off hand and used it to jerk the stake out of his leg. Then with an easy twist I heard the hollow crack of bone. Cliff let out a short cry of pain.

"Drop it!" Little Nick shook him and stake fell from his hand.

"Now. Boo to you!" I saw that same ripple of air that I had seen when Secret had charmed his father.

"Nooo!" Cliff screamed as Little Nick let him go. He

crumpled into a fetal position, still screaming. In the doorway Cindy stood utterly frozen.

"Stay there, oh, noble Knight, Enjoy the fright. I have plenty to share. Back to you soon, business to do." Nick stood and smiled at me. Huge teeth gleaming even in the dim night. "Should have stayed in the Dream, puppy girl. Taken her directly to the Queen, it would have spared you this night. Hee, hee, hee." Dark blood poured from the wound on his knee, but he took a step without a limp towards me.

I growled, but it sounded more of fear than threat. I made it to where Rey hid in the statue's shadow. Still had over fifty feet to the damn truck. "You can't have her," my tone more pleading than demanding.

Desperately, not having any other idea in my head, I pushed myself backwards as fast as I could, heedless of the way my blood rushed between my legs with each heave of my body. My heart thundered as it desperately tried to make up for the loss. Even if I made it to the truck, there would be no time to even get the door open.

I'm dead.

With that thought, I stopped moving. That was how this would go, wasn't it? Dreams and nightmares were coming into this world, and humans would have to fight to preserve their place in it. A disease, a plague, spreading into our world. The first victims rarely survive. It takes time to learn. Time to adapt.

There had never been a chance for me. We had all done our best. Even Secret had done what she could. Wish I could have said goodbye. I ripped my fingers from the wound and forced myself to stand.

Little Nick paused, giant lips pursing as if to say something but I didn't give him the chance. I flung myself forward, punching out with the horseshoe, aiming up for his belly. He grabbed my arm, stopping me cold with a grip like warm cement. With a flick of my wrist I tried to toss the shoe the last foot or so but the heavy thing just clattered uselessly onto the ground.

"Fuck." Was all I had to say as I waited for him to break my arm.

But instead he lifted me from the ground. I dangled by my arm as he grinned with a mouth big enough to swallow me whole. "You lose, puppy girl. Hee, hee, hee. Should have bowed, should have scraped."

"Put her down, you big meanie!"

My head turned as sheer dread grabbed me. Secret stood at the rear wheel of Big Red. Clasped between her hands and wrapped in a white cloth was the stake of iron pointed at her heart. "No! Run away!" I screamed at her and swung my foot at Little Nick, hitting him in the chest. The impact rippled along his chest but moved him no more than a stone moves the pond it's cast into.

"No Abby." She sniffed, eyes rooted on the spike, but one ear trained on me. "I'm tired of running. I'll make you a deal, Mr. Redcap."

"Hee, hee, hee, the time for deals is done, halfling." Little Nick sang. "I will take you to the Queen once I've had my fun."

"Put my Abby down and leave them all alone, or your task will fail. There will be no halfling anymore," Secret said.

"Do not toy with me, girl!" Nick growled.

"I don't bluff!" Secret touched the tip to her breast, setting her flesh sizzling, then arched her back, so the stake hovered directly over her heart. "If I drop it now, I'll die. Promise you won't hurt them anymore, and I'll go."

"No! Secret! No! You can't!" I tried to shout, but the words got tangled up in my breath. They were barely whispers.

"Heeeh." Little Nick snorted. "A deal today. You live, puppy girl."

"Promise?" Secret asked, her chest still smoking.

"On the Queen's name." With that, Little Nick set me down.

The horseshoe was right there and I reached for it. Nothing moved, everything numb as if I'd rolled in Novocain. Only my chest moved with my breath, and even that took effort. Little Nick walked up to Secret, and she tossed the stake away.

She looked at me. "Don't feel bad, Abby, this was always going to happen. I know you tried your best. I won't let it end like momma, or the goblin, or the pixie, or the troll, or the knight. You're only human, but I wish I could stay. I love you. Goodbye."

"No. Don't go." I protested as she took the bloated hand of Little Nick and walked into a growing darkness.

29

The darkness swam and Secret's goodbye floated through it like bubbles in the deep sea. Light pressed against my eyelids and they opened. Blurry white haze slowly focused into the textured plastic of a fluorescent light, its harsh luminance strained through tiny pyramids.

"Abby, dear. Are you awake?" someone whispered.

My head didn't so much turn as fall to the side. My Aunt Sybille clasped my hand in her cool bony fingers. Hard wrinkles accented the worry in her face even as she smiled with relief.

"What day is it?" I asked.

"It's Friday. Don't worry about work, your station's shut down for now." The tightness in her face meant that there were other things on her mind. Likely questions about a SWAT team and who knows who else.

"Are they okay? Cindy and Cliff?" I asked.

I got a sad smile in return. "Cindy's here, waiting outside. One moment. I'll get her."

"Goodbye." Secret's last word bounced out of my brain and across my lips. Aunt Sybille paused her rise and gave me a sharp look. When I didn't answer it, she finished standing and left the room. Cindy appeared in the doorway, her arm in a blue sling. She sat carefully to fit her frame into the chair Aunt Sybille had vacated.

We sat in a silence of shared pain.

I broke it with, "I have to go after her."

Cindy grabbed my hand and squeezed it so hard that pain bit through the numbness. "Abby, you almost died of shock. Cliff's arm is shattered and the only reason you're not handcuffed to that bed is that Victoria sicced a pack of lawyers on everybody."

"I'm sure they topped me up. Help me out of this bed." I said the words even as I knew she wouldn't help. Good friends don't help friends destroy themselves.

"No Abby, you have to rest. Tonight is the Solstice. Rey said at midnight the hunt may come. Whatever happens after that, in three months' time there will be cracks during the equinox." Cindy said with firmness.

"Not one day. We can't let them have her for one day." I grabbed the side of the bed and strained to move my body. So heavy, as if my veins were full of lead.

"Abby, she went with him to save you! She saved us all from being killed. I want to help her, too, but we're paramedics, Abby. We're not fighters, we're no good at it. Clearly." Cindy reached out and gently pushed me back down. "Don't make me ask the nurses to strap you down, Abby, because they will do it if I ask."

"We can get better at fighting." I said, knowing I'd lost. Lost rightly, but it still stung.

"Maybe, maybe we'll be a well-oiled military machine by the time of the equinox but not now. Now you stay in that bed and get better." Cindy said.

I sagged back against my pillow, "You're right. We're only

human. Let me get some rest." My tone came out far more bitter than intended.

"She's tougher than you give her credit for." Cindy countered and stood up. "Get some rest. They'll probably discharge you tomorrow. You're welcome to come back to my place if you don't want to go with your Aunt. I've got another room that doesn't leak, I could get a bed for it if you'd like." Her reflection walked towards the door.

"Thank you." I said, suddenly reminded that my apartment was still gone. All that remained of my material possessions were in my storage unit. My parents' things. Everything that I'd touched in the last ten years was ash. I had no home.

"Want me to tell your Aunt to come back?" Cindy asked, pausing at the door.

"No. I want to sleep." I lied.

"Goodnight, Abby." She said.

"Goodbye, Cindy." I said.

She hesitated the barest moment before flicking off the light. The room's reflection went dark, except the doorway, which shone like a rectangle moon hovering over the cityscape beyond. A few brave stars joined that false moon in the sky.

"Only human," I said to the empty room. "But I'm not human, not always."

If the moon had been full, would things have gone differently? What was the use of that? I hadn't even growled convincingly, like I had when Little Nick had invaded the apartment. "Did I offend you? When I decided that human weapons would work?" I said out loud.

The room did not respond.

"I'm not wrong. There're a lot of humans, and we're vicious fuckers." Being right wouldn't help Secret. I sighed.

How do you touch the moon? How does a human touch a god? And what did I fill my hand with in offering?

I laid there in the dark, turning the question around. I knew the answer, I had done it often enough when I had been younger, before Jimmy poisoned everything. Knitted my fingers together, closed my eyes, and asked forgiveness. Not to the God I had knelt before with Jimmy and my parents. Not the one who I had dreamed would punish the wicked and profane while taking us to a paradise.

Paradise was the furthest thing from my mind when I whispered, "Luna, please give me strength."

There was no answer; the room stayed still. I levered myself up onto my side. "I know I cannot do this alone. And I have shunned you unfairly, even as you guided me home in the Twilight and showed me the power of my rage in the Dream. Please give me the strength to rescue my child."

Nothing stirred, just the hushed fans of the monitoring equipment by my bedside. I pushed myself upright. The world spun, forcing me to close my eyes until the dizziness passed.

My veins were still filled with lead as I slid off the bed and my bare feet touched the icy floor. Pain gnawed on raw nerves as I forced the leg that Little Nick had chopped to accept the weight. "Luna, I am not a fighter by nature, but I am a warrior against death, a warrior against suffering. I have only myself to offer but I offer all of myself. I seek not a salvation, but the strength to protect those I love."

The pain did not lessen as I deactivated the monitoring devices one by one, muting their alarms. Reaching beneath my gown, I peeled the sticky sensors from my skin. Carefully I pulled out my IV line, clamped off the flow and arranged the tubing. "I don't know Secret well, but she fills a hole inside me. Let me carve a home for the both of us in your world. In your night."

Dragging my foot like Rey, I hobbled to the doorway. The lights in the hallway blazed. An emergency exit door taunted me from the end of the hallway. A nurse in pale blue scrubs crossed the hall without glancing in my direction. My lungs seemed shallow as I breathed through my teeth. I made a break for it, hopping on one foot towards the exit door, like a mad race at a family reunion. My injured leg screamed from the jarring impact, flesh straining against the stitches woven through muscle and skin. Adrenalin flushed the lead from my veins and I hit the door with a metallic bang and burst onto the emergency stairwell.

No alarm, no shouts of "stop there!" I gripped the railing as the chill of the air slapped me. "Thank you, Luna," I said as I peered down the square spiral and counted floors. Nine to go. Could be worse, could be better. The stairs were a little too wide to use both railings at once, so I put all my weight on the inner one. Praying with every breath I exhaled. "I thank you for this strength." With each step conjured, I grew more certain of Luna's touch. The pain did not lessen, but increased as my muscles burned, but my strength did not fail. I rested briefly on each landing to pray "Let me reach Secret. Let me take her somewhere safe."

The alarm sounded when I finally slammed a palm into the exit door and tumbled out into the night. The cold stung my sweaty skin as I fell to my knees.

And there in the sky above hung the barest sliver of Luna, my new goddess, smiling sideways as the Cheshire. "What now?" I asked her. "Show me the way... Please." The alarm blared like a wounded electronic goat.

I heard the distant howl of a coyote; it sang forth and stretched through the night. My goddess was not worshipped by humans alone. I hesitated, suddenly feeling silly, aware that I knelt naked but for a tissue-paper-thin hospital gown in the darkest season of the year. Really? Another howl drifted to the sky in answer.

And I tried, pushing a small breathy "awoo," past my lips, worse than a child's halfhearted imitation. My cheeks prickled with embarrassment.

My ears twitched as a howl answered my pathetic attempt, tone wobbling into and out of a puppy's range, mocking me gently. How did I know that?

I shook my head hard. No time for hows or whys. Just do it. You asked for a sign and she answered. Howl at the fucking moon, Abby, because you need help. I sucked in the damp air, filling my lungs until they threatened to burst. Then threw back my head and put every molecule of air within me into that howl. It sounded crude, drunken, but I made it loud, I made it mine and kept pushing it until I had nothing left. The concrete bit at my palms as they stopped my fall.

A chorus answered me. The coyotes howled notes of encouragement, inviting me to join the song. Human exclamations of surprise and fear yipped beneath. Whether a shouted, "Wha-the fuck!" or a breathy, "the hell?" I heard them all. Footsteps too, whether away or towards me.

I didn't get up as I labored to catch my breath. My upper lip trembled but not from the cold. Every hair on my body stood up as I felt her cool presence on my skin. Light shone from that pale sliver in the sky, bright enough to reveal the rest of her dark silhouette. Waxing or waning, she's always in the night. Again, She seemed to say, Show me how far you'll go.

Lifting my body up on my fingers and toes, I stood on all fours as an animal would. Drawing in a deep breath, I howled at the moon, another toneless but loud imitation at first, but midway through, a curtain fell away in my mind, revealing that the instrument I blew on had keys. And with that, my howl became a song. A song which I sang in prayer to my new Goddess. A wordless anthem of my need for her strength after mine had failed.

Then the men came, bearing shiny plastic on their breasts, which flashed in the beams of light they carried. They called out at me. "Ma'am, that's enough howling now."

I scampered back, snarling a warning in the language of all animals, the gravel of threat. The cluster of men fanned out into a line, choking off my escape. I could stand up, I could smile and use soothing sounds to indicate my surrender. Earnest or not. But no, these men would be the first to see my resignation from humanity. For while theirs is a terrible strength, with guns and black sticks, it would never save my Secret.

One of their number stepped forward brandishing a weapon, with the blunt end displaying a yellow square. I rolled to the side as it discharged with a pop of air, and sprang forward. He screamed as my teeth sank into his ear. He fell down beneath me. The sole man to not be frozen in shock and move to assist his fellow met with my heel to his groin.

Nothing stopped me after that. With a victorious howl I ran, ran as a wolf. Heedless of the human shape of my limbs, Luna surged within me, wild and strong. She answered me in the voice of the coyotes and sang of her ocean of fury for being shut away from the earth she loved. I invited her to touch the earth through me, and that narrow blade of light poured down through me. With each step she carved the humanity from my flesh and released the nightmare she had placed there. Claws scored the road I traveled over, my breath whistled over the fangs that pushed out my old, blunted teeth and let them tumble to the ground below. Winter's chill died away as blessed silver fur spread over my ugly skin.

The howls guided my path across the river, until my nose caught the redcap's murderous scent. His laugh echoed in the awful reek, but it only stoked my rage. Fury flowed through my heart as my paws left the road and plunged into the forest. The trail was old, diffusing into a cloud of half-remembered fear. My righteous run paused as I plunged my nose into the dirt. Here, the dank sweat of collected fear had sunk under the leaf litter, as if to hide away from my nose. Tracing a circle, I found the direction they walked. I howled, announcing my pursuit, and followed. The fey circle tried to shift the forest around me, my ears heard the trees slipping around in the dark. Closing my eyes, I focused on the scent and found another.

Secret, her scent a heady mix of earthy humanity and gossamer feline. The metallic tang of her blood guided me into the hidden circle. Luna's light, thin and sharp, penetrated the tangled cathedral of branches and showed me the scars of her passage. I paid a toll of blood, and the passage opened. For if Luna shone in all skies, her wolves hunted everywhere her light touched.

And this had become my sacred hunt.

30

On the other side She greeted me with the full force of Her light: no longer cool, but the warmth of her anger that penetrated my fur.

Go, was Her only command.

I ran.

She ran beside me, a wolf of shadow and light. We howled our hunger for the blood of the fearmonger, and this world answered. A great serpent slithered from the sky and joined with our path, its back a long forested path smelling of my quarry. My legs carried me on, heedless of the distance, ignorant of time and tiredness. The Goddess did not leave my side as she shifted through the night, a stag, a hare, an owl.

Her light revealed the castle of black stones and thorns that loomed in the distance. The forest around me grew cold: the ground beneath me hardened with frost as bitter winds buffeted my fur. I did not miss a single step. Black-feathered harpies shepherded flocks of birds that rose from the castle's ramparts and spread across the sky, circling above me in a ring of malice. In twos they dove down on me, trilling their sharp-edged cries of battle. Talons slashed at my back, beaks stabbed through my thick pelt. I sidestepped and rolled to avoid what attacks I could, but I would not let them drive me from my path. Blood soaked through my coat as they grew bold enough to dive at my eyes.

I struck then, snatching a half dozen crows from the air with my jaws. The flock's squawking turned to that of alarm, and they scattered. One harpy screamed in challenge, swooping down at me with talons that gleamed in Luna's light. I jumped up to meet her; the brittle bones of her wing broke like glass in my jaws. She shrieked as I bore her to the ground. With a twist, I ripped the limb from her shoulder before resuming my run. Her keening cry of pain doppplered like an ambulance's siren, and the flock dispersed in all directions.

The castle drew up its bridge and the portcullis slammed closed, even as its tower blocked the night sky. Defenses designed to stop armies of men.

I was neither. I did not pause to consider a battle plan nor search for a back way in. My legs propelled me across the moat and I clamped my jaws on the metal bars of the portcullis. The metal squealed with pain as it bent and tore. The bridge behind it yielded to my claws like balsa wood. A flurry of snow rushed around me as I entered the heart of the Winter Court.

Little Nick stood in the center of a clearing, bloated as a parade float. Secret huddled a distance behind him, her ears shining frosty white instead of black. Perhaps the Court possessed architecture of mind shattering beauty and opalescence. Perhaps there were thousands of soldiers standing on either side of Nick. I saw none of it. My world had narrowed to those two lights at the end of my journey.

"Hee, hee, hee," Little Nick laughed. "Have you come to

dance again, puppy girl?" His grin fixed on me as his blade twirled around his fingertips. "The girl's delivered, you're too late. Everything you've done is for naught, and every life I've claimed with this knife rests on you."

The photo of Mr. Gifford's corpse blew through my mind. Desecrated and mutilated, his last moments pain and pleading. A fate he did not deserve. How dare he? The growl rose in me.

"Ho, ho, ho, had you simply handed her over, it would have been fine, and the blood of your friends would not have had to run like wine." Little Nick's bulbous grin widened, and the blade stopped its whirling as he pointed it at my head, ridiculously small in his swollen hand. The balloon man wielding a pin. "Remember, puppy girl!"

A whirlwind stirred within me. The look of utter disgust on Cindy's face as she picked up the shotgun and asked how it worked. Cliff's "Shut up and pop, you fucking balloon." Fighting as I lay useless on the ground. The screams from the floor below as Little Nick lit the building on fire. Look at what I have done to you, the memories shouted, look at how I cast you and yours into a nightmare. They sought to smother my anger, but memory by memory, they only served as fuel for the fires within me. I had no room for his fear. One step became two, became three, and I charged for him. My bulk thundered across the ground.

"My blade is silver!" Little Nick proclaimed, headlight-sized eyes rounding from their vicious squint. "A bane you cannot stand against! You cannot prevail!" The chrome shine of it flashed with light.

As I hurtled towards him, carrying my slavering jaws nearer and nearer to his flesh, Secret stood in the flames of my mind, holding that butcher knife to her heart. Fire flashed as she bled onto the ring of mushrooms, braved seeing her mother and brought Rey to me as a guide. Her feline eyes shone as she, a child, bargained her life for mine. She'd been saving my life every step of the way. Why?

I faltered. That made no sense. I was a nobody, a stunted adult too busy punishing myself to live. Going through the motions for family and allowing myself joy ever so rarely. Only through undoing Jimmy's damage, or in the rare moments I forgot his name, could I be happy. In no way was I worth a seven-year-old's life. The fire in me sputtered as doubt blew through my bones.

Little Nick flew at me, a balloon on an angry wind, I dodged away, but his blade stung my side with a sizzle of flesh. "You're nothing but a ghost who forgot to die!" Little Nick cackled. "Time to fix that, Puppy girl!"

"She's not nothing. She'll never be nothing to me," came Secret's whispered voice.

"Quiet, girl! To bargain for mortal lives is to watch them be thrown away." A second voice creaked beyond my awareness as Nick and I circled.

Not nothing. She loved me. A grin spread across my muzzle. My vocal cords did not yield words as I breathed out a slow, low laugh, "Heh. Heh."

"It is funny," Nick chortled, floating from foot to foot. "To twist and bend and still fail."

He'd come so close. So close to convincing me to lie down and die. I wasn't nothing. I'd snatched one life back from the Twilight directly among the hundreds I'd pulled back from the brink over my career. Maybe it wasn't enough, but it wasn't nothing. I'd promised to protect Secret, and together we'd walked a hidden highway to the Court of Cats. Battled this abomination before me, and befriended a three-tailed fox. That wasn't nothing. Now I stood in the Winter

Court, no longer a woman, but a she-wolf with a new goddess at my side.

After all that, he had the temerity, as he quaked in his jiggly flesh, to suggest I was nothing. The hilarious part was that I had believed him. It's never nothing to try to stop a bleeding wound because sometimes, despite what it looks like, despite how cold they are beneath your lips as you breathe for them, you find that faint pulse.

My growl deepened and he tensed, blade pointed at my eyes. I would not be leaving Secret here, and he stood in my way. My claws bit into the hard floor beneath me, and I threw my body at the foul gnome. He thrust his little pin towards me, I opened my jaws and snapped down on both it and his hand.

His flesh burst like an over-pressured blister, his bitter blue-black blood splashing out of the sides of my long muzzle. Shrieking with pain, he tried to pull away, but my fangs hooked on bone buried in the blubbery meat. With a twist and a shake they tore free.

I spat the dagger, along with several finger bones onto the floor. Little Nick clutched at his torn stump of a hand. He shouted something I did not hear. It did not matter what words he used, the stench of his own fear said everything. He smelled of prey.

Wheeling around, Little Nick tried to run. For Cindy, I tore off his foot. As he fell, I grabbed hold of his side. For Cliff, I ripped him open. His foul blood gushed out in geysers of gore, drenching me in his harvested fear. Pixelated versions of his leering grin flooded into my mind, a thousand sparks of individual dread. I shook my entire body, clearing myself of his corruption. All that ended now..

Deflated, spindly like an insect as he was when he waltzed into the station, he still crawled away from me.

"Mercy!" He cried. "My Queen! Save your humble servant! Please!"

I didn't bother using my mouth. I placed my paw on the back of his head and pushed down. It popped like a meaty bug.

Little Nick lay still and quiet. For a moment. Then something squirmed beneath my paw pad. Lifting it away I found the broken pieces of Nick crawling. Thousands of tiny legs were sprouting from the shards of glassy bone as the blood congealed into squirming masses of worms. A parade of ants, roaches, and spiders were marching out of the sleeves of his ratty red robe. The unraveling. Little Nick was as close as the Fey got to being dead.

I howled in thanks and victory. Luna flared above me, bathing me in her light. My tongue burned and my side ached from where the blade had stung. These wounds she could not touch, but new breath filled my lungs. I stood, bones shifting in my hips, thighs swelling to hold my weight, thick padded digits stretching into fingers that bore sickle-like claws, and muscles rippling beneath my fur. Where I had ended my hunt a wolf, I now stood as a monster.

The air rang with the sound of flesh striking flesh. A solitary clap from a woman sitting on a throne of sculpted ice, clear as glass. She wore a delicate white gown and a glittering crown of frost. Deep blue lips and white skin gave her the complexion of a frozen corpse, but no corpse bore piercing eyes like hers or smiled as hungrily. Around her stood the Court of Winter, great pillars of ice flanked on either side of her throne, gold and gems frozen within them forming silhouettes of wolves chasing deer.

"Bravo, wolf," said this Queen, her voice echoing as if emanating not from her mouth but the hall itself. "You have conquered fear with your rage. You will be a worthy hound for my hunt. Welcome to the Court of Winter."

I bared my teeth and brandished my claws. The hunt had ended but clearly the battle had not.

"Your mistress holds no power here." With the snap of her fingers, clouds swallowed Luna and obscured her light. The heat of her light faded and bitter cold bit at my ears and nose.

31

"The girl is mine." The Queen said. "She has given herself to me and is my ward. I protect her as you did. If you wish to be with her, then kneel."

I shook my head no. I held out my hand and curled my fingers towards her in a clear gesture. Give me my Secret.

"You have given yourself to the Lady of the Night. I am Winter. We both work to hasten the end of the mortals' time in the sun. I ask you once more. Be my hound for tonight, wolf. Announce to the mortal world that their forgotten Gods have not forgotten them. Do this for me, and you may visit with the halfling while your mistress's light slumbers." She extended her elegant hand.

Secret was nowhere but she had been there, standing beside the queen, her fur white as frost, her lips almost as blue as Mab's herself. I wouldn't leave her here. Killing Little Nick had been a good step, but that wasn't why I had come. I didn't surrender myself to Luna to do it halfway.

I laid my ears back against my head and took an aggressive step forward. Queen Mab's eyes narrowed. "Don't let your mistress go to your head. I am Winter and even a wolf can freeze to death on the nights I am strongest."

We'll see about that, I thought, and charged. My body broke into a run, my knuckles slamming into the ground as I shot across it.

I had expected her to draw a sword of ice from the air, or a dozen soldiers to materialize before me, or simply freeze me solid in place with those icy eyes. Instead, she merely stood, glowering as I rushed towards her.

Only the barest corner of her mouth moved into the subtlest smirk as I arced downward, jaws opening to bite down on her thin form and tear her flesh. As my teeth touched her, she still did not move, but exploded into a howling blizzard. Cold struck my entire body and threw me backwards. My vision filled with a blinding torrent of snow. The world spun before slamming into my back with the crunch of ice.

Growling, I flipped up onto my feet, talons ready to slash but my eyes opened to only blackness. The wind screamed into my ears and clawed at my fur. So strong were its gusts that even with this monstrous body I had to brace against it. My ears folded back and I sheltered my nose in the crook of my elbow. Squinting into the dark I could only see the vaguest vertical shadows in the dark. I leaped towards one, slashing it with my claws. They scraped across its surface, tearing a chunk away. The shadow did not fall or scream. Placing my hand against it I felt the rough texture of tree bark.

Moving through rapidly deepening snow, I moved to another shadow, another tree. My head hit a branch and ice showered down. The next was the same. I stood in a forest in the middle of a blizzard. She had to be in here somewhere. Hiding among the trees. I sniffed hard, trying to find a scent: nothing but wet and cold greeted me. My heart hammered in my chest, but I could feel the jagged teeth of the cold gnawing at my tail and fingers. Unable to find anything moving, I howled a challenge into the wind's constant scream through the trees. Fight me!

"I am." Queen Mab's voice slithered down my ear canals like an ice cold tongue. "Do you not see the futility? One can face fears and defeat them but you cannot hunt a season."

Had I a mouth capable of speech I would have told her about the polar ice caps. Instead I could only growl and slog on. Could I find shelter somewhere? Endure the blizzard. How long could she keep this up?

Luna had changed me to this form but why? On four legs I'd be better off in the cold. My pawlike feet felt fine, but my fingers were losing feeling. Was there a reason, or had she expected a brawl as well? The God of my Sunday school knew all and did nothing. Perhaps Luna was more active but fallible.

I howled out to her, asking for her light. Seeking that fury I'd had in the hospital. She had given me power. It still lived in me in this body, built for death, but I had nothing to use it on here. No answer came but mocking laughter in the wind.

A shiver traveled up through me and I knew my miserable trudging was for naught. If Winter couldn't be defeated then I had to survive it. Sled dogs simply curled up and let the snow cover them. Could I do the same? I let myself fall into a snow drift. A glimmer of instinct guided me to curl up, my body didn't quite obey, my spine too stiff, but I could just cover my nose with the tip of my tail. Even with my back in the snow and my fingers tucked into my armpits I felt warmer. I shut my eyes to wait for the snow to cover me.

"Too bad it's the longest night of the year." I heard Mab

right in my ear and swung out a claw, only for a savage gust of wind to strike up under my tail. The deep snow around me evaporated as the cold tore through my pelt like iced needles. Stung, I leapt up with a yelp. The wind merely laughed. "The winter of the lone wolf is long and cold. Lean of prey and barren of company. My dogs get meat."

Hunger hit me like a fist in the gut. It doubled me over and my palms hit the frozen ground. The scent of bacon frying in a pan snaked into my nostrils for one glorious inhalation that flooded my mouth with drool. Then the wind snatched it away, filling my gaping maw with snow.

I tried to curse, but all that came out was "uc ou!" which wasn't nearly as satisfying as a good F-bomb. A longing for home gripped me. I wanted to curl up in front of a fire with Secret nestled against me, an empty mug of hot chocolate at her feet, the howling wind and the snow shut outside where it belonged.

Secret. I had to find her. I couldn't just freeze here. Taking a deep breath in preparation for standing back up into the storm, my nose caught the faintest scent. Young and feline. Secret and I were likely the only humans who'd been here in hundreds of years. I sniffed hard at the ground. Snuffling back and forth, I found the scent's thread and followed it.

The wind came thick with fresh snow. Trying to bury the scent, but I covered my nose with my hand, making a tunnel for my breath to warm the ground some. Mab raged at me, her wind pelting me with pebbles of ice. The roots of the trees beneath my palms gave way to rock-studded sod as I hurried on. The trail ended with my frozen fingers sliding over a plane of smooth ice.

"Give up, wolf." Mab hissed around me. "She is safe with me. No one can harm her here."

And let her live her life surrounded by creatures like Little Nick? No. I pried up a rock from the ground and slammed it into the ice. On the third strike, the ice shattered, and the pieces dropped down into a tunnel bored into the earth. Following the scent, I slid down into pitch darkness. Luna had provided thumbs for a reason.

Secret's scent hung in the stagnant air. The stone floor was still frigid, but at least there was no wind. I walked forward cautiously, wishing I could shout Secret's name into the darkness. Would she be able to hear me? I called forward with a whisper of a howl.

A sliver of the moon appeared but not Luna. It had teeth. Cheshire.

"Ahhh, Hello, there, Abby. In the dark again." His eyes opened, the feline slits glowing. "All alone without the barest morsel to offer poor lonely Cheshire." He did not loom as he did on the fence, his smile eyes stayed distant as they moved, as if he were a house cat prowling across the top of bookcases.

I growled.

"Oh I know, I know. How boring that the monster in you is a wolf. I would be very upset with Luna if you were me. You should be a tiger, or at very least, a mountain lion." He sighed.

I huffed noncommittally. Was he here to help? And more importantly where was here?

"Course, it's not a good idea to ask for exchanges on blessings. She might make you a squirrel instead, and then you'd need explosives to get anything done." He laughed as if his nonsense was funny.

My claws clicked on the floor as I walked. Cheshire stalked towards me, moving as if I were on a treadmill.

"Walking is not the way to go anywhere in Mab's heart.

Have you not had enough wandering, Abby? You have to know where you are going."

I stopped. We were in Mab's heart? She'd eaten me somehow? And Secret as well. How do you get out of a Fey's heart?

"Aaah, here we are. Give my regards to the Princess," Cheshire said, and I heard a clatter.

A soft light flared from beneath the cat, shining forth from a pile of broken glass at the bottom of a bookcase that held dozens of jars. I looked up only to see the whisper of the Cheshire's smile fade from view. By the light, I found myself in some sort of odd pantry. Shelves and shelves stored jars of all sorts, from mason jars to old-style flasks with stoppers. Most were cracked or their tops were pushed off by the expansion of ice. I looked down at the glowing pile, and found that beneath the glass lay a chunk of ice that had motes of light embedded in it. Picking it up with my claws, I saw they weren't motes, but tiny human figures, frozen in the ice like insects in amber. Minute bubbles clustered around the outlines of wings that extended from their backs. I turned the chunk and metal flashed within the ice. Each figure wielded a shiny fish hook with a wicked barb that dissuaded me from the idea of thawing them out.

Holding out the chunk of pixies like a flashlight, I walked to the thick door at the end of the pantry. Stooping so as not to knock my head against the door frame, I curled my fingers around the wooden door handle and paused. The Cheshire had said I shouldn't wander in Mab's heart. I had to know where I was going. Where would Secret be?

Secret was a princess and, in this world, Princesses belonged in castles. Closing my eyes, I visualized the banquet hall of a massive castle, its hearth fires roaring, men and women sitting at long tables gnawing on turkey legs, drinking from huge steins, as the babble of conversation made it difficult to hear the person next to you. My empty stomach twisted as my mind layered the scene with the savory scents of fresh cooked meat and sweat.

I pushed open the door and thrust the chunk of light ahead of me. No warmth of fires buffeted my nose nor did a tide of conversation wash into my ears but Secret's scent had gotten stronger. That warmed me, even as the light played out over long tables covered with frost. Sparse figures slumped with their heads resting on crossed arms. I stepped cautiously, my light refusing to spread to the walls of the hall, even as I held it high, creating a bubble of illumination. As I walked past one of the frozen corpses, I saw her sunken cheeks, and her arms were little more than skin stretched over bone. Little meat on there, have to go straight for the organs. I laughed to myself; did eating corpses count as consuming fairy food? A part of me churned with revulsion at the thought of eating human meat but it was surprisingly small.

At the edge of the room, I found one of the hearths, empty of everything but ash. I continued on. I found more corpses, not all of them human, some too big, others too small, with tails and horns and wings sprouting from them. But they were all as starved and frozen as the rest. Then finally I came to a table set on a dais raised above all the others. Its stout wooden chairs faced the hall, and in the center left seat knelt Secret. Watching me with mournful eyes. Her ears and hair white as frost and she wore a smaller version of the gown that Mab herself had worn.

"Abby, you-" she started, but I didn't give her the chance to finish.

32

A great joy propelled me into the air. I bounded over the table and swept her up into my arms. My tongue slathered across her ice cold cheek. She giggled as I cradled her, and happy whining noises rolled up my throat.

But on the second lick she hissed before crying out, "Owwwies! Too hot!"

The cold of her body radiated through my thick chest fur and chilled my sensitive spots buried below it. I ignored her cries and held her tight, striding back towards the entrance of the hall. The clinical part of my mind screamed frostbite on the edge of permanent damage. I needed to warm her up now! How to get out of here? I made it to the edge of the bubble of light before turning back with a snarl of frustration. The light chunk had cracked in twain. I had dropped it when I pounced on Secret. I stooped to pick it up.

"Abby owwwies! Stop! Let me go! I can't leave!" She sank a pair of burning cold fangs into my bicep, the shock of the sudden pain spasmed my arm, and she jumped away, scrambling beneath a table. I pounced, but only caught the tip of her frosted tail and she pulled it away.

Growling with frustration, I swatted the table onto its side, but she scooted under the next one. I wanted to scream at her about how stupid she was being. She was literally freezing to death here, but my lupine muzzle remained inarticulate. I threw myself down to her level, jabbed a claw at the floor and growled impatiently. Come here.

She shook her head. "No. Abby, they'll just come for me again. They'll send more knights."

I bared my teeth and pantomimed biting something. Then I'd kill them.

"Noo!" she mewed miserably. "I don't want you..." She blinked, a tear fled from her eye and froze midway down her cheek. "To be a monster for me. You're nice. You're kind. You help people."

With a huff, I grabbed my muzzle with both hands and tried to force it back into my face. If I could just... talk to her. I could convince her to come back with me. To stop hurting herself. She deserved the chance to grow up, dammit. No matter what she was. My muzzle refused to retreat, and I remained a beast.

"There is no place you can bring me that can help, Abby. Winter or Summer. One or the other. Summer killed my mother. So if I have to choose, I'll choose Winter." she said, breathing hard and looking up, "My Queen. I will open whatever gate you want, so long as you let Abby go home."

No! You can't just... give up. Couldn't say it so I howled instead, a mournful cry that shook the stone around us. There had to be a way to make this work. If Luna's blessing spread by bite then I could get back to Portland and create a huge pack of werewolves to protect her. No fairy could touch her. Or we could simply leave the city. Go somewhere with a thicker barrier. Maybe that wouldn't be forever but she'd have the chance to grow. I had no words to tell her these things, so I simply howled out the pain and my love.

My love. It didn't make sense. She'd never needed the promise and its teeth, not from the moment she hugged my side and told me she was bad luck. She had penetrated the wall I had built around myself without effort, and I had turned my demons into weapons to protect her. And now that little girl was freezing at least the human part of herself to death to protect ME. Without her human part, she wouldn't be able to open any gates.

The howl died only as I ran out of breath. Leaving me panting and my tears freezing in the corners of my eyes.

"Don't cry, Abby. Thank you." Secret said as she hugged my arm.

Hinges creaked, and I looked up at a doorway that opened back into a snowy night. "It's time to go home, Wolf." said the wind.

"Go on," Secret urged, petting my fur. "I'll miss you."

Slowly I climbed to two feet and stumbled towards the door. I paused in the doorway and looked back at Secret. She waved, her fingertips covered with frost. Swallowing, I trudged out into the snow. Up a flight of stairs. I emerged into the night. No stars or moon pierced the clouds, but still the light was enough for me to see by. No wind blew, and while the cold nipped at my ears and nose, it was perfectly bearable. The heaviness of my heart was so great it threatened to rip itself from my chest. A huge stairway of sculpted ice climbed into the clouds. Beyond it lay the forest I had wandered.

"Start your journey home, Wolf." The icy breeze whispered.

I stared at the stairway. Pondering my empty apartment, now burned. I had no home. Wherever I went, I'd have to build a new one. The loss of my stuff sucked but the thought of rebuilding while Secret stood here was worse. Or maybe Mab would let her out, and she'd live among the personifications of cruelties in the court of winter once I left.

Or...

"Heh, heh." The one human sound I could manage rolled through the eternal winter.

"Go." The wind urged.

Instead, I squatted and marked my territory. The fresh scent would lead me back here. Steam rose from the snow as I set off for the forest. The wind protested, but my thick coat allowed me to ignore it as I marked my travels through the trees, scraping my claws across the wood until I found a suitable one. Dead as a doornail but just a foot and a half around. The wind kicked up as I worked it back and forth, the wood crackling with the strain until it snapped at the base of the trunk and fell.

Snow buffeted me, but it couldn't hide my fresh scent trail as I dragged the thirty foot tree back to the entrance of the hall. The fury of the wind increased to the driving blizzard that Mab had first greeted me with, but I tracked through it with scent and purpose. I dug away the snowdrift she tried to hide the entrance under.

Secret's eyes went wide with horror as I pulled the tree into the hall. She protested, yelled at me, and even tried telling me I was a bad wolf, which I laughed at. I simply worked on breaking down the tree into firewood. It was easier than I thought. After breaking off the branches I split the trunk apart lengthwise, as easily as tearing cardboard. Once the trunk was in quarters I broke the wood into two foot long logs by bending them over my thigh. Then I hauled the corpses in the hall to a small kitchen on the side of the hall.

"You're making her angry!" Secret wailed as I returned to the hearth and began stacking logs in it. Her warning only made my tail wag. I combed some fluff out of my fur and set it beneath the twigs. Then I struggled with a striker I'd found searching the corpses I had carried into a kitchen off the side of the hall. Better if those didn't thaw yet. My long claws made handling the tiny tools difficult and they kept popping out of my fingers. "Abby. You need to go back. Go Home."

I looked over at her and gave a small wuff of agreement.

Her little mouth dropped open. I watched her moisten her mouth. "Leave!" She pleaded.

No, I shook my head.

Her little fangs dug into her lower lip and I went back to my struggle with the starter. Unable to speak, I could only do. A single spark flew as I found the right angle.

"Y-you can't stay here!" Secret stuttered.

I struck. Two sparks. One of them arced into the furball and smoldered.

"You'll die." Secret insisted.

Again I shook my head, as I leaned down and blew on the fluff ball with my nose. It smoked and then... flame.

"If you don't freeze, you'll starve." She said.

I blew into the fire until flames crept up into the sticks. Then sat back and pointed to a pot hanging above the hearth fire, and pointed at a corpse I hadn't moved yet. She looked at it and then at me, utter shock on her face.

"To stay here, you'll eat them?" Her voice a tiny squeak.

With a sigh, I nodded again. I doubted they'd taste any good, but I'd bet there were a lot of frozen corpses hidden in the Heart of Winter.

Secret wobbled, "Abby!?" her face screwing up she tried to hold back tears. I held out my hand towards her. This time she ran to me. I wrapped her cold little body in my arms and curled around her, enveloping her in my fur. I prayed my thanks to Luna as Secret whimpered against me. Her body thawed with the warmth of both me and the fire. The Goddess had sculpted me to not only survive in the Heart of Winter but to make it my home.

"Owwwies," Secret whispered and shivered as the frost melted from her hair and fur. Instead of running away she snuggled closer. Slowly, the fire spread up into the logs and threw off heat that I could feel with more than my nose. The white glitter of frost that covered every surface in the hall retreated away from the fire, leaving a glistening wetness in its wake. As Secret fell into an exhausted slumber, I found myself contentedly awake and making plans. Christmas was close. I'm sure there was an unfortunate corpse out there with vaguely clean socks to serve as stockings. Perhaps that forest would host some game if Mab calmed down some. I didn't know how she worked, was she merely the bitterest, coldest parts of winter? Or was she all of winter?

If she were all of winter, did that not include snuggling up by the fire, wrapped in your favorite werewolf? Or enjoying hot chocolate with coworkers at the Starbucks? After all, Portland winters are pretty dang mild, more rain than snow, despite the dark. Two inches of snow is annoying but few people die of the cold anymore.

With the warmth of the fire flowing over me, I shifted onto my back to stare at the beams that stretched overhead. I'm not a huge Christmas person but those beams were begging for some decoration; rip some branches off some pine trees and twist them together to make garlands? Is that how they did it in the old days?

A command shot through the air. Stop.

What's the matter, Queen Mab? I thought back. If I'm

going to live here I'm going to make it as homey as possible. Gotta make up for the whole "living on frozen carrion" thing. Carrion sounds a lot tastier than corpses. Secret shifted on top of me, head moving to rest on my breast, which I was surprised I still had beneath the thick fur of my chest. But there was no arguing with that somewhat uncomfortable squishing sensation. They weren't very big, but they were there. Actually, as I thought about it, I felt a similar but lesser sensation beneath her bony little shoulders.

Swiftly abandoning that line of thinking, I forced myself to think more about Christmas decorations; it had been a pagan holiday originally. Right? A tree would be a good first step. Although maybe in a room without an open firepit. Immediately my thoughts strayed to Christmas at my parents' house, which was tangled up with Jimmy, so I moved on to New Year's. Drinking. Mostly alone in recent years. But if I had made it back, I'd impose on Cindy or Cliff. Cindy occasionally showed me pics of twenty or so trans women looking quite trashed. If I had to do it here, I'd probably light some candles and howl at the moon. Personally, I watched Hallmark movies and dodged invitations from my aunts. Sometimes it worked.

Ahh the Hallmark movie, there's a winter tradition for you, Mab. You don't get internet in here, do you?

I swear the floor shuddered as I started running through all the sappy winter wonderland plots I could remember. Dedicating each to Queen Mab, ruler of all things Winter.

By the time I finished, the heat of the fire had chased away all the frost in the room. In addition, the beams that crossed the room looked... waxy. Perhaps it was simply the wet of melted ice.

Perhaps not. I inhaled, and I smelt it. Very faint but the smell made my stomach howl all the same. Careful of

Secret, I slowly sat up. She gave a soft murmur of protest before folding into her cat form and nestling herself in the corner of my arm. Like this, I could hold her in the palm of my hand with room to spare. Petting her with two clawed fingers, Secret purred as I went to the door. Cold darkness greeted me beyond the doorway. Closing my eyes, I inhaled the scent of pork fat, and while holding all the wintery ways that smell can occur in my mind, I stepped through the doorway. The stone sloped downwards. I got the sense that the path I followed wound its way deep into the earth. Into Mab.

33

I heard the sounds of cracking and shifting around me. Frozen things struggling to move. When I paid them any mind, the scent faded sharply, but strengthened as I turned my imagination to wintry delights: the Saturday market at Christmas time, mugs full of hot chocolate, the neon garden of the winter lights festival, the laughter of a crowd, and the scent of frying food so heavy in the air that you can taste it.

Snow crunched under my foot.

Opening my eyes, I found a festival stretching out before us. Not Portland's Ode to Winter, but one out of a storybook. Small wooden huts clustered together in the gently falling snow. The air was heavy with spices and meat. The babble of a merry crowd lapped at my ears. Shadows of people walked the paths of packed snow, lit by lanterns hung on posts and on the corners of the stalls.

"Mew?" Secret stirred and poked her feline nose out between my fingers. During the walk I had held her close. Within a blink, I heard the rustle of her transformation, and I found her humanish in my arms again. Her little black dress was gone, replaced by a thick black coat trimmed with white fur, black leather boots, and a knitted, white, cat-eared cap. She grinned up at me. "Nice collar, Abby," and giggled.

My hand went to my neck and something jingled. I had to bark a laugh as my fingers curled around it. A wide leather collar encircled my neck, studded with jingle bells. I set Secret down, and she wrapped her hand around one of my fingers as we walked into the market. She stuck close to my side, watching the shadowed people as I tracked the scent that had led us here. A stall at the edge had a sign that depicted a pig on a spit. Words were unreadable scribbles carved into the wood. They were unneeded. The shadow inside offered me up a skewer of meat, and I took it with a rumble of thanks.

"You shouldn't..." Secret's warning trailed off as I ripped into the meat.

So good. Tender lean meat marbled with melting fat. My tongue ached with its memory after I swallowed. I gave a small howling prayer of thanks to Mab. The ground shivered beneath me hard enough that the bells around my neck laughed. The vendor offered more meat and I took two, offering one to Secret.

"But... The rules!" she protested, gripping the stick with both of her mittened hands. A slice of tenderloin folded around the skewer longer than her head. Her eyes watched me devour mine before she took a tentative nibble. A surprised mew escaped her as she chewed and then attacked the rest of the meat with savage vigor, making adorable noises of feline pleasure with every bite, until she was curling her tongue around the bare stick. "Thank you." She eventually said, handing the stick back to me.

I shook my head and pointed at the ground.

She blinked in confusion. "Thank you... Queen Mab."

Again the ground shook. My bells jingled and I kept

them jingling, bouncing up and down on my toes, well, paws, they were one and the same.

A giggle escaped her, and she covered her mouth.

I kept jingling, settling into a very ancient rhythm.

More giggles, and then she burst into a song that even her odd life wouldn't be able to escape. "Jingle bells! Jingle bells! Dashing through the snow..." She didn't know much of the words but she skipped around me humming as I made my way to inspect other stalls, jingling all the way.

If it smelled good I ate it, although mulled cider proved to be a challenge. Secret laughed and danced with a cat-eared doll she'd gotten. The ground's pulses began to come more frequently; I could see them coming as ripples in the untrampled snow. Finally, with my stomach warm and full, the stalls ran out and we came into a center circle. Statues of ice guarded the four cardinal directions, Swans east and west, Reindeer north and south. A throne of crystal-clear ice sat with its back to a pile of wood as tall as I, waiting to be lit into a conflagration.

On that throne sat Mab. Her long-fingered hand clutched at her chest. Those blue lips had warmed to scarlet, and she looked wet with sweat in her icy raiment. Her lips peeled back into a defensive snarl. "Leave. Go back the way you came, wolf. You can take her. I do not wish to see this part of me anymore!"

"Yay! Thank you!" Secret cried out, attacking my thigh with a hug. "We can go home!"

I squatted down to all fours and gathered my thoughts as I filled my lungs.

"That's not ness..." The Queen sputtered.

My mind reached back into that moment when the coyotes had sung with me, imagined them snuggled in their dens, bellies full of fattened squirrels, and sang out a howl to her. Of all the good things the cold can bring.

"Stop it!" Mab shouted. "I command you to stop this instant! I rule a court of cruelty, wolf! Do not cross me!"

The ground pulsed, and as I opened my eyes from the song, I saw that Mab had stood from her throne, pointing a trembling finger in my direction. Smoke rose from the wood behind her. I stood.

A wave of her hand and a stairway spiraled up from the ground between us. It reached into the sky. "Go, before I change my mind and freeze your heart solid, wolf! I am cruel and cold. Starvation and loneliness."

She was that. It was true.

I stood, my bells jingling. She was so much more than that. Bursting into a loping run, I ran around the stairway. Making the bells ring with every step. She watched me come to her. Maybe she could have frozen me but she didn't. It's hard to kill something that's in your heart; it's almost as hard to push something out. I've never managed to get Jimmy out of mine. She had no more words as I wrapped my arms around her thin body. The burning cold of her sliced straight through my fur and we both screamed with agony.

"Let go!" She pleaded as we both ran out of breath.

But I couldn't; my arms had frozen around her. Ice threaded across my skin, locking me in place. I whined as the ice encased my muzzle. I got a final whiff of pine smoke as the cold threaded into my nostrils and stopped my breath.

Then, through the ice that covered my eyes, I saw the orange of a rising fire. A thunderous and gentle *Thoom* pulsed through me, and the ice cracked. A pause. *Thoom.* Warmth pushed out from my own heart, but it wasn't the origin of the pulse. It came from the woman in my arms; it came from all around me.

As quickly as it formed, the ice melted away from my body as the bonfire crackled and popped. Drawing in a grateful breath, I clutched Queen Mab tighter as she grabbed fistfuls of fur and screamed into my shoulder. Howling out happiness to her only made her pant harder as the pace of her heart increased. She remained ice against my skin but her cheeks gained a rosy flush as her clothing melted away. "I should... make a coat from your pelt for what you've done to me." With that, I felt her lips on the underside of my jaw, a cold little kiss as she relaxed against me. Her hands slid up through my fur and found my ears. Time wobbled for a moment as her fingers made little circles at their base. "You've ruined me now, Wolf. After I had finally frozen out this part of myself."

I let her go, but she held herself to me, rubbing her cheek against mine like a cat claiming territory. "Not so fast. You had your chance to escape, and I will let you go on my own time. You've made your home in my heart, you've celebrated in my name, and eaten of my food. A piece of my heart is in you and this entitles me to a piece of yours." We parted, just enough for me to look into her still-frozen blue eyes. They shimmered with tears she did not shed; her long fingers held my jaw closed as her other hand pressed through my chest. I shivered as she caressed the flesh of my heart, letting it pump against the cool flesh of her hand. A light tingle of pleasure spread from her touch. With a sharp pinch, my heart skipped a beat, and her hand withdrew. She showed me a mote of pulsing silver light trapped between two fingertips.

She kissed it with her red lips, and a wind whipped through my chest. Every inch of my skin prickled, my fur puffing out in vain to ward off her cold. A shadow bearing a satin pillow the color of forest stepped up, and Queen Mab placed the mote upon it as I slowly sank down onto my knees. She spread her naked arms as a swarm of shadows rushed around her, dressing her in rich folds of dark green velvet, her thin form thickening to fill its rich bosom and hips. A hooded cape of cloud-white fur draped across her shoulders, hiding the deep plunge of her neckline as she tugged on white leather riding gloves. The tips of her pointed ears were as red as her cheeks. No longer simply embodying cold's cruelness, that aspect now confined to a mere blade of ice belted around her wide hips, instead she thrived with the warmth of the bonfire behind her. Her heartbeat pulsed through my body, sparking waves of hot and cold. My ears ached in the absence of her fingers, as the waves eddied into a core of want that reached into my loins. Her scent, the promise of passion and warmth in the dark.

Never in my life had I desired anyone as I wanted her in that moment.

Those eyes, still ice-blue, stared into mine, her expression skeptical before those gorgeous lips broke into a warm smile. Suddenly, my fur became so warm I had to pant, and my goddamn tail started wagging. "The first of Luna's wolves is a winter wolf." She decreed with pride.

"Abby's mine!" Secret's voice rang out, tiny but fierce. "You can't have her! She came for me, not you!" Small arms encircled my wrist and she tugged on my arm that had been hanging limply at my side.

Queen Mab put her hands on her knees and squatted down closer to Secret's level. "Child, I hold a piece of Abby Night's heart, a tiny speck compared to the swathe of soul she has pledged to Luna for your rescue. And yet that is but a single snowflake in a blizzard compared to the portion of her heart you hold, young halfling."

If she moved to hurt Secret I'd rip out her throat, but short of that, I continued to kneel, aching for touch, a kiss, anything.

"Let her go," Secret demanded with the imperious tone only a cat can muster. "Abby owes you nothing; she's reminded you of all you are. That's a boon granted, not a debt."

"And for that I extend my favor to you both, but child, you still partook of me. Because of this contest we have waged, my court will go hungry for another year and Summer will gain the first foothold in the mortal world." She sighed a with light hmmm. "I still starve for these celebrations. I must insist on my due in this lean time."

I managed a warning growl and stilled my stupid tail for a half second.

"I'm not going to harm her in any way; be a good wolf." Mab favored me with her smile, and my insides started to melt again. A needy whine crawled up my throat as I tried to stand. Secret's firm tug on my wrist held me back.

"Queen Mab. Stop that." Secret hissed.

"I'm doing nothing, child. You'll understand when you're older." With that Mab held out her gloved hand. "Give it here now."

Secret glared at the hand. "I don't need the solstice to open the way. I could take you to the holiday markets, just you. No court. I could do it three times."

Mab laughed a little sadly. "I am my Court, child. You have changed my heart, but hearts can change with the wind. Change outside the heart takes time. Feed me now with yourself, and I promise I will have the strength to begin those changes."

The ears on the knit cap folded back and her tail curled with uncertainty. "My momma wouldn't-"

"You mother's life was stolen to feed the Summer Queen!" Mab snapped. "If you wish to see her restored, it will be through me. I will accept nothing less than my due." Her fingers beckoned.

Secret's tail lashed with clear frustration, but she took off her mitten, reached into her chest, and twisted. A grimace of pain flashed across her face and disappeared. She pulled her hand out, and it had gained a dusting of black fur. Whiskers sprouted from her eyebrows and above her lips as she held her fist over Mab's outstretched hand. "To reclaim?" She asked.

"Join my hunt on a solstice and bring me the beating heart of a mortal to replace this piece of yours." Mab said.

"Promise?" Asked Secret.

"I swear it as an oath," Mab said, and a shimmer passed between them.

Secret's hand opened, and a small spinning mote of both light and darkness dropped into Mab's hand. It snapped closed as soon as the mote neared the palm. Mab brought her closed fist to her nose and sniffed deeply, savoring the scent. The fire behind her climbed higher, and she released her breath in the manner of a junkie feeling the high coming on. "I name you Princess of Winter."

"I am Princess of the Cats." Secret crossed her arms and pouted.

Mab opened her eyes and handed the mote off to another waiting shadow. "If your lifetime proves long, you will collect many titles. Best get used to their weight now. Give me a moment with your wolf, and I will bring you back to the court."

"No. Take us back to the court now. She's given enough to you." Secret said.

As they had talked, my wits had started to collect themselves, and I managed to pull my tongue back into my mouth and look a little less like a tame dog. Until Mab said, "I'm not taking anything, I'm giving her a treat." Then she slid into me, warm lips on the underside of my jaw and icy fingers burrowing through my pelt to claw across my skin. We kissed, I'm not sure how it worked, my jaw opened and things happened. Things that left me panting with heat and shivering with cold afterwards. I held her or she held me, one ear being delicately stroked by two finger tips inside and out while her lips murmured in the other. "I am the winter born of your desires, wolf. Whether or not you reclaim your heart piece from me, you will remain winter's wolf. Summer will forever be unkind to you. Outside, your mistress's light will find you. The cost of her favor is higher than you can imagine, wolf. Luna is not sane; her madness will leach into you. When you need rest, come home to me."

"Enough secrets!" Secret called out and my ear twitched out of Mab's fingers. "Stop being gross with... Evil. She's evil, remember."

Mab let me go with a laugh that rang like bell chimes.

I shook myself out, mind raking itself back together after Mab's touch had applied a leaf blower to my conscious thoughts.

"Oh, child!" Mab continued to laugh, "I was evil, but you two have gone and made me complicated." She waved at the still-waiting stairway, now decorated with pine garland and holly. "Start your journey back."

34

How much heart did one person have? And precisely what part of my heart did Mab take? These were the two questions that sat on my long inarticulate tongue as I climbed stair after stair up through Mab's heart. Had I been able to talk, I would have peppered Secret with these questions. Although as we finally emerged from the countless layers of frozen dark into a snow-covered forest that smelled familiar, I would have given Mab another heart helping to explain the modern concept of an escalator to her. Secret lay nestled in my arms, definitely not purring, almost as if her very slightly rigid body were broadcasting an anti-purr of silence as her tail flicked from side to side with annoyance.

I paused for breath as we approached the dark hole that had been sliced into a cloud. A quick swallow to realign my tongue between my teeth. The crisp air felt good on it. I peered down at the forest below, blanketed in inviting fluffy snow; the dawn made it all shine bright.

"Keep going," Secret said, rousing me from thoughts of running through that forest.

With a nod, I trudged up the last three spirals and into

the cloud. Wind swirled around us and the bright day dimmed to darkness. One more step and the packed snow of the Winter Court's floor greeted the pad of my paw.

I found myself in an amphitheater composed of ice; a fan of nine almost-empty seating areas looked down at me. At the top of each, figures clad in black armor sat in thrones. Some alone, some with three or four others at their feet. I recognized the thin form of Damocles in one but none of others.

"Behold!" Boomed Queen Mab from behind us. "Two new members of the Court. The Princess of Winter and her wolf."

I turned my head to look at the throne. It was as we'd left it. The two pillars framed the throne on which Mab sat as a pretty frozen corpse. Unchanged. Had it all been a trick?

No. I smelled the hint of cinnamon and mulled wine drifting through the air. Mab's eyes, too, had a shine.

"That's it!?" Screeched a voice, one of the figures standing from her throne, well, surging at a leash. Her lower torso was a mass of long segmented legs, like a spider's but far more of them. "The night is nearly over, my Queen. We have missed the hunt. For whaaaaat?" She scuttled down to the railing of her section and hissed, the mass of tentacles that covered her lower face like a veil lifting to reveal the sharp beak of an octopus.

"Lady Phoebe," drawled Damocles, popping open his watch. "That wolf bested Giggles while he was bloated with a meal and the halfling child will hand us the city itself. The hunt will come again."

So Damocles was a suck up. Interesting.

"Want Smash!" Shouted a huge knight whose muscles had burst the seams of his armor. "She strong. Come, doggy." He pointed at a seat below him, next to two other armor-clad figures who bristled with weapons.

I shook my head and started for the way I had come in.

"SHE MUST SERVE A KNIGHT OR BE A KNIGHT!" The floor shook, and my fur blasted sideways from a creature with the voice of a foghorn. Little more than a mouth with arms and legs.

"The wolf serves the Princess and will, in time, serve me." Queen Mab said in a soft voice that carried everywhere. Her knights stilled. "Go, Wolf. Till the Spring Equinox when we do battle with Summer. Perhaps then is when the Court of Cats shall be reclaimed."

That set the knights murmuring. Whispering to each other, despite the fact that none of them sat next to the others. The door I walked through was little more than an arena entrance carved in the ice.

Outside, Luna greeted us, her thin crescent low and large on the horizon opposite the sun. Her light shone with a tired pride. A sharp click drew my attention to the side.

Damocles lounged against the black brick of the castle and twirled his watch around his fingers. I heard him yawn. "An interesting time. Not how I read the gears turning at all. The gears slip, the teeth wear down, but still turn towards the inevitable."

I gave him a short, impatient growl.

Chuckling, he picked up a package bound in brown paper that had been at his feet. Tossed it into the air and caught it. "She's a sprocket," he pointed at Secret, who glared back at him like a cat who'd found a dog in her turf. "The Moon's a spring," he continued. "But you... Are you gum in the works? Or a sandy grain grinding the gears? Or do you turn on things I do not see? A mechanism thus unknown in the design?"

I stepped out onto the wooden drawbridge. "Apologies. I digress." With a flourish he held out the package to me. Both Secret and I eyed it warily. "A gift I give. An oath of no strings attached to this mundane thing."

He tossed it, and I snatched it from the air instinctively and sniffed it. It smelled of postal funk. In fact, it had an address on it, one that wasn't mine or that of anyone I knew. I narrowed my eyes at him.

"It never reached its intended owner, but will not be missed. An accident occurred." He shrugged, and I noticed that his armor had a shine it had not possessed before. Limbs still long and thin, but not quite as skeletal as when he had stood in Cindy's path. "So sad, but not really, everyone knew how that story would end. Open that when you need it. Give my regards to the reaper." He paused, opened his watch and glanced at the time. "I must go." Something shone in the dark of his eye slits. "Tick Tock, ladies."

We set off along the road into the forest. When we got to a fork, Secret pointed in the same direction that my nose pulled me. The lightest whiff of decay that seemed foreign to the dark, silent forest surrounding us. The path led to the sky road I had run here on. It greeted us with a jogging path, studded with benches and the occasional darkened street lamp.

"Abby?" Secret asked as I watched the path. "Why didn't you run up the stairs when we had the chance?"

"Whuff," I said noncommittally, glad for once that I couldn't talk, mainly because I didn't know what I would say to that. Queen Mab had offered us passage out of her heart, but I had to hug her instead. She had needed it. I had needed it.

Secret hopped down from my arms. The clothes she had

worn in Winter's heart had disappeared, and she stood in her little black dress, less human than she had been; thick black fur covered her hands and feet, her tail was heavy with fluff, and her straight hair had gained a wave to it. She'd become a long-haired cat, a winter's cat. For a time, she simply stared down the road, her hand pressed against her chest. Perhaps she felt the same kernel of cold that nestled in my own chest.

I asked in a mental prayer for my words back, but the goddess's answer was apparently "not yet." I worried that the real answer would be: "never". So, with a huff, I padded up beside Secret on all fours and nudged her.

She hugged my muzzle. "Abby?" she asked. "Did we lose? Next year we'll have to hunt with her."

The image of her frozen and white, the human side of her dying of cold loomed, and I shook my head hard.

"Hey!" Secreted protested, staggering back from my whipping ear. I followed it up with a kiss across her cheek. "Ewwww!" she mewed with distress, "Dog drool!"

She wanted dog drool, huh? I'd show her dog drool. With a playful pounce, I delivered a lick from chin to forehead.

"Mrrowl!" she cried, "I'm slimed!" and ran. I chased her in a circle, slavering her with kisses, until her squeals gave way to happy giggles. That sound only made me sink further into lupine joy. Tail wagging, I scooped her up and hugged her tight.

"Moooom!" She protested.

And we both froze. A look of mortification on Secret's face as I gently placed her down onto the ground. She turned away, breathing hard, but held onto my monstrous thumb.

"You're not my momma, Abby," she whispered, giving a

sniffle. "But.." She looked up, eyes shining, "You're the second best thing. Can we go home now?"

I'd take it. Maybe I'd ask her to call me Auntie. When or if I ever got to talk again, O Goddess of mine.

No response from Luna, although I still felt her attention and... amusement. So I nuzzled Secret, pointed at my back, and lay down beside her.

She scrabbled up without hesitation, her hands grabbing fistfuls of skin and fur. I wasn't exactly sure where home would be but it definitely wasn't here. Stretching out like a cat, I sang a howl to Luna.

I ran. On my back, Secret let out a peal of laughter and it made my entire heart sing, the little cold bit singing right along with the rest of me. It felt so good to run, not for my life or anyone's peril; simply for the joy of my paws and legs carrying me onward. Secret hunkered down as the air rushed around us. My perceptions narrowed to only the road: I barely saw the islands of the fey floating beyond, although I could feel their eyes. Hungry.

In the future more battles awaited. More roads to travel, tolls to be paid. But this day, this season maybe, had been won. Secret was worth the cost. So what if I wasn't human? So what if I'd joined the Winter Court? For the first time in ten years, my future felt more important than my past.

Remember this moment, my first wolf, Luna whispered into the back of my mind.

I howled in thanks. Secret laughed and added her own little "awoo" to the mix.

As the road sloped down towards west Portland, Luna let herself down over the horizon and yielded the sky to the sun. My gait faltered as my bones began to shift, painfully contracting with hesitant slowness. I managed to make it to the entrance of the forest before my front legs gave out entirely, flopping me down onto the dirt. Secret rolled off me with a laugh and up onto her feet.

It gave me something to smile at as my entire body filled with sharp needles.

"Come on, Abby!" Secret gestured for me to hurry towards the forest, her other arm carrying Damocles' package. "We're almost there."

Growling with effort, I stood up on still-shifting legs, my ankles pressing my weight into the ground without heels. Secret didn't wait, trundling off in the direction of the fairy circle. I shuffled after her, on feet that were approaching a human shape but remained stretched, the fur and muscle shrinking away faster than my bones could compress. Every few steps I had to spit out another couple of sharp teeth. It sounded like a swarm of caterpillars were gnawing on my skeleton, a constant grinding from every crevice of my body. When we reached the circle, I flopped down, grateful for the excuse to stop standing. As Secret performed her ritual, I watched as my nose slowly pulled back to the point where I couldn't see it, no matter how hard I crossed my eyes.

Portland's wet chill greeted us.

35

Back and very naked. Quite cold, too, in the gray of morning. Piece of winter in me or not, I shivered as I looked down
over my body. I felt oddly compressed, but everything
seemed as it had been. The slight roll of my stomach
remained, apparently Luna's light wasn't an easy ticket to a
supermodel bod. A fresh scar cut across my ribs, where
Little Nick had cut me. The other scar I didn't remember
receiving. A crescent shape rose above my left breast, its
flesh pale and white against my tan skin. I'd have to be
careful wearing anything low cut. "Turn into a werewolf and
all I get is a lousy tattoo." I muttered to myself. My legs
needed a shave, too, but they usually did. The fact that all
my body hair had turned white simply made it more
obvious.

"Want this?" Secret offered me the package, now
partially opened with three parallel rips across the side.
Pink terry cloth pressed out.

I took it and ripped it open, pulling a soft pink, but very
plush, bathrobe from the paper. Monogrammed with the
initials RL on the tag. I pulled it on. Better than being

naked, but I did worry about doing these walks of shame every time there happened to be a full moon. Secret nodded and we walked out of the fairy ring and into the forest. I kept on trying to dig my claws into the slick ground, but it doesn't work well when you don't have claws. Trees provided hand-holds. I kept trying to smell the air, and getting almost nothing compared to what I had gotten used to. Just the wet of Portland air and the reek of sodden earth.

"Abby!" Someone called my name. My gaze lifted from the ground to see Cindy and Rey waving from outside an ambulance parked on the street. Cindy waved her arms. Rey waved her three fox tails. I waved back, and then remembered I had lost the lupine muzzle. "Cindy! Rey!" I called back, more out of curiosity than any need. My voice sounded a little husky, but the words came out fine.

"Hi, Cindy!" Secret hurried towards them and gave my partner a hug. Well, either it was a hug, or Secret simply crashed into Cindy's hips. "Miss us?"

Cindy laughed. "You bet, kid." And patted her head, only slightly awkward. Meanwhile, I breathed my own sigh of relief as I reached the pavement. I said nothing until I, too, had gotten a hug from Cindy.

Rey bowed deeply to me, "Welcome home Miss Night," and then to Secret, "And you, too, Princess."

Secret put a finger across her lips and shushed Rey. "That's a secret!"

Rey gave a half shrug. "Not a well-kept one."

"Okay, How'd you know we were here?" I asked Cindy, who simply looked to Rey.

"Daylight crossings are difficult to miss." Rey looked reproachfully at the kitty princess.

"I needed to do it fast." Secret said with a slight sulk. "I didn't wanna wait."

I growled in approval. Then blinked and remembered words, "You did great. There room for us in that bus, Cindy?"

"Yep, that's why we're here. Borrowed it from Cliff." She pointed at her sling. "Got another week of desk duty." There was a bit of pain in her smile.

"Get in the bus." Cindy moved to the driver's side and popped open the door. I followed to the passenger side, Secret allowed Rey to guide her to the back of the ambulance. "We don't want to stay here," Cindy commented as we fastened our seatbelts. She took out her phone and handed it to me before starting the engine.

"What am I supposed to do with this?" I asked, confronted with Cindy's very pink Zelda-themed lock screen.

"Code's 1234. I got a playlist for you." Cindy said, already guiding the ambulance from the curb.

Refraining from commenting on Cindy's lock code, I unlocked the phone to see a video player already open. Looked like the local news clip. I hit play.

"Police are still looking for a local woman who assaulted officers at the OHSU last night." Blurry security footage showed a circle of men in dark clothing getting blasted through by a streak of something. Me, I remembered, then my employee ID photo appeared on the screen. "She's wanted in connection with the Santa murders. Police warn that she might have suffered a psychotic break, and consider her dangerous."

"Shit." I swore.

"Gets worse." Cindy responded. "Might need to get you a fake mustache."

Next video. "We have better footage of what witnesses are

describing as a huge wolf running across the Burnside bridge last night." The perspective changed to inside a car. Off-camera occupants shrieking "ohshitohshitohshit!" as a massive beast tore by as if they were standing still. The footage was blurry, but the loping gait of a canine had been captured in the movement. A news anchor cut back in, "No wolf has ever been reported to be that size. Experts speculate that the animal might have been a confused polar bear or perhaps a strange prank. Internet conspiracy theorists are... howling about a werewolf loose in Portland." He gave a hollow laugh, clearly bemused that his teleprompter would posit the existence of werewolves.

The video rolled into the next clip, flashing the title, "Abby Night? Victim of the Santa Murderer or werewolf?"

I swallowed so hard that my tongue almost went down my throat. Then the smiling face of Slade Higgins appeared on the screen. "That fuck nut!" I cursed and then did it again. I had totally missed cursing.

"Let me tell you!" Slade launched into a rant, "I've met Abby Night, and she is a total crazy lunatic. Totally into some deep occultist shit. She's got a black cat and a friggin' fox. I've got fucking footage, ya'll. Can't show it due to legal mumbo jumbo." Slade rolled his eyes. "Non-consent and all that jazz. But let's give her a shadow of a doubt, right. But let's review the facts." A map of east Portland pops up. "Abby is a patient at legacy hospital. Why? We don't know. But this is a level-one trauma center; something fucked her up. Rumor is she's wrapped up with this Santa killer dude. Maybe he knifed her, maybe she's helping him. Again, we dunno, alright? Here's the goddamn facts. Seven or eight pm, Everybody around the Medical Center hears howling. And you know it's Abby howling like a wolf. She's nearly butt naked. Bunch of security guards go to try to calm her down. And like, she attacks them. Mauls one. Runs away on all fuckin fours."

"Five minutes later, bam, over a hundred people see a giant wolf run across the Burnside bridge. That's not hard evidence of anything. Maybe she had a huge fursuit or something stashed somewhere. But according to the police, she's been missing for three days now. Fair, I say. I wouldn't want to show my face around here no more, either, after mauling a dude."

"Oh gods," I said about to close the video.

"But you know what's also fair? We gotta assume we got werewolves now. We've had zombies for like a year or so. And-" I moved to flick it off.

"Keep watching." Cindy urged,

I restarted the video. "We gotta defend ourselves, right?" Slade continued, holding up a red shotgun shell. "So I've been making these babies." He twisted the cap and a dozen pea sized silver balls rolled out. "One hundr'd percent sterling silver shot in these. If ya got werewolf troubles, you won't have one after firing one of these. Now I know, 'this wasn't a full moon or nothing, Slade, how'd we know that the whole silver thing actually works?' And you know what? That's fuck'n fair. But if you're facin' down something the size of a bear, pumping round after round and it's not doing nothing, you're gonna wish you had one of these to try, right? I molded the shot last night. The silver's not cheap, and I got twenty, got them on my store for a hundred bucks. Just in case, right?" I swiped up. The video had nearly thirty thousand views. Far more than most in the account, and it linked to a dozen other accounts with similar headlines and much higher viewer counts.

"Congratulations, you went viral." Cindy said as we drove onto the Marquam Bridge.

I sighed and looked down over the water. "Shit. I don't know what to say to that. I can tell ya what happened."

"Save it. More at the house want to hear it." Cindy said, "I was really worried about you, but Victoria insisted you were alive. So Rey's been watching for you."

"Listening," Rey corrected from the back. "When the worlds come together it's... still crunchy. And I knew she'd be back, too. Luna is not one who chooses poorly."

"Are you dangerous?" Cindy asked. "Do we have to go buy a bunch of chains?"

"Uh," I laughed nervously, "Maybe?" I had been a monster, but I had been in control. Mostly. In the back of my mind, I remembered that anger that had seized me in the times before. What had happened with only Luna's touch from the Twilight. "Might not be a terrible idea for the first time." Especially if Slade and his viewers would be out there hunting for a new wolfskin rug.

Cindy nodded to herself and looked at me. "We'll deal with it. You're back." She reached out, and we fist bumped. "That's the important thing."

She turned off the highway, and I knew she was taking us back to her place. I took a deep breath. "Cindy... Thanks, Secret and I, we'll stay for a while and oh, Rey, too, I guess. Until we figure out where we can go." I said.

"When this all started, I told you I'm not much of a fighter. Proved that." She laughed, "You can stay as long as you need. That and I could really use a renter to help afford the repairs. Nor would I mind the company."

"Rent requires a job and... not being arrested." I said.

We turned the corner and saw Cindy's house, the blue tarp gone and the roofing tiles gleaming with that just-put-on shine. "I think Cliff might have some ideas on that front,"

Cindy said. We pulled up, and the door opened, Cliff and Victoria stepping out onto the porch.

I shot a quizzical look at Cindy.

She smirked, "I called them both as soon as Rey heard you coming." Cliff came out towards us as I opened the door, arm in a white cast from elbow to wrist.

"Did you get him?" He asked.

I nodded, "Yeah, I did." I started to add details, but he held up a hand.

"That's all I need. The rest is just paperwork."

I laughed, "Gonna be a lot of paperwork, then."

"I'm learning how to do all of it, but let's leave it for tomorrow." He said.

We hugged, somewhat awkwardly.

"I'm good with tomorrow." I admitted.

"I'm not!" Victoria called out from the porch as she stood in the doorway. "Tell me everything right now!"

"Tall order, Vicky! Real tall order." I laughed. "How 'bout some food, first?"

"I'll order Chinese," she declared. "It might be a bit, being Christmas Eve and all."

"Christmas Eve?" I blinked and looked at Cindy.

"It's been three days," Cindy shrugged. "Merry Christmas on top of it all. Looks like we're not working it, for once. Won't that be weird?" She grinned, "Come on I've got cookies and hot chocolate while we wait for the food." It turned into a long day. We laughed, ate and drank. I painted the trip in broad overviews, wary of the costs Secret and I had run up. When I out-ate Cliff, we all joked that my Aunt Sybille might have to get a bigger turkey this year, but a bit of fear from all three humans mixed with the scent of the food. Cindy fussed over Secret's new appearance, called her adorable, and she preened. Victoria kept staring at my eyes while Cliff wore his nice grin a little forced around the edges.

Victoria and Cliff said goodbye with the setting of the sun. Cliff promised he'd be reopening the station soon, while Victoria told me to call her if I needed legal advice. Then there was a very long call with two very worried Aunts. I assured them I was okay, blamed the hospital escape on a bad reaction to painkillers. The only thing that prevented them from showing up on Cindy's doorstep was that they didn't know where she lived. They both demanded I go back to the hospital; we went round and round. It got harder and harder to keep a growl out of my voice, and I had to hang up on them when I noticed that my claws had peeled up a tile from Cindy's countertop.

"Woof." Cindy said as I handed her back her phone. She stared at my clawed hands, with their thickened fingers. After a moment I forced them back to normal, well not normal, human-looking. I had the sensation that my body was stuffed inside of a can and pressed against every surface.

"Sorry," I said.

"It's a new moon tonight, Abby." She frowned worriedly.

"Doesn't matter," I said, and knew I spoke the truth. Casting light or not, she loomed above, not a rock in the sky, but part of me, an external heart. She made no demands, whispered no words, she was simply present and making my skin feel too tight for the both of us.

"The moon doesn't matter, then?" she asked with a flush of sweet fear.

"She matters, she's my goddess. But the phases? I don't know yet, Cindy. There's no How to be a Werewolf guidebook, as far as I know, and I haven't had a chance to ask Rey if she knows anything."

Cindy didn't hide the skepticism and wariness on her face. It didn't take a mind reader to tell she had second thoughts about me staying with her. I let her ponder as the silence stretched between us. Her gaze drifted downward and she contemplated her nails. Sky blue today, a color we hadn't seen overhead in months. I wasn't sure if she was waiting for me to offer to go find somewhere else, but I didn't want to.

"Wanna see the room?" She looked up and smiled with clear, unclouded blue eyes.

"Yes!" I said with almost a bark of enthusiasm.

Secret jumped up from the floor, where she'd been lying in a semicircle of coloring books for the last hour.

Cindy laughed, "You, too, huh?"

Secret nodded enthusiastically.

"Follow me." Cindy turned and led us farther into the house, the fear scent gone. The room was across from her own at the edge of the second level. She unlocked it with a key, and handed it to me. "Just don't jump up and down too much or you might wind up in the kitchen. Once I tackle the water damage we can give Secret her own room, but you'll have to share for now. That okay?" She asked Secret.

She giggled, "I'm good with Abby."

"You have no idea how loudly she snores." Cindy pushed open the door, revealing a bedroom twice the size of the one in my apartment. The queen-sized bed with its black walnut frame was scratched and tired but stood solid. The small twin on the opposite side had a screaming pink headboard shaped like a cat's paw.

With a high pitched eeeeeee! Secret streaked into the room and pounced on the bed. "I love it!" she squeaked.

Cindy and I shared a laugh. "So that's why you had to let us stay? You already found her the perfect bed?" I asked.

"Partially," Cindy blushed, "Also... Rey's staying in my room."

I bristled and suddenly the cuff of my sleeves tightened. "Cindy she's-"

"Dangerous?" Cindy smiled nervously and whispered, "Do you even know what your eyes look like right now? Rey, Cliff and I had a bit of... an adventure while you were gone. She knows what she is. What she can and can't do." Together we looked down at my clawed hands. "I don't think you have any idea what you are now Abby. That's scary."

"I won't hurt you, Cindy. I promise," I said, trying to pull the claws back in, but they refused to go back in the can.

"Why don't you get a little rest, Abby." She backed out of the doorway. "I'll make dinner in an hour or two while you get yourself back together."

I nodded, "Thanks." And closed the door. The latch clicked and I leaned against the door, listening to Cindy's footsteps retreating away. With a heavy sigh, I pulled off my clothing. Secret watched, but didn't say anything as the top of that can in me came off. It hurt as my spine extended and my rib cage expanded, but only in the same way that popping your spine hurts, its momentary and the sheer relief is worth it. With first breath in through my long nose that cramped feeling dissipated entirely. The air of the room echoed with the distant scent of the humans who had stayed there and the far more recent stink of the mice that sheltered in the walls. I padded around its edges, feeling the weight of my body, appreciating the ease of it as I replaced the scents with my own.

"You're very pretty, Abby," Secret said as I found we had a mirror on the rear of the door. A wolf blinked back at me, her coat white with the slightest dusting of gray, silver eyes glinting well above the doorknob. A winter's wolf. I felt a pang of loss for the woman I used to see in the mirror, knowing that when I saw her again, she'd be a lie. At least in the nighttime, this beast would always be beneath her skin. Would I be able to show this to Cindy without her freaking out? I smiled, and was shocked by the size of my own fangs. No smiling, then. Moving back, I found Secret looking up at me. "So, can we stay? Please? Can this be home?"

Course, silly. What do you think I just did? This room was my territory now. Couldn't say it, though, so I licked her cheek instead.

This got a giggle, she staggered back, and I followed up with a playful nip at her tail. She shrieked and ran. I chased her. We made it four rings around the room until I put a paw through the drywall.

We froze. I pulled the misplaced paw from the wall.

"Bad Abby! You shouldn't chase cats!" she chided before erupting into a fit of giggles. I curled up around her and she hugged my neck, muffling her laugh in my fur. She had a sweet laugh. I stuffed myself back into that human can just far enough that I had fingers again, and immediately put them to use tickling her. "That's cheating! Bad Abby! Bad Abby!" she cried out and I relented, letting my fingers slip back into paws.

She forgave me quickly, and huddled against me, the beds forgotten as we dozed on the floor. When I woke up, a moonless night hung outside the window. A new night that I'd given myself over to. There were fights and dangers out there. Humans who would object to the trades I had made. We all had to adjust. At that moment, in my new territory, in my new home with Secret resting against my side, it was all worthwhile.

ACKNOWLEDGMENTS

Dear Reader,

Thank you for reading! If you've enjoyed *Emergency Shift* please leave a review.

I love writing Abby and her friends. Every day I wake up excited to create more of their stories. As soon I sent a draft of Emergency Shift to the editor, I was already planning the sequel the next morning in the shower. It's a great feeling and I hope you have fallen in love with this fledging family too, because I plan on putting them through the wringer.

There are many people who aided in this book's creation. First of all, my spouse, Amanda, for their support in all aspects of our life together. There is no other person who would tolerate being trapped in the same space with me for seventeen years, let alone a year of pandemic. Then Seria who has tutored me on paramedic procedure, life, and outlook in addition to beta reading. My editor Andrea Johnson who goes beyond the call of duty and lets me bounce endless ideas and what ifs off her. Big thank you to my beta/sensitivity readers, Carissa Vixen, Ash, Nathan and Jo. Friends play an important part in keeping me sane.

Thank you Paul and Michelle for dragging us outside no matter how hard it's raining, and to Chris and Megan along with the rest of the nebula crew for pulling us into your awesome family and friends circle.

Many cheers to my Patreons, the regulars of the Familiars Freehold Discord server, and members of the Fluff Pile Facebook group. (Links to all in my newsletter)

Normally I'd shower you with links about all the wonderful places above but with this being the first book in a brand new series I have only one request for you.

Please leave a review on Amazon and one other place: Good Reads, r/Fantasy on reddit, Facebook, or Twitter. That would be a huge help in getting this series off the ground. Thank you very much!

ALSO BY DANIEL POTTER

Freelance Familiars Book 1: Off Leash

Freelance Familiars Book 2: Marking Territory

Freelance Familiars Book 3: High Steaks

Freelance Familiars Book 4: Aggressive Behavior

Freelance Familiars Book 5: Pride Fall

Rudy & the Warren Warriors (a Freelance Familiars short story)

* * *

Rise of the Horned Serpent Book 1: Dragon's Price

Rise of the Horned Serpent Book 2: Dragon's Cage

Rise of the Horned Serpent Book 3: Dragon's Run

Rise of the Horned Serpent Book 4: Dragon's Siege

Made in the USA
Las Vegas, NV
24 April 2021